THE NIGHT SHE DIED

DEIRDRE PALMER

Storm
PUBLISHING

Ebook ISBN: 978-1-80508-300-9
Paperback ISBN: 978-1-80508-302-3

Cover design: Lisa Horton
Cover images: Trevillion, Shutterstock

Published by Storm Publishing.
For further information, visit:
www.stormpublishing.co

ALSO BY DEIRDRE PALMER

The Wife's Revenge
The Girl in the Dark
The Night She Died

To my fellow 'Write Romantics' – Jo Bartlett, Jessica Redland, Helen Phifer, Jackie Ladbury, Helen Rolfe, Sharon Booth, Rachael Thomas, Lynne Davidson and Alex Weston.

ONE

Layla Mackenzie glanced up at the image of herself, capped, gowned and scrolled, standing on the wide, stone steps of the city hall. Her gaze was focused a little to the left of the camera's eye. Her smile, though genuine, had been tugged from a darker place. Each time she came here, she tried to avoid looking at the photo. She was never successful.

She hadn't minded much at first. After all, she had given it to them, even though she'd thought it a little strange that they'd asked for it. Now it felt more than strange. It felt completely wrong. The photo was an imposter, stealing the place of the one that should be on this wall, in this house.

Except that the rightful image didn't exist. The evidence of Danni's achievement slept in the drawer of the beechwood chest, below. Layla knew that because she'd seen it one day, when she'd gone to fetch a pen.

No photograph. Just a posthumous degree diploma inside a brown envelope with the university's postmark.

Melody was back from the kitchen with the topped-up teapot. 'More toast, Layla? There's jam, marmalade, honey.' She pointed unnecessarily to the pots grouped in the centre of the round table. 'Or perhaps you'd like another egg? The hens are popping them out like crazy, aren't they, Reece?'

Reece gave a curt nod without looking up and continued dipping toast into his own egg in silence.

'No, that was just right, thanks.' Layla smiled. 'Another drop of tea and I'm good to go.'

Melody's own smile dipped, then returned, though with less confidence. Her mouth had a slightly forced look about the corners. Her eyes were too bright, her posture too solicitous. Her hand quivered as she held the teapot over Layla's mug.

Layla sighed, more obviously than she'd intended. All she wanted now was to be on the road, away from Melody's walled-up desperation, the veiled entreaty for her to stay a while longer.

'Oh, go on. A bit of toast won't hurt. Honestly, you girls and your figures!' Melody smiled, stood the teapot on its mat and resumed her place at the table.

'Leave her alone,' Reece said, coming to life. 'It's not her fault you've cut up half a loaf.' He winked at Layla.

Melody gave a little laugh. At the same time, a shadow passed across her face. Layla relented, took a triangle of toast from the silver rack and spread it with honey. Melody sat back in her chair, for the moment satisfied.

'Now then,' she said, looking pointedly at Reece, her husband, and reaching across to the windowsill. 'We have a little something for you.'

Layla was puzzled for a moment, until a large cream envelope appeared on the table in front of her. *Her birthday.* She was surprised they knew when it was; she couldn't remember telling them. She supposed it was okay if they wanted to give her a birthday card, except that Melody seemed to be making a big deal out of it.

'Thanks. That's really nice of you.' She smiled at them both but left the envelope where it was.

'We know your birthday isn't until tomorrow but you can't trust the post to deliver on time, even with first class...'

'Mel, let her open it, for pity's sake.' Reece raised his eyes at Layla. 'What is she like, eh?'

Open it. No point in saying she would rather keep it for the actual day – one look at Melody's face told her that. They were only one day adrift, so it was reasonable for her to open the card now, under normal circumstances.

But these weren't normal circumstances, and she'd far rather have done it in private, in her own time.

Melody was waiting. Layla wiped her fingers on her napkin and picked up the envelope. Peeling open the flap, she edged out the card. The picture showed a girl dancing in a garden; a girl with long dark hair, like Layla's, hiding her face. *To a dear daughter on her birthday,* said the raised purple lettering.

Her stomach fought against the food she'd eaten. This was a first. Just when she'd thought there could be no more firsts, another came crashing down. Glancing up, she caught Reece giving his wife a thunderous look before his expression settled into controlled neutrality.

As she opened the card, a cheque fell out. A cheque for five hundred pounds. She swallowed. They shouldn't do this. *Couldn't* do this. And yet they had. She didn't know which was worse, the wording on the card or the money. She glanced hopelessly around, longing to see the glimmer of a ribbon-tied package enclosing her favourite scent or a book – anything that spoke of almost-normal.

Anything other than this. *If only they knew...*

'No, please. I can't accept this; it's miles too much.'

'Nonsense, of course it isn't. Money goes nowhere these days. We thought you might like to put it towards a nice holiday,' Melody said brightly, before Reece interjected.

'You must do whatever you want with it, Layla. No strings.'

Reaching for his wife's hand, he closed his own tightly over it. Restraining, not comforting, Layla thought.

'No strings. Absolutely none.' Melody pushed back her hair with her free hand.

Thoughts pressed rapidly into Layla's mind, one after another. This wasn't fair. They were pushing the few boundaries that were left. No, not pushing them, whacking them to kingdom come with a swinging demolition ball. Outside the window, a black crow was perched on the fence post. Tilting its head, it shrieked to the wide blue sky. It echoed how she felt.

'No, honestly, it's very kind of you both, but it's too much.'

She stood the card up on the table in front of her, angling it slightly so she couldn't see the purple lettering. Then she put the cheque back inside the envelope and set it pointedly aside.

Melody looked as if she was about to cry. Pulling away from Reece, she gathered up a corner of the white tablecloth, bunching it in her hand below the edge of the table.

Could she really do this, reject their generosity with its illuminated subtitle – *we have no one else to do this for* – without causing them pain? She didn't want to hurt them; they'd suffered enough already.

She picked up the envelope. 'How about I keep it for now, but I won't cash it unless I need it for something really important?' Something that would never happen. 'Would that be okay?'

A look passed between Melody and Reece as they checked in with each other. The gesture seemed automatic, hollow as an Easter egg.

'Yes, of course,' Melody said. 'If that's what you'd rather do, it's fine with us, isn't it, Reece?'

'It is indeed.'

'Well, then, thank you. Thank you both very much.'

Layla stood up and stooped towards Melody, brushing her cheek with a kiss that didn't quite connect.

It wasn't really fine with them, of course, and sometimes she felt she was making things worse by coming here. Would they wake up one morning and realise that? Realise they'd be better off without the constant reminder she must surely bring every time she rocked up at Foxleigh Farm, with her weekend-guest gifts and her heart full of secrets? Somehow she doubted it.

The treads creaked under Layla's feet as she went up the narrow staircase to the bedroom under the eaves. Although Melody called it the guest room, it was obvious no one else had stayed in here since she'd been visiting.

The room was fresh and pretty, with pale blue-grey walls and white painted furniture. A golden oak beam, like a stick of toffee, ran from side to side beneath the vaulted ceiling. A pale blue towelling robe hung on the back of the door. There were slippers in her size beside the bed and books by her favourite authors stacked on top of an old sea chest. Behind a low, latched door was a tiny shower room with a shelf full of expensive gels, shampoos and creams. She had used the robe and slippers and plunged into a couple of the books, but the toiletries remained with their discreet packaging intact; she preferred to use her own stuff which came in lime green plastic bottles from Super-drug. A line had to be drawn somewhere, even if it was a shaky one.

At least they hadn't put her in Danni's room. The closed door at the end of the passage on the floor below had a firm look about it, as if it hadn't been opened in a long time.

Her rucksack packed, she sat down on the bed beneath the slope of the ceiling, gathering her thoughts, then rose and smoothed out the cover. After a last check to make sure she'd left nothing behind, no clue to her occupation of this room, she took a deep breath and went downstairs.

The Morlands stood outside the back door as Layla stepped

into the ancient blue Fiesta and started up the engine. She glanced in the rear-view mirror. Melody's arms were wrapped around herself, her hands rubbing at the sleeves of her grey sweater as if she was freezing cold, even though the March day was mild and sunny. Reece stood apart from her, buttoning the cuff on his denim shirt. They waved as she moved off. Layla gave a single wave back, then drove past the pond, the orchard and the old stables, now converted to holiday lets, then turned onto the road which would take her from Sussex to Kent, and home.

TWO

'Hang on, Layla! Don't come in yet!'

Several voices penetrated the closed door to the room which Mum called the 'through'. Layla scuffed out of her shoes and sank onto the cream-carpeted stairs. She felt tired and anxious, not at all ready for this.

Eventually, the door opened, letting out the acrid smell of burnt matches and a collective 'ta dah!', as if this was a big surprise. She was pleased to see her friend, Seth; he would take the heat off. Layla didn't particularly enjoy being the centre of attention, even within her own family. She smiled across at him and a connecting smile bounced back. She felt a little better.

Her mother, April, gave the signal by way of a raised fore-finger and everyone sang 'Happy Birthday', some coming in later than others so that the last line was repeated at least three times, ending with a croak and a coughing fit from Nan.

'Come and blow your candles out then, darlin',' April said, squeezing past the others to kiss her middle daughter on the cheek and hustle her to the table.

Layla gazed at the square, pink-and-white cake – the size of a hockey pitch, with her name picked out in silver balls – and felt her stomach tighten.

'Funny time of day for cake, isn't it?'

'I don't expect the Queen would turn her nose up at a bit of cake at eleven o'clock of a Sunday morning, would she?' April addressed her question to no one in particular. 'It's not easy, getting everyone in the same place at the same time.'

There were murmurings of assent at this.

'It's an amazing cake, Mum. I love it.' Layla gave April a hug.

Already, this was too much. The trials of the weekend were too fresh and raw, the emotional toll too heavy. It wasn't Mum's fault, though; she mustn't take it out on her. It was nobody's fault but her own.

'Thanks, Mum. And everyone for being here.'

She smiled round at them all.

'Aw, go on,' April said. 'Where else would they be?'

Jadine, her younger sister, was beside her now, her boyfriend, Alex, abandoned on the sofa. She nudged Layla in the ribs.

'Get on with it, then, before we all die of starvation.'

'Somebody should have got up in time for breakfast.' April nodded towards Jadine, crystal earrings swinging, catching the light.

'Let me blow the candles!' Finn, Layla's nephew, cavorted round the table, puffing out his cheeks and sending out a spray of chewed crisps to land on the newly vacuumed carpet. 'It's my birthday on Saturday!'

'Then you'll have your own cake, won't you?' Rowan clamped a restraining hand on her son's shoulder. 'Layla, for Pete's *sake.*'

One sweep of breath and all the candles – only ten, thankfully, not twenty-five – were snuffed. A round of dutiful clapping and cheering, then Mum set to with the pearl-handled cake slice, liberated from its velvet-lined box for the occasion.

Seth drew Layla to one side. 'So, how was it, *chez Morland?*'

'Like you wouldn't believe.'

'That bad, uh?'

'Tell you later.'

Seth gave her shoulder a squeeze and went across to talk to Jeff, Rowan's partner. The chatter went on around Layla. Her rucksack was still in the hall, the Morlands' card hidden at the bottom. She would take it to work later and feed it into the shredder in the hotel manager's office.

To a dear daughter. So much more was contained in that phrase than the innocent letters spelled out. The more she thought about it, the more apparent it became that Melody alone had been responsible for the monumental aberration; Reece, when he'd seen the card, had seemed as shocked as Layla. She wondered if he had taken Melody to task over it later, then decided he probably hadn't. His wife was his priority; he wouldn't risk upsetting her over something that couldn't be changed.

Layla squatted down beside her grandmother's chair and gave her a kiss on the cheek. Nan was wiping a finger around her plate, dabbing up the last crumbs of cake and posting them between her lips with a sucking sound. One of the silver balls had lodged itself between her bottom front teeth, like a misplaced tongue stud.

'All right, Nan?'

'Right as ninepence.'

'You'll be saying that on your deathbed.'

'I won't. I'll be saying thank the Lord I'm going somewhere I don't have to take me shoes off every time I come in the front door.' She lifted a foot, wiggling her stocking-clad toes.

Seth came over and leaned on the arm of the chair.

'Fancy a cup of tea, Mrs Foster?'

'None of your Mrs Foster business. It's Mary. Don't stand on ceremony. There's enough of that around here already.'

Seth grinned at Layla over Nan's head. 'A nice cup of tea then, Mary?'

'Ooh, yes, please. You are a good boy. Isn't he a good boy, Layla? Especially for a Jew.'

'Nan!'

Seth was already on his way to the kitchen, chuckling to himself. Layla followed. She closed the kitchen door and stood silently while Seth filled the kettle and flicked the switch. He turned towards her.

'Must say I've seen you looking brighter, sunshine.'

'That's no surprise, is it?'

'I'm only looking out for you, that's all.' Seth raised his hands.

'I know you are. Sorry.'

'Doesn't matter. I'm used to it. You're always like this when you've been with them.'

Layla felt close to tears. 'I'm turning into this horrible person I don't even recognise half the time.'

'Come here.' Seth held out his arms. Layla folded herself into them, ducking her head so she was closer to his height.

'You'll have to put a stop to it,' Seth said, after a moment. 'Tell them you can't go there any more. Now, for preference.'

She didn't reply. He was right; she would like nothing more than to step away from Danni's parents, put some distance between them before the whole thing overwhelmed her completely – if it had not already done so. But Seth didn't know the truth – nobody did, apart from Layla herself. To him, it was black and white, a simple decision begging to be made. *If only.*

The visits to Foxleigh had been all right – kind of – at first. The old red-brick and tiled farmhouse with its rambling cottage garden and chickens in the yard was a joy, the Morlands welcoming and sweetly eager to make everything perfect for her.

The first weekend she'd spent there had been at the beginning of August last year, six weeks after Danni died. Melody had phoned out of the blue. Layla hadn't expected to have any contact with Danni's parents once the funeral was over. There were obstacles, of course, her own ambivalence at the invitation being one of them.

Being in Danni's home, with Danni's parents, without Danni, had threatened to stir up more emotions than she knew how to cope with. But for some reason they'd seemed to want her there, especially Melody, and she'd pushed through, for them – for Danni – and trained herself to relax and enjoy their hospitality. How could she refuse them, under the circumstances? How could she refuse them anything?

She hadn't seen the warning signs – but could have seen them, had she chosen to. Then that morning, the debacle with the card and the cheque had forced her to confront the truth. The wires had tightened. She was caught, like a rabbit in a trap.

She broke apart from Seth. He nodded towards the door. 'Something's kicking off in there.'

'Doesn't it always?'

Raised voices carried the gist of the argument: Jeff's, demanding to know why Rowan was going out again; Rowan's informing Jeff – and the neighbours two doors down – that all he did on a Sunday afternoon was snore in the chair, so it was no wonder she wanted to go out and have a bit of fun. Nobody reasoning, nobody backing down.

The kitchen door opened and April came in.

'Why they always have to start I'll never know.' She turned to Seth. 'What must you think of us?'

Seth shrugged. 'Families. It's par for the course.'

'It certainly is with us.' April ripped open a bag of Doritos and shook them into a bowl with a rattle of bracelets, then turned to Layla. 'It's a shame we couldn't do this on the day. You'll have your presents to open tomorrow, though, so it's like having two birthdays. Did you have a nice time, love? I didn't have the chance to ask.'

'Yes, thanks, Mum. It was fine,' Layla said, crossing her fingers behind her back.

'That's good, then. It's kind of them to keep inviting you. I can't imagine what they've been going through. If anything happened to one of you girls, I don't know what I'd do…'

'Mum, don't.'

April's face cleared. She smiled. 'No, quite right. No good looking on the black side.' She scrunched up the empty Doritos bag and dropped it in the bin. 'That's it, then.'

'Shall we get out of here?' Layla whispered to Seth.

'Do we dare?' Seth whispered back, glancing at April.

'Sure we do. Mum…?'

'Yes, love?'

'Would you mind if I went out with Seth for a while?'

'Of course I don't mind. This is your day, such as it is.' April gave a conspiratorial nod towards the door. 'They'll be going soon, with any luck, but best nip out the back.'

'Thanks, Mum.' Layla kissed her cheek. 'And thanks for the lovely cake and everything. I won't be long.'

'What about Nan's tea?' Seth asked, when the kitchen door had closed on April.

'Someone else'll do it.'

More raised voices. The argument between Rowan and Jeff had broken out again.

'That's it. We're gone.' Layla opened the back door.

Seth cleared his throat and glanced down at his socked feet.

'Hang on.'

Layla grabbed the front door keys from the hook, hopped out of the back door and ran barefoot round to the front.

Seconds later, she'd retrieved their shoes from the hall and they were away.

THREE

Seth drove his little yellow Citroen down the winding length of Warbler's Way, along Robin's Lane, past Thrush End – much sniggered over by Layla and Rowan when they were teenagers – and out onto the main road.

'Melody's doing my head in,' Layla said.

'As you are doing mine.'

'I burden you with my problems, you keep yours to yourself. That's the deal.'

'Bloody car's like a homing pigeon,' Seth muttered as they passed the elegant stone-pillared entrance of Tidehall Manor where they both worked as chefs.

'Speaking of which,' Layla said, 'what time are you on duty?'

'Whatever time I damn well like.' Seth gave an innocent cyclist an unnecessary blast of the horn.

'Five, then, same as me.'

It was all bravado with Seth. He had to toe the line as much as anyone else, more so if he wasn't to be accused of having special treatment because he was the boss's son – the big boss, the owner of the hotel chain of which Tidehall Manor was a very small part.

'Where're we going?' Layla asked, as Seth took the road leading out of Maybridge.

'Just driving. Thought that's what you wanted.'

'I did. Now I need a big cold glass of Pinot. Let's go to the Swan.'

Lifting an imaginary chauffeur's cap, Seth reversed the Citroen smartly over the grass verge and headed back towards the river turn-off.

The Swan, its white-painted walls strung with coloured lights which gave it a festive appearance and drew in the tourists at night, stood at the head of the bridge over the May. A wooden deck was fastened to its upper storey, giving a scenic view of the river. Layla headed out there now. She chose a table at the far end and sat with her arms resting on the rail. Below, the water flowed fast and high, carrying with it a detritus of leaves and the occasional crisp packet. She stared at it through screwed-up eyes until she felt quite dizzy with the motion. But her mind wasn't on the river.

Her weekend at Foxleigh had been the worst yet, not only because of the birthday thing. The tension between Melody and Reece had been way off the scale. For all their efforts to act normally in front of her, she'd felt stranded between them like a bird caught in telephone wires. Their brave show of togetherness had lasted until after dinner last night, when Reece had finally given in and retreated to his study, leaving her and Melody watching a film on TV. Layla hadn't taken in a word of the film – no more, she suspected, than Melody had. Instead, she'd sat in a room that seemed empty, no matter who was in it, wondering for the hundredth time what she was doing there.

She was so lost in thought that she'd almost forgotten about Seth until her glass of wine appeared in front of her.

'If you can't tell Melody to her face, then phone her or write a letter,' he said, sitting down on the opposite bench, 'but whatever you do, make it soon, otherwise you'll end up as demented as she is and that I don't fancy coping with, if it's all the same.'

'Melody isn't demented; she's grieving for her daughter. So is Reece. Grief makes people irrational.'

'Yes, I know it does, especially in their situation. Sorry, I just meant... Well, you know.' He shrugged.

'They don't talk about her when I'm there, Seth. I don't think they do even when I'm not there.'

If Melody and Reece spoke of Danni all the time, they wouldn't stop because she was there, would they? It felt unnatural, not bringing her into the conversation; she'd been Danni's best friend, which was surely the reason they'd wanted to keep up the contact with her in the first place. But, as she'd said to Seth, grief had its own agenda. It struck in different ways, and not always as you'd expect. She must take her lead from them, especially when she was a guest in their house.

She thought back to when her father, Doug, had died of a heart attack. It was ten years ago, but April's frenzied cleaning bouts were as sharp in her mind as if it were yesterday. Her mother hadn't been able to keep still. Whirling through the house like a dervish, she'd attacked every surface with her sprays and cloths, and cooked mountains of food none of them had the stomach for.

Then there were the photographs. Virtually every photo of her dad they possessed had made its way into a frame to be propped on every available surface and dusted twice a day. It was as if April was afraid that she, or her girls, would forget what he looked like, otherwise. As if they ever would.

And then, as suddenly as it started, everything stopped, the photos snuggled their way back into the album and life in

Warbler's Way continued as before, but without Dad. The same, but different.

'They gave me money for my birthday. Five hundred pounds,' Layla said. She daren't mention the message written on the card.

'Bloody hell. You didn't take it, did you? Please tell me you didn't...'

'Yes and no. I said I wouldn't cash the cheque unless there was an emergency, which there won't be. I didn't have any choice, Seth. You should have seen the look on Melody's face when I tried to say no.'

'Even more reason to stop seeing them. Post back the cheque with a letter. Cruel to be kind.'

No, just cruel. They so looked forward to her visits, never wanted her to leave. At least, Melody didn't. She couldn't do it to them. Danni had only been gone for nine months, which was nothing in terms of such a loss; the wounds were still raw. It was too soon.

Perhaps it would always be too soon.

The house was blissfully quiet by the time Seth dropped Layla home. A note in April's neat handwriting told her that she'd taken Nan home. Everyone else had gone apart from Jadine, who was lying face down on her bed, fists curled on the pillow like a baby's.

Layla's old bedroom had morphed into her mum's en suite within weeks of her departure for university. The main bathroom was downstairs, tacked onto the back of the house, beyond the kitchen. The night-time trek wasn't popular with anyone, especially April. Her solution to the problem had only succeeded in creating a new one. Now, Layla shared Jadine's room and slept on a bed as narrow as a ladder, with her belongings in boxes in the loft.

She could live-in at Tidehall, like Seth and the Romanian waiters, or find a flat-share or a bedsit, but after she'd finished uni at the end of last summer – after Danni – Mum had gathered her up and brought her home. She'd had no thoughts of moving out again. Home was safe, in so many ways. Besides, it wouldn't be forever.

At first she thought Jadine was asleep, until she rolled over onto her back, flinging her arms out to the sides. Her cropped blonde hair formed a half-circle on the pillow, like a lopsided halo on a fallen angel.

'Are you working tonight, Layla?'

'Yep. Five till eleven. Why?'

'Just checking.'

A sly smile strayed to Jadine's lips. Mum would be out tonight, too. The Maybridge Arms had karaoke on Sundays. A group of them went – women from round here, mostly from Warbler's Way. April always sung that Queen song while she was getting ready, the one about having a good time. Now it seemed as if Jadine would be having a good time, too, along with Smart Alec.

Jadine's boyfriend had earned his nickname the first time he'd set black-socked feet inside the 'through', wearing his work uniform of black trousers, white shirt and a red tie with the bank's logo. Alec's job was a big point in his favour as far as Mum was concerned. She could be amazingly naïve at times.

Jadine rolled off the bed. 'D'you want the bathroom?'

'No, it's all yours.' Layla skirted Jadine's bed and lay down on her own, beneath the window, intent on taking a nap.

Jadine stripped down to her knickers, threw on her pink dressing gown and banged out of the room. Most of Jadine's clothes were pink, if they weren't denim. It suited her looks and her personality, fitted her baby-sister role to a T. Only nineteen and looking younger, Jadine was the afterthought; the last-ditch stand; the happy accident.

You'd have thought she might have felt the odd one out among the sisters because of the age gap, but if anyone felt that way it was Layla. She looked different, for a start, because she took after their dad. She was taller than the others – five feet eight in her socks – with glossy dark brown hair, skin that tanned easily and strong, even features that were most often described as striking rather than pretty, whereas Mum, Rowan and Jadine had the kind of retroussé-nosed fluffy blondeness that attracted indulgent smiles from total strangers. Stand them together and they looked like a row of dolls waiting to be taken home and loved. A classic example of deceptive appearances.

Her sisters rushed at life without so much as a sideways glance. They refused to be sidelined or overlooked. They arrived in rooms with a bump, as if they'd slid down the banisters, and primped and preened constantly, like contestants in a beauty contest. Both had romped out of school as soon as they were legally allowed, but they weren't without talent or ambition.

Rowan was the manager of a hairdressing salon housed in a listed Georgian building which, because of its proximity to the cathedral, was captured for posterity on numerous picture postcards. Jadine 'did hairdressing', too. The salon where she worked was situated in a blank-faced parade of shops, sandwiched between a betting office and a launderette.

Of the three Mackenzie girls, Layla was the one who'd had to be reminded to brush her hair, sew up the unravelled hem of a skirt and have her bedroom light switched out at two in the morning when she was found to be still reading. And then, at thirteen, as if she'd suddenly woken up from a dream, she'd announced she was going to be a top-class chef, as if it was some kind of mystical calling.

It was Mum who'd insisted she have what she called a proper education to go alongside the cookery, when Layla would have been happy to work her way up from being a hotel washer-up if necessary. When she'd got a place on the hospitality degree course, Mum couldn't have been more excited than if she'd won the lottery and had raced around telling all her friends that she had a daughter who'd got into university.

Layla and Danni had laughed over that the first time they got together, raising their eyebrows at the untoward behaviour of mothers in general. It hadn't taken much to set them off in hysterics. Oh, she missed Danni so much...

Deprived of her nap by the familiar rush of anguish, Layla sat up on the bed, drawing up her knees and gazing out of the window at the uninspiring vista of Warbler's Way, with its snaking rows of pebbledash houses. She wondered what the Morlands were doing now. Reece might be reading, or marking his Maths students' coursework and longing for Monday morning when he could escape to the university; Melody sewing in the conservatory, pruning the roses, or feeding the hens, their Sunday afternoons running parallel to one another, intersecting occasionally with distant smiles and cups of tea, but otherwise staying within the boundaries of the worlds they'd created for themselves. It was how they'd learned to live.

Her phone beeped inside her jeans pocket. Melody. Of course. It was as if she had a hotline to Layla's mind.

Did you get home safely?

She'd meant to message her as soon as she got home, but with the party and everything, she'd forgotten. She thumbed a reply:

I did, and thanks again for a lovely weekend.

And here again came the tide of unalterable feeling, crashing down like the sea against rocks. She lay down again, turned onto her side and closed her eyes. Seth's words came back to her. Seth, who – as any sensible person would – thought that she'd more than done her duty with the Morlands and it was time she walked away. He couldn't understand why she didn't.

But he didn't know the truth about the night Danni died; nobody knew, except Layla.

And they mustn't. Ever.

FOUR

Melody put the phone down. She remained standing in the same spot in the kitchen, pen in hand, reporter's notebook open on the counter in front of her. She stared at the empty page. It felt wrong to have written nothing down. Adopting a businesslike stance, she wrote 'Layla. Cancelled.' Then she picked up the notebook and flung it across the room. It smacked against the wall and slid down to land on top of the vegetable rack.

Her breath came in frighteningly uneven bursts, cracking hard against her ribcage. Leaning both hands on the counter, she fought to control it. Her mind groped for a new thought, a good thought to replace the bad one and break the association with the pain, as the therapist had taught her. The therapist, however, didn't understand that the pain was necessary. How else would she know she was still alive?

The phone rang again. She grabbed it, thinking it would be Layla calling back to say she'd made a mistake with the dates, that of course she was coming at the weekend and she wouldn't miss it for anything. It wasn't. Instead, Melody heard herself reciting the off-season rates for the holiday lets as hope dripped away.

The call ended; she retrieved the notebook, straightening it out and placing it back on the counter with the pen, then went out of the back door and wandered down to the rose garden. The garden was protected on three sides by powdery, rust-coloured brick walls, with a low box hedge on the fourth. More bricks formed a narrow path between the beds. Breathing deeply, letting the sights and scents of the garden calm her, Melody walked along the path, avoiding the puddles left by last night's rain.

A shrivelled red bloom, left over from last year, clung to a thorny stem. Melody reached for it. Straight away, the fragile, brown-stained petals disintegrated in her hand. Every year she marvelled at the tenacity of the roses. Month after month they clung on, through rain and wind and dipping temperatures. And then, as now, new leaves began to swell and break, bringing the promise of summer and new flowers, like a well-kept secret.

Her own perfect little rose, her beautiful daughter, would not bloom again. For Danni, summer was over forever...

Stop.

Melody left the rose garden and headed back to the house to fetch the keys to the holiday lets.

As she crossed the garden, the keys in her hand, her mind returned to Layla. The girl had other calls on her time; she must remember that. The hotel trade could be unpredictable; staffing was difficult. People came and went, especially the foreigners. Naturally Layla had to be flexible, step up when she was needed, and they had a wedding on at the weekend, she'd said. Layla loved her job. She was hardworking and ambitious; it came across clearly in the way she spoke. It was one of her qualities that Melody most admired.

Layla hadn't been specific about when she would be free, though; a troubling thought. No other date was ringed in red on the calendar, to be eagerly awaited. Her heart beat faster, sweat broke out on her forehead. It happened every time she thought she might be losing Layla altogether. And then she realised that Layla probably intended coming the weekend after, only she hadn't said so, either because she'd forgotten or she thought it was obvious. Yes, that would be it. Melody's mind latched onto this belief and filed it. The anxiety passed.

The three former stables – named Willow, Hazel and Larch – sat at right angles to one another around a paved courtyard. Last summer, after it happened, Reece had thrown himself into their long overdue refit and redecoration, almost to the point of obsession. Melody remembered endless hours spent alone in the house while he worked on until darkness fell. For some reason, it had never occurred to her to go out and join him. Instead, she would sit, inert, in front of the TV, or take a long bath and go to bed.

Eventually, Reece would return and fall, exhausted, into bed, his face an impenetrable mask, his hands a landscape of scrapes and bruises. Refurbishing the holiday lets had been his special project, his way of coping. She'd understood that and tried not to feel abandoned.

Melody had been granted compassionate leave from her job as an IT systems trainer. She had never gone back. Like everything else, it seemed pointless and, in any case, she was far too tired. She'd lapsed into a state of inertia then, but once she'd managed to pull herself out of it, the holiday lets had become her domain.

A woman from the village came to clean and do the laundry between bookings. Melody took care of everything else. It gave her a small measure of relief to discover that in some corner of her life she could still be reliable and responsible, that it hadn't all run away from her entirely. Reece, she suspected, was even more relieved, though he never said.

There were two middle-aged couples from Manchester staying in Hazel. The women were sisters, Melody thought. She had overheard them arguing good-naturedly over which couple should have the bedroom and which the sofa-bed in the living area. Larch had an elderly couple from Portsmouth and their dog, a little white terrier with a brown patch over one eye.

All was quiet as Melody crossed the courtyard. The cars were gone; everyone would be out for the day. Willow, unusually, was unoccupied until Saturday. Letting herself in, Melody passed through the chain of rooms, checking soap dispensers, hanging mugs on hooks, plumping cushions and replacing spent tea lights. Wild daffodils had been left wilting in a jug on the windowsill. Melody threw them in the bin, washed out the jug and replaced it on the sill. Some of the leaflets on the coffee table were dog-eared and out of date. She threw those away, too, making a mental note to drive to the tourist office in Foxleigh and pick up some more. She could do that this afternoon.

The corner of something poked out from beneath the sofa. She stooped and pulled it out. It was a child's colouring book, probably belonging to the little girl who'd stayed last week. Danni had loved colouring, had gone through any number of these books. She'd got very cross if she crayoned over the lines. Melody felt the sting of threatened tears. She swallowed them back.

And then, as she'd known would happen, Layla swung back into her mind. Sitting down, Melody took out her mobile and scrolled through her contacts. She mustn't just let things happen to her. She must take control, accept the unacceptable, as her therapist, Kate, had suggested in that clever, turn-around way of hers that made the words come out of Melody's own mouth. If she wanted to speak to Layla, there was nothing stopping her.

Hi, this is Layla. Please leave a message and I'll get back to you.

Melody waited a moment, then clicked off the phone.

In the end she didn't drive to the village. Instead, she slept the afternoon away in the conservatory, her book on her lap. She seemed to need so much sleep. Kate had not responded when Melody asked why this should be. She had let the question fall into the silence.

That day the session had overrun, which was Melody's fault because each time Kate had begun her summary, she had panicked and started talking about something else. It didn't faze Kate, of course. Nothing did. Except when the keypad on the door had clicked and buzzed and a tall, fair-haired, rather good-looking young man put his head round, muttered 'sorry' several times and closed the door again. Colour had flown inexplicably to Kate's cheeks. Letting the pen she'd been holding fall to her lap, she'd grabbed a strand of that glorious red hair and twisted it around her finger, quite manically. Melody's instinct had been to ask if she was all right, but the focus shifted again, dramatically and expertly, back to Melody herself and the moment was gone.

The bereavement counselling she'd had at the beginning had helped a little, but the effect hadn't lasted. The extra therapy sessions had begun six months ago, suggested by Melody's GP – in desperation, she suspected – as she sat silently before him and waited for a miracle. The clinic, attached to a large district hospital, was twenty miles south of Foxleigh, on the outskirts of the seaside town of Haverstone. It might not be on the doorstep, but it had the best reputation. And Melody was lucky to get an appointment so soon, as her GP had pointed out when she'd seemed doubtful.

'Yes, I know. Thank you,' Melody had said.

She hadn't felt lucky though. She hadn't felt anything. Reece hadn't had counselling or therapy. He had never inferred that Melody was in some way weak because she needed these things, but that didn't stop it being the truth.

If Reece was disappointed that Layla wasn't coming on Saturday, he didn't show it. It might have helped if he had, but Melody had learned not to expect it. He was a bit quieter than usual for a while after she told him. Then, while she was standing at the kitchen island, slicing onions and carrots for a casserole, he approached her as he might approach the dentist's chair, put his arms stiffly around her and said she wasn't to worry because Layla would be back, if not the following week, then soon.

Even in Reece's dutiful embrace, Melody felt his absence more strongly than if he'd been out of the house.

Later, she said, 'We must think of something we can do for Layla.'

Reece looked up from his newspaper and frowned. 'How do you mean?'

'She comes from nothing, which means her opportunities are limited.'

Reece put the paper aside and looked hard at Melody. 'Where do you get these ideas, Mel? They don't come from Layla, that's for sure.'

'Not directly, no, but you've only got to listen to what she says.' Did Reece ever listen to what Layla said? He seemed so preoccupied, sometimes, that he might as well not be in the room. 'Her mother works on a supermarket checkout; those sisters of hers sound like nothing but trouble and they're only hairdressers. She wants to work in the States and get some really good experience, then eventually open her own restaurant. What kind of help is she going to get from that sort of family? Precious little, I should imagine.'

'Imagine's about right,' Reece muttered, getting up from his chair.

'What's that supposed to mean?'

'Nothing. Look...' Reece sighed. He looked tired and bewildered.

'Oh, I'm sorry. I don't know what's got into me today.' Melody reached up and touched his arm as he stood uncertainly beside her chair. 'You feel the same as I do about Layla, though. I know you do. You want the best for her, the same as me.'

'Don't try to run her life for her, that's all I'm saying, Mel. Anyway, I thought we just did something for her. Five hundred quid, remember?'

'Which she won't use. She made that pretty clear.'

'There you are, then.' Reece raised his hands in a gesture of exasperated triumph. 'She doesn't want our help. She doesn't want anything from us. Why should she?'

Melody felt drained and near to tears. 'It was the birthday card, the words on the front. It wasn't only about the money; it was the card. I didn't set out to buy it. I saw it on the rack in the shop and it spoke to me. I knew it was a mistake as soon as I saw her face when she opened it, but I wanted her to know how we both feel about her and that we love her almost as if she was our own daughter.'

'Yes, well, that was a shock for me, too. For Christ's sake, Melody, what were you thinking? I couldn't believe it when I saw what was on that card. I'm fond of the girl, of course I am. I like her coming here, she brings a bit of life to the place, but don't pile on the pressure. Don't make her feel guilty, otherwise she won't come at all.'

'Don't lecture me, Reece. I'm not one of your students.'

'I'm not...' Reece ran a hand across his head. He lowered his voice. 'I'm not lecturing you. I'm only trying to stop you being any more hurt than you already are, that's all.'

'Sometimes I think I'm hurting for both of us,' Melody said.

Reece backed away, his eyes narrowing. 'Oh no, Mel. No. Don't ever say that.'

Shaking his head in disbelief, he crossed to the door.

'And so you run away,' Melody murmured, half to herself.

'I'm going to do some marking, as it happens.'

The door closed firmly behind him.

FIVE

Reece closed a second door – the one to his study on the other side of the hall – and dropped into the tapestry wing chair that had weathered the storm of Melody's threats to take it to the council tip and emerged, victorious, to continue its shabby existence.

Sinking further into the upholstery, he felt the comfortingly familiar graze of scratched threads as he rubbed his palms across the balding patches on the arms. He could swing for that girl! Didn't she realise how much worse she'd made Mel's life by cancelling next weekend, and how much worse his would be as a result? He'd a good mind to get her on the phone, tell her to get her backside over to Foxleigh and stop being so bloody self-ish. What did mere work matter compared to the agonies brought on by her thoughtlessness? And, to add insult to injury, she was now sitting on a cheque for five hundred big ones, cour-tesy of yours truly! Honestly, he could kick her, he really could.

Raising his hands in an exaggerated gesture, he slammed them down again, hard. Dust erupted from the chair arms in volcanic spurts. He took a long breath, letting the adrenaline rush subside, then sneezed as the dust reached his nostrils.

Right, that was that. All over. He hadn't meant a word of his internal tirade but it had done its work. The wire stretching between his shoulder blades melted away and his facial muscles relaxed. He got up out of the chair and went to sit down at his desk by the window.

He could never admit to Melody that a black cloud now hovered over his forthcoming weekend as well as hers. Someone had to strike a balance. Layla was such a sweet girl, and attractive, too. He'd go so far as to say she was beautiful. She was thoughtful and kind. No wonder Danni had been so fond of her.

Kindness was Layla's strength. It was also her downfall. Reece had fully expected the girl to stop coming to see them before now, for contact to dwindle to the odd phone call or email, then to a Christmas card, then to nothing at all. He'd prepared himself for it. He just wished Mel would see what was right in front of her and do the same.

Layla had her own life to live. It wasn't her fault – Reece flinched at this point – that Danni didn't. Even now it pained him physically to say his daughter's name, even inside his head. As for saying it out loud, especially in front of Mel, it wasn't happening. He wondered if Mel spoke her name in those sessions with her therapist. If so, the woman was favoured. She was a stranger, though, relatively speaking, so it didn't count.

Reece sat, hands behind his head, staring across the yard at the side of the house towards the wiry compound in which the hens wittered and scratched. Nearby was a blue-painted rabbit hutch, empty and silent. For a second Reece could almost believe he saw a furry white head with pink-lined ears emerge, as if to sniff the evening air. It wasn't a real rabbit. The original, live, occupant of the hutch had been a rather ugly grey rabbit called Smokey which had escaped, probably to meet a gruesome end. His daughter, with heart-squeezing perceptiveness beyond her nine years, had replaced it with the toy

because then, she said, she wouldn't have to face losing another
pet.

Tugging his gaze away, Reece dragged the pile of coursework towards him, found his mark sheet and opened the top
script. He peered at the writing which contained mainly
English, of a sort, with a smattering of the Greek alphabet
thrown in for added colour and confusion. At least with mathematics it was mainly figures he had to decipher; other lecturers
of this bunch of civil engineering students weren't so fortunate.

He had marked seven scripts when he caught muted sounds
coming from the kitchen; Melody, making tea. Wondering if she
would bring him a cup, he thought about what he might say to
her if she did. The time passed and she didn't come.

He couldn't pinpoint the moment when their roles had
reversed; the realisation had stolen up on him, unannounced.
At the beginning, he had clung to Melody, literally and figura-
tively. His need for her had raged through him like a forest fire,
but the flames could only lick the edges of the impervious
stronghold his wife had built around herself.

Denied access, devoid of the continued strength required to
break through the barrier, he had drawn back into himself,
removing himself as far as possible from her physical and
emotional presence; refurbishing the holiday lets had given him
reason. Then later, when Mel was ready and had turned to him,
seeking him out with the same kind of urgency, he couldn't
respond. It wasn't that he didn't want to. The moment had
passed. He simply didn't have it in him to give her what she
needed. Whether, subconsciously, he wanted to punish her, he
had never been able to work out. Not that he had tried; he was a
mathematician, not a psychologist. He would leave that one for
the experts.

His thoughts winged back to that night last summer; a night
of ringing phones, car headlights pooling on brickwork, lowered
eyes, thick-soled shoes scuffing politely at the doormat and tea

left to go cold. He remembered the smooth, cold feel of the steering wheel trapped beneath his hands, Melody in the passenger seat and the quaking shudder of her silent, dry-eyed sobs. He remembered raising a hand in greeting to the driver of the tractor they'd passed in the dawn-drenched lane, as if it were an ordinary morning. And he remembered that, on their return the following afternoon, they discovered they'd left the front door unlocked and the back door wide open. They'd quipped to one another about how lucky they were not to have been cleaned out, because there seemed nothing else to say.

He remembered all the tiny, unimportant things, but not the actual event, the culmination of the two-hundred-mile drive. In theory, the journey had been unnecessary because by the time they arrived, Layla had already formally identified her. The police had wanted to hurry things along. Layla was there; she was Danni's best friend.

But they had wanted to see her, even though the formalities had been completed. Of course they did; she was their daughter. To go away without seeing her would have felt like abandonment of the highest degree. In the end, having made their intentions clear, they were kept waiting for what seemed an extraordinary length of time, during which he felt he'd entered some kind of parallel universe. The woman who kept friendly guard on the bench beside them wore sparkly earrings, as if she'd forgotten to take them off after a night out; miniature silvery cascades that swung to and fro as she glanced up and down the grey corridor. The woman offered Melody her hand to hold. Melody had smiled unhappily and kept her hands firmly to her sides.

Reece remembered all these things but nothing of how it was, what he'd seen, once they were led inside the room; it had been wiped clean from his memory.

The television went on in the other room. The level tones of the newsreader brought Reece back to the present. If Melody

was waiting up for him, she was in for a disappointment; he had
at least a dozen pieces of coursework left to mark and he
planned to finish them tonight. Mentally kicking himself for the
mean thought but with no desire to retract it, he jotted a figure
in the mark box against the student's name on the sheet and
turned to the next script.

SIX

Morgan Hampshire stared out of the window at the churning waves and felt the familiar stab of anxiety. What was it about the sea that made people crazy to live within spitting distance of it? It was only a body of water, mostly empty of anything interesting.

It had been Kate's choice, this flat on the third floor of a sharp-edged block with nondescript double-glazed windows and aquamarine frosted glass balconies. He kind of understood why she liked it. Kate's family home was in Milton Keynes, and she'd lived in London for a fair amount of time; the sea view was a novelty for her. Morgan had been brought up in Suffolk, in a house literally yards from the beach – the ideal playground for a child. But for some reason he couldn't quite fathom, he really didn't like the seaside any more. He would much rather have moved somewhere inland – there were plenty of other places within reasonable distance of Kate's work – but he hadn't said anything because he loved her and wanted her to be happy.

Rivers, now they were different. There was nothing daunting about them. He liked rivers, especially the May, at Maybridge, for which he'd developed a slightly embarrassing fondness. The loft above the disused boathouse, its view of the river obscured only by willow fronds, was the only place he made any real progress with his writing.

There was something about the flat that deadened his creativity. Perhaps it was its bland, boxy shape, the constant stomping of the two blokes overhead, the agoraphobic view of endless sea, the perpetual shopping list pinned to the fridge by a heart-shaped magnet, or a combination of all these things. If Kate thought he was being pretentious, she kept it to herself.

Kate was a staff nurse in the mental health unit of the district general hospital, a few miles north of the town. Mostly she worked on the psychiatric wards, but now she'd qualified as a psychotherapist, she spent part of her week dealing with her own outpatient caseload.

Kate worked so hard. Her dedication outshone anything Morgan might accomplish, which was why it was a surprise when she'd peeked out one day from behind the edifice of her career and exhorted him to make a start on his own. Not his job in the bookshop nor other vague ideas that smouldered quietly in the background, but his ambition to be a writer.

And then she'd gone a step further, surprising him even more.

'Why don't you take a year out? Stop flogging books to other people and write your own? I'm earning enough for both of us. You owe it to yourself to give it your best shot, Morgan.'

Shoulders tense, eyes shiny with anticipation, it was as if she'd handed over a massively exciting Christmas present and couldn't wait for him to open it.

Morgan had been tempted, he couldn't deny that. A year to sit with his feet up – or under a desk, at any rate – and spend all day, every day, doing what made him happier than anything he'd ever done in his entire life. Apart from being with Kate, of course. What was there not to like? Well, being a kept man for a start. Kate didn't see it that way but Morgan did. The idea didn't sit easily with his conscience, or his pride. Besides, being – or trying to be – a writer was a lonely business. His job at the bookshop may not qualify as a lifetime's career, but he enjoyed it. He liked chatting to the customers about the books they'd come to buy; he liked tracking down the books they couldn't find on the shelves and the least amount of information they could provide, the better – it added to the thrill of the chase. He liked the other staff; well, most of them. He even liked the sheer physical toil of shifting and sorting crates of books, finding satisfaction in their final arrangement on the shelves.

After much debate, they'd reached a compromise. Morgan would reorganise his working hours to allow him two clear days off a week, Friday and Saturday, days he would dedicate to his writing. He'd known his manager would agree. Others had done it; a precedent for flexible working had been set. As for potentially busy Saturdays, he only worked one in three of those so getting people to fill in hadn't been a problem. If he wrote in the daytime, he and Kate would still have their evenings together, when she wasn't on duty. Kate had thought it was sweet of him to consider that aspect. Morgan had thought it was essential.

Much later, he began to wonder, probably unfairly, whether there was an element of wanting to be in control in Kate's offer to support him. It was hard not to think that way at times.

Three months on and already he felt like a con man. The book wasn't going well. After a decent spell of reading and meticulous research, he'd stopped procrastinating, taken a deep breath and faced the blank page. At first, the words had chugged out of his brain faster than his fingers could record them. And then he'd hit a number of problems, none of which he was anywhere close to solving. It happened, he knew that. Any writer would tell you. This wasn't first-hand knowledge since he didn't know any other writers – apart from his father, who wrote academic books on geology – but he'd built up a satisfying wodge of information from creative writing hand-books and the internet.

For reasons he couldn't now recall, he had thought his psychology degree would be useful for his writing. It wasn't long before he'd discovered that his limited understanding of the human condition was nowhere near enough to see him safely across the landmines of character and structure and plot. He had quickly learned that writing, for which he could quietly boast a certain talent, was one thing; writing a novel quite another.

Hopefully, his determination to crack this would see him through. Besides, he couldn't stop now, even if he wanted to. He was addicted. Writing had become a perpetual itch that demanded regular and thorough scratching.

It was Tuesday today, not one of his 'official' writing days, but he'd taken the week off as holiday and the luxury of the extra time stretched enticingly before him. Turning his attention back to the computer screen, he scrolled through the pathetically short distance to the end of the document and began to type. If he produced some words straight away, it was a usually a prelude to more words, whereas if he began by reading what he'd written previously it could be ages before he got going, if at all.

He'd added two hundred words to his latest chapter and was about to read them back to see if there was any danger of them moving the story on when the front door opened and banged shut again.

'I'm ill,' Kate announced, coming into the room and dropping onto the sofa. 'And before you say it, I know I shouldn't have even tried to go in.'

Morgan stared at her, momentarily baffled, until he remembered she'd said something this morning about feeling lousy. Through the thick wall of leftover sleep, he had registered the mention of a headache. Clearly he should have taken more notice, been more sympathetic. He watched her now, tearing impatiently at clips and elastic bands, finally releasing a frenzy of Titian curls that billowed out in a crazy halo before settling around her shoulders. Kate had so much hair. It got everywhere, on the carpets, in the plugholes, everywhere.

He got up from the desk and sat down beside her, cupping her face gently in both hands, turning her towards him. She looked paler than usual, yet her skin felt hot to his touch.

'Poor Kate. You do look awful. What do you need? Aspirin?'

'Took some before I left.' Extricating herself, she stood up. 'I'm dead on my feet and I ache all over. I'll go to bed, if that's all right with you.'

There was some kind of side to her tone, as if he'd done something wrong.

'Okay,' he said. 'I'll bring you some tea later.'

'Don't bother. I expect I'll crash out.'

The door closed decisively behind her.

Back at his desk, Morgan heard the muffled jangle of voices as the television went on in the bedroom. Daytime telly always sent Kate to sleep, she said.

He typed a few more sentences, read them through, deleted them, then leaned back in the chair, hands behind his head. After a while, his hand strayed to the bottom drawer of the desk and felt inside for the crumpled edges of a photo wallet. He brought it out and opened it, letting the small collection of photos fan out onto the desk. They'd been taken last December during a pre-Christmas visit to Suffolk to see his parents, who conveniently happened to be under the same roof at the time.

Separating the pictures with his thumb, he picked out the one he always looked at first, of him and Kate on the beach in front of the house, grinning, watery-eyed, at the camera while white-plumed waves whipped up behind them on a sea the colour of spat-out chewing gum, and ragged clouds chased across a threatening sky. Morgan's arm was round Kate's shoulder. She was leaning in, with both arms around him. The wind was grabbing her hair, whisking it into a frenzy below her green beret – the beret that moments later he had chased and eventually caught as it bowled towards the sand dunes.

Kate had doubled up with laughter, her hands on the knees of her cord trousers, and they'd carried on laughing as the wind grew even stronger. They'd clung to one another, struggling to stay upright as they staggered back to the house, his father and his partner crunching up the beach in front of them, his mother behind, hand-in-hand with hers.

They hadn't laughed like that since, not that Morgan could remember. To him, the photo was truly significant because it was of the old Kate, the Kate whose open face laid bare every nuance of every feeling she'd ever had. The Kate so full of love and life she made him dizzy. The Kate who, when he looked into her eyes, gave him his inner self reflected back.

Perhaps, Morgan thought, Kate had changed because nature and the passing of time decreed that she should; that this was how it was meant to be when you were firmly settled into life as a couple. It wasn't her fault that he had not changed along with her.

Without looking through the rest of the photos, he pushed them all back inside the wallet and replaced it in the drawer then, on impulse, got up from the desk and went to the bedroom. Tapping lightly on the door, he put his head round. The TV was still on, with the sound turned down. Kate was on her side, half lying down beneath the nautical-striped duvet, facing away from him. She had changed into an old grey T-shirt of his. She turned as she heard him.

'All right?' he asked.

'Yeah.' She smiled wearily.

'I was thinking, if you're better by then, I might go up to Maybridge on Friday instead of Saturday.'

'Of course. Go on Saturday as well if you want to. I'll be

asleep most of the day, anyway. I'm down for a shift Friday night, covering for Tracey.'

'Oh, okay. Sure?'

'It's cool. I said.'

Pleased, although slightly puzzled at the casual, almost disinterested, response, Morgan padded back to his desk. Kate had a problem with Tracey, said the reason she took so much time off was because she was such a dimwit at managing her personal life and if she was given an inch she would take a mile. So why was Kate, Tracey's senior, covering for her? And why had she not told him about the extra shift instead of waiting until he'd prompted it? It wasn't like her.

SEVEN

On Friday morning, Morgan parked in the potholed yard behind the riverside outbuildings and went to find his mate, Connor. There was no sign of him in the office, nor anywhere outside. He walked towards the little jetty and met Ted, Connor's grandfather, coming out of one of the outbuildings with a coil of rope over his shoulder.

The old man was Connor's closest relative, his parents having died in a road accident when he was twelve. He had family in Ireland who would gladly have given him a home but he hadn't wanted to go, so his grandparents had taken him in. Connor and Ted were close, as close as grandfather and grandson could be, and even more so since Connor's grandmother died five years ago.

Ted and Connor held the franchise of the riverside enterprise which included the pleasure boats, the café and gift shop and the kiosk which sold teas and ice creams, as well as issuing daily fishing permits and tickets for the river cruises.

The older man peeled a flattened roll-up from his lips and raised a hand in greeting.

'Hey, Morgan. Good to see you. Con's taken *Princess*

Delilah out. Got a load of Spanish kids on board. He was well chuffed.'

Morgan grinned. 'Tell him I'll do a turn later.'

Ted tapped the side of his nose. 'Keep your head down till this afternoon, I would, lad. The kids'll have gone and it'll be all creaking old dears filling in time between their lunches and their cream teas. Nice and quiet, like.'

The old man went to walk away, then stopped and turned back to Morgan. 'I'll stand you a pint in the Swan, lunchtime, if you're about. Be good for you to meet some of the locals. Game of darts, too, if you like.'

'Thanks, but I'll be busy. Another time,' Morgan said.

He gave Ted a cheery wave and headed along the path towards the boathouse.

It had been a close run thing, getting to Maybridge today. Kate's illness had turned out to be quite a virulent bug and she'd stayed in bed all of Wednesday and most of yesterday until she'd emerged, whey-faced, around six and said she thought she could eat something. He'd fed her pasta and ice cream, neither of which she finished, and they'd had a quiet night in front of the telly.

Not wanting to seem too eager to get away, he'd casually asked if she planned to go to work today, as if it didn't matter to him one way or the other. She'd looked at him as if he was mad. Of course, she said, and she'd be doing the double shift. She couldn't let Tracey down.

Oh no, we mustn't let Tracey down, Morgan had felt like saying. He had no idea why he felt resentful because he'd really wanted to come up here today. Perhaps it was because she'd made it so easy for him.

Heaving the plastic container of water from the floor, he filled the kettle and threw the switch, then set up the laptop on the old trestle table in front of the window which served as a desk. The laptop blinked into life and the page sprung up, giving him his constant companion – a middle-aged, spectacle-wearing man whom he'd named Poodle Chafferty.

Poodle was a private investigator – the nickname derived from the large, woolly brown dog that was his constant and devoted companion. He hadn't so far given the dog a name, nor had he revealed his master's real one, deliberate omissions which, Morgan considered, added a nice touch of mystery. Sometimes he pretended the dog was his and was right there beside him whenever he took a walk along the riverbank in search of fresh inspiration. Kate would think he was mad if she knew. Quite possibly, she'd be right.

Kate. His mind drifted back to the first time he met her. It was the year before last, July. He and a bunch of university mates had been in Brighton celebrating their graduation. Kate was there on a hen weekend. The two groups had converged on the bumper cars on the pier at the same time. Somehow, he and Kate had found themselves jammed together in the last available car. She had wrested the wheel from his grasp as they slewed around the track, forcing a crash at every obstacle. The girls shrieked and the boys jeered at one another while the poles sparked a manic light show above their heads.

A shred of pink candy floss had been stuck in her hair. The sugary smell of it, combined with the hot, oily smell of the cars, was intoxicating stuff. It seemed the most natural thing in the world for his arm to sneak around her bare shoulders. And there it stayed for the rest of the day and long into the night, until he left her on the steps of her hotel, which was when he'd kissed her.

He felt inexplicably sad, remembering. He reached for his phone, intending to send her a text but he couldn't think what to say. Besides, she'd be busy and unlikely to read it, let alone text back. Unlike him, Kate wasn't prone to distraction; she couldn't very well be, given the nature of her work. He should leave her alone to get on with her day.

He shouldn't be thinking about Kate, anyway. Not now, not here. The boathouse wasn't about Kate, or about life in the flat in Haverstone. Sometimes the boathouse was about Connor or Ted, or the benign troupes of river trippers, or the soft green edges of the small, landlocked city. But mostly it was about Morgan himself. The boathouse was his space, his time, his chance to do something worthwhile with his life, and he mustn't waste it.

Despite the internal pep talk, he didn't feel like starting work yet. He made a mug of tea and drank it, then sat with his elbows on the makeshift desk and gazed through the smudged window at the river. He liked the way the water changed colour, from olive green to navy blue and pewter, always slicked with silver. Today, with the sky dull overhead and rain clouds banked up behind the cathedral spire, it was a gleaming khaki. A light wind parted the reeds on the opposite bank and a pair of moorhens emerged, circling on the water before busily paddling away.

Watching the river soothed him, as it always did. Feeling more settled in his mind, he turned back to the laptop and began to type.

Kate wasn't in when he got home around five. He hadn't expected her to be – when she worked a double shift she usually ate in the hospital canteen and crashed out in the staff room – but the flat felt empty and forlorn and he wished she was there.

Dumping his laptop on the table, he took out his phone and sent her a message:

How are you feeling? xxx.

The reply came back almost immediately:

OK. x.

She must be on her break.

He waited for another message to appear. Sometimes she sent a second, longer one, as if she'd just remembered something she wanted to say. Nothing came. Perhaps he shouldn't go up to Maybridge again tomorrow. She had only said she was okay, not fine or much better. She would need to sleep after the night shift. He could stay around and do some work here, make her a nice meal for later. But Kate wouldn't expect that. She seemed to need so little from him.

Morgan woke the next morning to the sound of the loo flushing, then the gush of the shower. Rolling out of bed, he padded to the bathroom.

'Hi.'

'Oh, hi.'

She seemed almost surprised to see him. She peeled off her knickers and dropped them in the laundry bin. Her badge and nurse's watch were on the bathroom shelf, the rest of her clothes slung over the edge of the bath.

Shooting him a provocative smile, she stepped into the shower cubicle. 'Coming in?'

'Yeah.'

Morgan flashed a smile back, already half out of his boxers. He'd hardly closed the door of the cubicle when she pulled him to her, locking her body against his and engaging him in a deep, ferocious kiss that sent a great surge of desire through him. His mouth moved down her neck, across her shoulder, then to her breasts, his tongue finding her nipples, until she pushed his head away and raised herself up against the wall of the cubicle, her body undulating beneath his, while the powerful jet of the shower cascaded down.

Minutes later, they collapsed together onto the floor of the cubicle in a slippery tangle of limbs.

'Wow,' Kate said breathlessly.

He smiled, and scrambled to his feet, pulling her up after him, feeling pleased that she still had the capacity to surprise him, that they could still surprise each other. He stepped out of the cubicle, leaving the door open.

'Kate?'

'What?'

'Nothing, doesn't matter.'

She paused, frowning, the shampoo bottle tilted in her hand. 'No, go on. What were you going to say?'

Morgan pulled a towel from the rail. 'I love you. That's all.'

She gave him a look he couldn't interpret. 'Me too.'

The cubicle door closed with a quiet click.

EIGHT

Climbing the external wooden staircase of the boathouse, Morgan noticed a piece of paper flapping on the door of the loft. Unpinning it, he unlocked the door and went inside, reading as he went. It was a note from Connor asking if he would take out *Lady Tabitha* at two o'clock.

The boats didn't run during the winter months, but the beginning of March brought the annual arts festival to Maybridge and the influx of visitors made it the ideal time for the season to begin. Early April, and already business was starting to pick up, despite the chill in the air.

It had been Morgan's idea to help out. Neither Connor nor Ted expected it of him, but he wouldn't have felt comfortable using the loft and not giving anything in return. Besides, he enjoyed taking the helm of the little cruise boats and gliding along the river with a mixed bag of expectant tourists on board. It reminded him of an idyllic summer he'd spent with relatives in Devon after A levels, when he'd divided his time between surfing with his cousins and helping to operate the ferry across the river. Connor had been working there at the time; that was how they'd met.

Footsteps sounded on the stairs and Connor appeared. Standing at over six feet, Connor had to duck his head to avoid collision with the doorframe.

'Not interrupting, am I?' He glanced at the laptop, saw it was still closed. 'Not, then. All right for this after?'

'Yeah, no worries.'

Glancing down, Morgan saw that Connor had a paintbrush in his hand and his elderly combats were splashed with bright blue. Connor held up the brush.

'I could give you a bit of this as well, if you like. Got a couple of rowing boats in the shed wanting a makeover.'

Morgan laughed. 'I think I'll pass, if it's all the same.'

Connor looked serious for a moment, lowering his eyes and running a hand through the black wavy hair that fell almost to shoulder-length.

'Grandad had another dizzy turn yesterday so I took the painting off him. I had to hide the tin. He's such a stubborn old fool.'

'I've noticed. Seriously, though, I could do a bit of painting if it would help.'

'No, you're all right. Just *Tabitha*, if you wouldn't mind. There's a party of ten booked, for a kid's birthday. It's a one-way trip. They'll be getting out at the zoo.'

Bookings in advance for the cruise boats weren't usually necessary, but sometimes people booked if they wanted to be sure of seats at a certain time. The little zoo, which contained mainly domestic animals, a children's play area and an animal-themed restaurant which hosted birthday parties, was the last stopping point on the forty-minute trips. Before that, the river wound its way past a row of Elizabethan cottages mentioned in the guidebooks, the sloping gardens of a Georgian manor house and a Victorian rope factory now housing an art gallery and a warren of artisans' workshops.

There was a fine view of the cathedral from the river, much

painted by local artists. Other than that it was mostly trees, water meadows and wildlife. The gasps and little shrieks when the punters spotted a family of ducklings or the velvety back of a water vole made Morgan smile.

At half past one, he set off for the jetty. Nipping aboard *Lady Tabitha* to check that all was in order, he collected an empty Coke can and a couple of chocolate wrappers from beneath the seats, slung on the canvas bag in which the tickets were collected, and stepped off the boat to wait.

Before long, a sizeable group appeared round the side of the kiosk, obviously the party Connor mentioned. Heading the group was a shortish, middle-aged woman in a black trouser suit, her bright blonde hair neatly pinned up. She held aloft a blue balloon with ears and a bear's face, across which it said: 'Birthday Boy!'

There were three young lads among the group, one of whom was presumably the boy in question. The kids jostled one another as they went, yelling at the tops of their voices. Morgan hoped they'd quieten down a bit when they were on the boat; there were two old women with identical Brillo-pad hair waiting by the rope now, as well as a family with three stoical children and an earnest-looking couple in matching anoraks and serious walking shoes. The couple exchanged dubious glances with the women as the jetty began to fill up with the rest of the birthday party.

'Finn, and you others, for Pete's sake keep away from the water! We don't want no accidents, not today.'

The woman who had spoken was a younger version of the one with the balloon. She wore skin-tight jeans and heels destined to vanish down the cracks between the planks the moment she set foot on board. Beside her slouched a resigned-looking bloke with a buzzcut and a nose stud, followed by a fresh-faced skinny guy holding hands with another petite blonde wearing denim shorts over black tights and a pink filmy blouse with a black bra underneath.

'I thought we'd be closed in. It's gonna be freezing.' She gave *Lady Tabitha* a scathing look, shaking her head. 'Nightmare.'

'I'll keep you warm, babe.' The skinny guy gathered her up in a bear hug and moved in for a quick snog.

'I wanna sit up front with the driver!' yelled one of the boys.

'You'll sit where you're put, Finn,' the older woman said, in a firm but kind voice.

'It's my birthday and I'm eight. I can sit where I want.'

The boy scowled, unhooked the rope that guarded the gangplank and began swinging it round in circles, making his two mates squeal with excitement as they tried to wrestle the rope from him.

Morgan reached for it and returned it to the hook.

'It's all right.' He smiled at the woman in the heels who appeared to be Finn's mother. 'Overexcited, I expect.'

'Overexcited? I'll give him overexcited in a minute.'

She looked Morgan up and down appreciatively, as if she'd only just noticed him, then smiled provocatively, tossing back her long blonde hair and flashing china-blue eyes at him. Buzz-Cut immediately stepped up to stand close to her.

Morgan smiled back, then cleared his throat. 'Right then. Everyone aboard.'

He turned to the older woman who was holding out a bunch of tickets. 'Is this all of you?'

'Yes. No. Hang on.' She scanned the jetty as the others pushed past her, and past the women, the couple, and the other family, to bag seats in the covered part of the boat. 'Where are they? Where's Layla?'

'She's taken Nan to the loo, Mum,' the girl in shorts shouted back. 'Here they come.'

Morgan waited, looking round to check that the kids were under control, then stooped down to retrieve a ticket that had missed the bag and gone under the steps. When he stood up, he found himself facing a small, elderly woman with a determined expression and, linked to her by a supportive arm, the most beautiful girl he had ever seen.

NINE

Layla pulled the tray of rosemary sauté potatoes towards her and spooned portions onto three plates of lamb cutlets and creamed spinach. Finishing them with a whirl of redcurrant sauce, she wiped the rims of the plates clean and lifted them onto the service counter.

Out of the corner of her eye she saw Big Barry, the head chef, checking the plates over before giving a satisfied little nod. Layla allowed herself to breathe. That should be the last, thank God. The clamour of the kitchen had simmered down to a tired buzz.

Glancing round to check that Barry wasn't watching, Layla slipped out of the kitchen and along the passage to the airless box that passed for the staff room. She opened her locker and felt in her coat pocket for the note. Crumpled from so much handling, the small square of paper felt as insubstantial and meaningless as a bus ticket. She smoothed it out and read its brief content for the hundredth time. *Would you give me a call some time?* it said, then gave a mobile number and his name, *Morgan Hampshire.*

Nothing had been said, not a word exchanged apart from

his half-whispered 'Bye then' as she and the rest of her family had piled off the boat at the zoo.

He might have been saying goodbye to everyone. He might have. But he wasn't. He was speaking to her alone, as if they knew one another already, which she almost felt they did. Then, as he'd helped her unnecessarily up the steps and onto the jetty, he had pressed the note into her hand with an awkward smile in answer to her questioning look.

Was it some kind of game he played, a joke? Did he keep a supply of similar notes and hand them out to any passable female to see what would happen, like sending a message to sea in a bottle? If so, he knew exactly what he could do with it.

That had been her first thought; she'd soon dismissed it. He didn't seem the type to get off on that kind of behaviour. Her rapid summing up told her he was too quiet, too unassuming. And the note itself, with its polite question was, Layla felt, an indicator that this wasn't something he did often, and possibly never had before.

She'd been drawn to him – it was useless trying to deny it. He was tall – five-ten? – and slim but with a solid strength about him. Mid-brown hair, shortish at the back and sides, longer on top. Blue-grey eyes, kind of almond-shaped. Ridiculously long, curled lashes, for a bloke. Not that she had looked closely, not for more than a second, anyway; she'd long ago trained herself out of that.

She wasn't going to call him, no question about it. No good could come of it; she had proved that. Several times she'd taken the note out with the intention of throwing it away. Each time, something stopped her. There was an unusual twist, an ambiguity about the whole thing that intrigued her, and no matter how hard she tried not to think about it – about him – her mind kept switching pointlessly back.

'What've you got there?' Seth asked, coming up behind her.

Layla drew in breath. 'D'you have to creep about?'

'Not creeping anywhere, my little fruit bat. Wondered where you'd got to, that's all. Big Barry's wondering, too.'

Bang on cue, the head chef's voice thundered down the corridor. 'Lay-laa!'

'Make him wait,' Seth said. 'Give.'

He held out his hand. Obediently Layla dropped the note into it and watched with a sinking feeling as Seth's face lit up.

'Morgan Hampshire. Is that a human being or an investment bank?'

'Very funny.'

Layla reached for the note. Seth waved it in the air, out of her reach.

'Who is he, and why don't I know about him?'

'Because there's nothing to know.'

Seth was waiting, his patient expression in place, the one that said he would wait all night if he had to so she might as well tell him now. And so she did, what little there was to tell, minus the bit about her instant attraction to Morgan. She also said she had no intention of doing anything about it.

She went to turn away. Seth put a hand on her arm. 'There's a whole world full of blokes out there. You can't avoid them all. You can't cut that part of your life away permanently, pretend it doesn't exist.'

'We have to get back,' Layla said, shaking him off.

Reaching into the locker, she pretended to straighten the sleeve of her coat to avoid looking at Seth. He touched her arm and held out the note. She took it wordlessly, stuffed it into her coat pocket and locked the metal door.

She would have been content to let the silence linger as they left the staff room and headed back to the kitchen, but Seth, never one to waste a good chatting opportunity, moved on to familiar territory.

'Are you off to the Morland Mansion on Saturday?'

'It's not a mansion, it's a farmhouse. And no, I'm not.'

'Not? Blimey, that's a first. Do they know?'

'Yes, I rang Melody this morning and told her I was working.'

'No text, eh? I'm seriously impressed.'

'I owed her that, at least. I hated lying to her, though.'

'How did she take it?'

'Okay, actually. She was cool about it.' Layla frowned, as if her own answer surprised her.

'There you are, then. That wasn't so hard, was it?'

Layla shrugged and walked on ahead, into the kitchen. Seth didn't need to know about the three missed calls from Melody that had come through on her mobile.

Easter had come and gone, and Haverstone was rapidly coming to life with the start of the holiday season. The shops in the small town centre had shifted the basic necessities aside in favour of local scenic prints, Haverstone pottery and boxes of fudge. The bed-and-breakfasts were starting to turn a profit, and chilly campers occupied the caravans up on the clifftop site.

What you saw with Haverstone was precisely what you got – a relentlessly efficient holiday machine with hotels, pubs and cafés at every hundred paces, themed playgrounds for the kids, a swimming pool, crazy golf, and deckchairs on the prom for the less energetically inclined.

The beach, Morgan always thought, must turn out to be something of a disappointment to some when they discovered that the fawn-gold stretch of what appeared to be sand in the distant tourist brochure shots was, in fact, entirely shingle. Not that it stopped them packing onto it in all weathers.

Morgan strode down the main street that led towards the seafront, deliberately averting his gaze from the stretch of sea that was visible between the buildings. It was only ten past nine and the air felt pleasantly astringent against his skin. At this time on a Friday, he'd usually be well into his writing, but this morning he was on an errand. Over his arm in an awkward bundle hung Kate's green duffle coat which she'd asked him to take to a certain dry cleaner's before the half price end-of-season offer ran out.

The purposeful way she'd cut the voucher out of the paper with the nail scissors had struck a discordant note, reminding him of his status as second-fiddle breadwinner. The feeling was entirely down to his own stupid pride, of course. Kate would never knowingly make him feel that way, any more than he would have done when he'd supported her throughout her psychotherapy course.

They were living in a glorified bedsit in south London at the time – their first home together. Having given up his own post-graduate course because he'd lost sight of its purpose, he had taken a job as a warehouseman. It had suited him very well; it built up his muscles without his having to set foot inside a gym and left his mind free to indulge in dreams of literary stardom.

Standing in the dry cleaner's shop, waiting his turn, an image came to him of the girl from the boat, the girl who had mesmerised him so completely that he'd gone right ahead and handed her his number with no qualms, and no guilt whatsoever. He couldn't even claim it was a spur of the moment act of madness. During the forty-minute river trip he'd thought of nothing but her, sneaking as many backward glances at her beautiful face as he dared while his mind went into freefall.

What had he been thinking? Not of the danger, certainly, nor the possible consequences.

He clutched Kate's coat to him, folding the familiar woolly material between his fingers as if by doing so he could wipe away his betrayal. Kate deserved so much better.

He was at the counter now. Letting out a slow breath, he deliberately turned his thoughts to his novel while the female assistant spread Kate's coat out on the counter and examined it with a concentrated frown, as if she was searching for forensic evidence.

Poodle Chafferty had apparently had enough of languishing on the page while Morgan laboured over the plot and had begun to steam ahead with the action of his own accord. Naturally, the guy would need a little direction – he couldn't be allowed to have things all his own way – but there was a promising feel about it. He began to write the next chapter in his head. He was looking forward to getting home and banging out the first rough draft, then tomorrow at the boathouse he would knock it into shape.

His escape to Maybridge this week had become a done deal when Kate had announced her intention to visit her parents in Milton Keynes. 'Going home' was how she always referred to it, as if the flat was a temporary stopover. It annoyed him slightly. He'd never taken her up on it; he would only be subjected to a long-winded rationalisation that he'd be expected to understand at once. That was the thing about Kate. Everything she did had a reason. Sometimes his life seemed purposeless in comparison.

'That your mobile?' The assistant nodded towards Morgan as she passed over the ticket for the coat. Smiling his thanks, he pulled the phone absently from his pocket as he left the shop, his mind half on his plot and half on Kate. He answered without looking at the screen.

'Yep?'

'Is that... Morgan?' a female voice said. 'It's... I'm Layla. From the boat?'

He almost dropped the phone. Fumbling with it like an inept juggler, he stepped back into the shop doorway and briefly closed his eyes.

'Are you there?'

'Yes, I'm here.'

'You did mean me to ring? That's what the note said, right?'

She sounded almost accusing. He felt wrong-footed; he'd

convinced himself she'd simply screwed up the note and dropped it into the nearest litter bin.

He thought about Kate, deliberately pulling an image of her towards him, but she slipped away, vanishing into the brickwork like an apparition.

'Yes, that's what it said.' An uncontrollable grin spread across his face. 'It's just that I didn't expect... You took me by surprise.'

'Look, I'm at work. I haven't got long. What was it you wanted?'

Morgan opened his mouth and closed it again. A woman pushed past him in the doorway, tutting as she entered the shop. He stepped out into the street, pressing the phone to his ear against the roar of a motorbike.

'Traffic. Sorry,' he said, playing for time.

He could hardly change his mind now, tell her he'd made a mistake, could he? Now it seemed he was about to make an even bigger one. Dodging into a quieter side street, he stood with his back against the darkened window of a closed antique shop.

'I'd thought perhaps we could meet up. Bad idea, though, probably.' He attempted a laugh.

'You did ask me to ring so presumably you didn't think it was such a bad idea at the time,' she said, though less brusquely than before.

'Yes. I mean, no.' He tried to gather his scattered wits. 'What I mean is, I'd really like to talk to you.'

'Talk?'

'Yes.'

'I'm not in the market for a relationship, or anything like that.' Her voice carried a heavy note of warning. 'You need to understand that.'

'I do, and it's fine.'

'But do you? Understand? Because if you think...'

'Yes, yes, I do. I get it. Totally,' Morgan said, wondering if he'd ever 'got' anything in his whole life.

What the hell had he thought he was doing, writing that stupid note and passing it over discreetly as if they were twelve-year-olds in the middle of a maths lesson? And why, if she was suspicious about his intentions – and who wouldn't be? – had she bothered to respond? She must already think he was a nutjob. Morgan listened to the silence at the other end of the phone, a silence that seemed to go on for ever. The phone felt huge in his hand, swollen with its own importance.

'Okay,' she said eventually. 'Let's do it. Let's meet up.'

TEN

Layla walked along the river path, veering left and right to avoid the Saturday morning procession of kids on bikes. The wind swooshed through the trees, ripping apart the ragged curtains of the willows, pitting the surface of the brown water and ruffling the feathers of a pair of swans sailing along with the flow. Her hands were buried in the pockets of her hooded top, the zip pulled right up to her chin. She wished she'd worn her parka instead.

It was an omen, the grey, cold day. She shouldn't be doing this. It was all wrong. It wasn't too late to turn around and make a run for it. He wouldn't be able to contact her; at least she'd had the presence of mind to phone him from the anonymity of the hotel reception.

He hadn't been as she'd expected on the phone. Without an audience – she'd assumed he was alone when he took her call – she'd expected a line of well-versed patter, a confident spiel designed to have her eating out of his hand. Instead, the awkward, clipped conversation had turned everything on its head and she'd ended up feeling as if she was the one doing the asking. As a result, she'd been unintentionally curt, but it hadn't seemed to put him off.

Nervous as hell she might be, but there was an element of challenge in what she was doing. Whether she was challenging herself or him, wasn't clear.

She reached the café and the kiosk. The two pleasure cruisers were moored by the jetty, a string of rowing boats rocking on the water behind them. The café was busy but the kiosk was deserted; the boats wouldn't be doing much business on a day like this. The path curved, following the bend in the river. Layla walked on and suddenly, right in front of her, was the boathouse he'd described.

At some point in its past the building with its A-shaped roof had been painted white, but was now weathered to silver-grey. The bare dark wood showed through in places where the paint had peeled away in ragged folds, like skin after sunburn. A life-belt, once red, now faded to a muddy pink, hung loosely from the wall by a fraying rope. The door to the boat storage area had slipped in its frame so that one corner dipped into the water; it looked as if it hadn't been opened in years.

Stopping on the path a short distance from the boathouse, she looked up at the row of blue-framed windows for signs of movement but saw only the swaying branches of the trees reflected in the darkened glass. The place seemed deserted.

Then a door opened on the upper storey and there he was, beckoning her towards the steps. 'Hey, come on up.'

Layla crossed the patchy grass and stopped by the steps. Morgan smiled down at her, rubbing his chin. He looked pleased to see her, but a little uncertain, as if, now she was here, he didn't quite know what to do with her.

She swallowed her own nerves and helped him out. 'The café, you said?'

'The café, yes. I'm not quite ready, though.'

Layla walked up the steps, feeling the treads bow slightly

under her weight. In other circumstances, she would have suggested that she wait at the bottom, but Morgan's quietly unassuming manner told her there was no need for caution; or if there was, it was a risk she was prepared to take.

The loft was more spacious than she'd imagined from the outside. The white paint on the walls was intact, if a bit scuffed and grubby in places. Rush matting covered part of the bare wood floor. A trestle table was set up in front of the window overlooking the river. It held a laptop, pens and a notebook. An old-fashioned leather-seated office chair sat in front of the table. The rest of the furnishings consisted of a small cupboard with a kettle and tea things on top, and a taller cupboard in the corner with layers of newspaper wedged underneath the front, presumably to keep it from toppling forwards. There was also a large plastic container of water and some kind of oil heater, and a rusty drawing pin secured an old calendar to the wall above the cupboard, its yellowing pages curling at the edges.

Morgan stood quietly, allowing her time to make her inspection before he marched up to the table, spun round and flung out his arms.

'Welcome to my humble abode. Not literally, of course,' he said, seeing her questioning smile. 'There isn't much scope for abiding, as you can see. I'm up here a couple of days a week, weekends usually. Working.'

He nodded towards the open laptop. She wasn't sure if he was inviting her to take a look, but she did anyway. While he seemed a bit embarrassed, he didn't try to stop her.

'It's a story,' she said, looking up from the screen. 'Your story? You're a writer?'

'Well, yeah.' Morgan turned a bit pink and shuffled his feet. 'It's kind of what I do here. At least that's the theory.'

'Are you famous?'

Well, he could be. Layla felt defensive in the face of Morgan's laughter. Lots of famous authors wrote in all kinds of odd places, including squalid little sheds. Not that this was squalid, just basic, and sort of cosy, despite its bareness. She could see the appeal.

'It's nice in here,' she said, deliberately changing the subject. 'I like it.'

'Do you? Good. So do I.' Morgan rubbed his hands together and smiled.

'Yeah. Smells a bit funny, though.'

She wrinkled her nose.

'It's linseed oil, from the boats. Still hangs about. I smelt it when I first came but now I don't. I've got used to it, I suppose.'

He explained that the loft had been used in the past as the office for the boatyard, before the owners of the site developed it into a tourist attraction and put up a new office next to the café.

'Which is where we're heading now, right?'

It was starting to bother her slightly that he was making no move to leave, other than to shut down the computer and pick up his wallet. She didn't know him, did she? The open face, the expressive eyes, the ready smile, they were all surface dressing. And yet the more she tried to dredge up an element of self-preservation and remind herself of the stupidity of coming alone to this hidden place on this hidden part of the river to meet a strange man without telling a single soul, the more reassured she felt. He was all right, this Morgan. She didn't know how she knew that. She just did.

The room darkened. The sky beyond the window had turned to charcoal grey, the piling clouds a dramatic shade of purple.

'It's coming on to rain,' Morgan observed unnecessarily, as the first fat drops hit the window.

He cast a concerned eye over her. 'You're not wearing much.'

'I'll be fine. We can make a run for it.'

They both turned to look out as the rain suddenly pounded

the window, rattling the glass. It cascaded through the trees and sleeted down on the river, a mini-monsoon.

'Or, we could stay here. I have tea, I have milk, I have sugar. I even have biscuits.'

He opened the cupboard, brought out a round tin and held it up. It had toy soldiers on it.

'Yes,' Layla said, nodding. 'Tea sounds good. Thanks.'

Morgan switched the kettle on. It crackled into life, loud in the sparse surroundings. Layla sat down in the office chair – the only chair there was – and swivelled gently to and fro while she watched, with some amusement, Morgan's attempts to drop teabags into mugs without missing the mugs altogether. There was a tension in his shoulders, a sudden shyness in his smile as he stood, arms folded, waiting for the water to boil.

'You don't look very comfortable on that,' he said, regarding her appraisingly as if she was an exhibit in a gallery. He held up a forefinger. 'Tell you what...'

Turning on his heel, he went to the tall cupboard in the corner. It rocked as he opened the door. He put out a hand to steady it and dragged out a green and orange checked blanket, unfolded it and shook it out, sprinkling the floorboards with dust and a tobacco-like mix of dead grass and leaves. Spreading the blanket carefully over the rush matting in the middle of the room, he looked at Layla for approval.

'Picnic?'

Smiling, she got out of the chair and sat down, cross-legged, on the blanket. She watched Morgan make the tea while the room filled with a peculiar half-light and the hammering rain drowned out the sound of the rushing river.

It had seemed less like a picnic and more like a weird tea-drinking ritual as Morgan had sat facing her, mirroring her cross-legged position, two chipped mugs in front of them and the toy-soldier biscuit tin placed dead centre on the blanket.

They had talked about home and family, school and university, work, and Morgan's writing. They'd discovered a shared taste in books and, to a lesser extent, music. Talking about travel and holidays, they'd realised with exaggerated delight that they'd both been in Spain in the same week in August two years ago, Morgan in Barcelona, Layla in Benidorm. Layla told him she'd love to work in a New York kitchen, in a proper high-end restaurant – Candy, an American friend from her course at uni, had given her the idea and it had crystallised into a real ambition.

At some point in the conversation she'd learned that Morgan had a girlfriend and that she was called Kate. He'd thrown the name in a couple of times without making a big deal out of it. He wouldn't have needed to; clearly, he had taken in what she'd said on the phone about not wanting a relationship and she was grateful for that. The faint dip of disappointment she'd felt on learning of the existence of Kate was automatic, and as such, easy to ignore.

But in the midst of the conversation, something indefinable had happened; a kind of connection had grown between them, an extension, perhaps, of what had happened on the boat. She'd felt it in the boathouse, rising like smoke through the easy chat and laughter. She felt it now as she walked back along the riverbank, holding a shabby old black umbrella that Morgan had found in the cupboard and insisted she take, even though the rain had almost stopped by the time she'd left.

She'd imagined it, of course. The peacefulness of the boathouse, its scenic setting, the sense of isolation and the thunderous skies had all conspired to create an air of intimacy as they'd sat enclosed in a half-lit world that extended no further than the edge of a picnic rug.

Clearly, she was overthinking this. Morgan was a nice guy

whom she happened to strike up a rapport with, that was all. He might be a genuinely good person whose intentions were, as Mum would put it, entirely honourable, if a touch off-kilter. Or, bringing the girlfriend into the equation, he might not.

Well, it didn't matter either way because she wouldn't be seeing him again; the risk was too great. Already she had pushed herself a stage too far by agreeing to meet him in the first place. It may have been the start of a beautiful friendship – an unusual start, remembering the way they'd met – but friendship, nevertheless. And that was fine, if that was the way it turned out.

The problem was that as they'd sat in the boathouse loft and talked about innocuous things, she'd felt the protective layers she'd built up so carefully beginning to lift away, threatening to leave her raw and exposed, and receptive, potentially, to the kind of feeling that could turn the world around in a heartbeat.

The kind of feeling she'd experienced with Harvey. The kind of feeling she would never have again, because she wouldn't let it happen.

ELEVEN

Harvey was a sportsman. Football, cycling, running, surfing, skiing – when he could afford it – and rugby, especially rugby, the numerous scars of which he bore with martyred pride. He couldn't get enough of it. And he couldn't get enough of Layla.

They'd met at the university Freshers' Fair, held in a marquee on the campus. She was about to enter her final year and he was one of a group of newly-enrolled sports science students queuing noisily at the desk where Layla was helping to hand out free condoms and leaflets on sexual health, something he reminded her of incessantly and with great merriment during the course of their intense eight-month relationship.

Harvey had a great sense of humour, a bit juvenile, and definitely twisted at times, but he made her laugh and she liked that. That and his overtly handsome blond looks, his unbelievably perfect body, and the things he did to hers that made her feel as if she'd died and gone to heaven. He wasn't her type, he wasn't her age – he was two years younger – and on the face of it they had nothing in common. He was, however, impossible to resist, and Layla didn't even try.

By the end of that winter, she had her own collection of

rugby scars. Shivering on the touchline with a clutch of other girls most Wednesday and Saturday afternoons, she acquired a hoarseness of voice from all the shouting, thread veins on her cheeks from the cold wind and a permanent cough that developed into full-blown bronchitis at least once every six weeks. But she didn't care about any of that because Harvey Donohue was, if not the love of her life, then a very close runner.

Apart from Harvey, the person Layla spent most of her time with was Danni Morland, a student on the English and journalism course. Thrown together on the same corridor in the scuffed 1960s block – the first-year halls of residence – they had spent their first week consoling and commiserating, and cooking up massive amounts of comfort food in the kitchen they shared with four other new students. And then they had come round to thinking that perhaps it wasn't going to be that awful after all, and they'd gone out and started having fun.

In their second year, they moved out of halls and into a gloomy maisonette in a converted, crumbling Victorian villa, where they shared a vast bedroom and stuffed newspaper up the chimney and into the window frames to keep out the cold. The modernised terraced house they shared in their final year with three other students, all male, felt luxurious in comparison. They had a bedroom each, proper heating and a well-equipped kitchen which mostly they had to themselves; the boys merely passed through in order to empty the cereal packets, or pinch all the forks for mammoth takeaways that stank the place out for days afterwards.

The summer term began, their last, and already their lives were changing. A low- level sense of panic hiked into being and rose to a crescendo when the exam timetables were published. Layla and Danni looked at the screen, then at each other, thinking the same thing. This was real; it was happening, whether they were ready or not.

They weren't. Layla's practical cookery exams were out of

the way but there was a mass of revision to get through for the theory exams. Still, as long as she put in the hours and struck lucky with the questions, she should be just about okay. Danni, though, seemed to have a death wish where finals were concerned. She hadn't read half the books she was supposed to for her English course – according to her, anyway – and crammed them in, night after night, in hugely indigestible chunks. By day, she tackled the rest of her revision in frenetic bursts of energy which did her no good at all, because it was never long before she was off the case and onto one of an entirely different nature: a geography student called Nathan.

Danni's unrelenting major crush on this guy had sustained a fatal blow when, after several dates and one ill-judged night of passion, he dropped her without warning or explanation. Danni was distraught – unnaturally so, in Layla's opinion. It wasn't like her to be so upset over a bloke, especially one she'd known for such a short time. Her calls and messages unanswered, Danni made regular reccies of Nathan's favourite haunts, hoping to bump into him, but she never did. Layla was secretly glad. Rumour had it that Nathan had moved on and was busily souring the atmosphere behind the campus library loans desk while he worked his way through the coterie of young, pretty assistants.

Danni refused to believe a word of it; nor did she lose faith. Nathan was working his way up to asking her to take him back, she'd said, plucking another tissue from the box beside her bed. Arguing was pointless, even though there was no evidence to support Danni's theory. Layla could only pray that Danni's priorities shuffled themselves into the right order before any serious damage was done. Meanwhile, she did all a friend could do by way of offering distraction and comfort, and an endlessly listening ear, even though her patience had begun to wear thin in the end.

Unfortunately for Danni, Nathan was not her only problem; there was obviously some sort of ongoing argument with her parents at the time. Layla didn't know the details because, unusually for Danni, she refused to talk about it. She only knew that Danni had returned from a weekend visit half a day early with a slam of the front door and an exaggerated cheerleader bounce, switched on the exact moment she set eyes on Layla. It was impossible to miss, too, the unprecedented number of calls from home Danni fielded, which she would either dismiss without answering or conduct fierce, back-turned conversations just out of Layla's range.

'Why can't she just get it?' Danni pleaded, cutting off a call from her mother as she and Layla were queuing in the chippy one night, having left the nearby pub just before closing time. Her eyes were fixed on the blackboard menu, giving the impression she was talking to herself rather than Layla.

'Get what?' Layla shot back, but they were at the counter by then, and either Danni hadn't heard above the clash of metal and the hiss of hot fat or pretended she hadn't. Whichever it was, Layla felt she couldn't ask again. She'd just wished that whatever it was would sort itself out soon. She hated to see Danni so unhappy.

When someone in their year invited them to a pre-finals party, it seemed the perfect way to relieve some of the pressure. Danni said she wasn't going; she wasn't in the mood and had far too much work to do.

'Haven't we all?' Layla said.

Excuses. She wasn't giving in. Danni needed this. They both did.

She waited until the evening of the party, then cornered Danni in her room with a last-ditch throwaway plea.

'Well, I'm going to this party, with or without you.'

Danni wriggled out from beneath the laptop and narrowed her eyes at Layla. 'Will it be a girls' night?'

'Girls' night. Totally.'

'Promise?'

'Scout's honour.'

'Gotcha! You weren't a Scout.'

'Brownie's honour then.'

Beyond the window, the sun had slipped lower, reaching between the half-drawn curtains to paint Danni's face ghostly white and brush deep shadows beneath her eyes. Her forehead gleamed unhealthily with sweat. *Forget the party*, Layla wanted to say, regretting her strong-arm tactics. *Catch an early night instead.*

But before she could say it, Danni was off the bed, kicking off grubby pink ballerinas, sashaying out of grey trackies, shooting a smile. 'Fine, you win. Let's do it.'

Raking through the hangers in the wardrobe, she hooked out a black silky slip of a dress, still with the tags on. It had Nathan written all over it. 'This do?'

The house was in a dilapidated Georgian terrace, in an unfamiliar part of town. It was four storeys tall, including the basement, with a pillared porch, large sash windows and a short flight of steps, clad with chipped black-and-white tiles, leading to the peeling front door. Layla rang the bell but it had no chance of competing with the bass boom coming from within. Danni shoved the door with her foot. It opened onto a once-grand hallway with several doors leading off it. Most of the doors had felt-tipped keep out notices taped to them in language ranging from politely funny to downright filthy.

Following the direction of the music, they squeezed along the teeming passageway and down the stairs to the communal area in the basement. At the kitchen end, a row of mismatched tables formed the bar. Layla unscrewed the top of one of the bottles of wine they'd brought with them. There were no glasses, only plastic tumblers. She half-filled two, but Danni grabbed the bottle, necked a mouthful, then frowned at the label.

'I don't fancy this much.' She stood the bottle down, reached for a litre bottle of vodka – 'Ah...' – and tipped a generous measure into a tumbler. 'Up yours.'

Above the ear-splitting din, Danni's voice shrilled long-lost-friend greetings to people she'd seen in the last week, if not the last day. Layla watched her blonde head bobbing through the horde with a nervy fascination. Usually, it took a while for Danni to embrace the spirit of a party, become part of the action. Tonight, it was as if she had cast off her persona at the door like a pair of muddy shoes and become somebody else entirely.

Layla danced, laughed, mouthed words at friends and drank wine. Danni was right, it was rank, but it would do the job. It was some time before she realised she'd lost sight of her friend. She scanned the heads, then pressed between hot bodies to search further. The basement was almost pitch black apart from firework flashes from the lights on the sound system and the quivering stars of fairy lights strung around the walls. Peering through the gloom, she attempted a systematic search. No sign of Danni.

Then, suddenly, she appeared, grabbing Layla by the arm.

'I told you! Didn't I say he'd come crawling back?'

'Who has?' Ah. Danni was looking back, over her shoulder. Layla followed her gaze towards a guy in a white shirt and sunglasses. Despite the sunnies, Layla recognized Nathan. He was looking in Danni's direction, as far as Layla could tell.

'What did he say?'

Danni flicked her hair back. 'Oh, that he was sorry, he was an idiot – well, I knew that – and he really missed me, he'd made a mistake, blah blah blah. The usual pathetic excuses.'

'You're not getting back with him,' Layla said, having to half mouth her words as the music rose in volume. 'Tell me you're not. He wasn't good for you. He'll never make you happy.'

'No, of course I'm not. You were right. He's an arse. I don't know why I let him get to me.' Danni grinned, and glanced back over her shoulder. 'In any case, what would be the point? Another couple of weeks and I'll be out of here. I might make him sweat for a bit, though.'

Layla put both hands on Danni's shoulders. 'No. Tell him, once and for all. We don't need those games, not tonight.'

'Yeah, you're right as usual. Okay, I'll make it super-plain he hasn't got a cat in hell's chance. Happy now?'

'Yes. Make sure you do.'

Leaving Danni threading her way back towards the luckless Nathan, praying she wouldn't give in, Layla pushed her way to the makeshift bar where a group of friends from her course were gathered.

A while later, she decided to head upstairs, mainly to check on Danni, whom she'd not seen since their conversation earlier. Music riffed out of a room off the hallway, trying its best to compete with the bass boom from the basement. She pushed in through the half open door. If anything, it was even darker in here than downstairs, the atmosphere less full-on, more intimate. Stumbling through the crush, she found Danni in the corner, lounging half on a chair and half across the lap of a boy Layla had never seen before.

She grimaced into the darkness as the two of them leaned in for a lengthy snog. 'Don't mind me.'

'We won't.' Danni giggled, and kissed the boy again, her arms looped around his neck. 'This is Art,' she said, releasing him. 'Well, not art as such, not like in a painting, obviously. It's his name. Art. Funny, isn't it?'

'Hilarious.'

Danni giggled again, a falsely high-pitched sound. Her eyes were all glittery. Layla caught a whiff of something pungent and saw the glowing end of a spliff pinched between Art's fingers. He offered it to Layla, holding it high above his head as if it was an Olympic torch.

'Want some?'

Layla ignored him and addressed Danni. 'Let's go back downstairs.'

'I'm all right here, with Art. Have a puff, go on. Don't be a wuss.'

Danni took the spliff from Art, drew deeply on it and passed it to Layla. She took it and put it to her lips, avoiding drawing on it properly. Passing it back to Art, she tried to work out her next move. It was useless reminding Danni that this was supposed to be a girls' night – she doubted she'd even remember the last half hour, let alone anything that had gone before. At some point, though – preferably before dawn – she would have to get her home, unscathed. By the look of her it would be more a case of damage limitation.

Layla began to feel a little bit lonely. She was missing Harvey. Seriously missing him. It was impossible not to, in the face of all this amorous activity. She half wished she'd given in to his puppy-dog appeal and brought him along, but she'd held firm. This was a finals party. Besides, tonight was supposed to be about Danni, to help her loosen up before the exams. It was a pity her friend had interpreted the intention in a different way entirely.

Art was struggling to his feet now, pulling Danni up with him to merge into one shadowy shape swaying roughly in time to the music. Perhaps it wasn't so bad. If Danni wanted to bring out her wild child, who was she to stop her? She wasn't her bodyguard, or her mother. She took a last look, averting her gaze from Art's hand caressing Danni's thigh below the hem of her dress which had ridden up almost to thong height, and left them to it.

. . .

It was after one a.m. when Layla gave in to the undertow she'd been kicking against all night and rang Harvey. Bored with dancing and drinking, and watching people beginning to pair off, like Danni and Art, she needed to hear his voice.

Harvey was in bed but he hadn't been asleep. 'Jump in a cab and get yourself over here. You know you want to.'

She could see his eyes shining narrowly in the semi-darkness of his room in halls, his naked chest and the perfect curve of muscle in his forearm as he held the phone.

'I do want to, but I can't. I have to look after Danni, get her home safely.'

But already the riptide pull of Harvey was proving too strong. He sensed her weakness, knew she'd give in. He didn't even have to try.

'Layla, Layla, Lay-laa,' she heard him sing softly into the phone as she stood on the doorstep beneath a navy-blue sky pierced with stars.

'Okay, you win. I'll be there.'

In her mind she saw his victorious smile. She felt light, happy and loved.

Back inside the house, she made her way to the room where she'd last seen Danni. She tapped her on the shoulder, hard, twice, before Danni looked round.

'Hiya!' she said, as if it was the first time she'd seen Layla all night.

'Danni, I'm going now. Will you be all right?'

'Going?' Danni stopped dancing, without detaching herself from Art. 'No, don't. Stay. Have some fun.'

Layla hesitated, but only for a moment. There was a taxi rank on the corner. She could be there in five minutes, in Harvey's arms in fifteen.

TWELVE

Morgan was writing at home in the flat, trying to make up for the time he'd lost yesterday. The window was partly open and the growl of idling engines drifted up as the procession of beach-goers nudged its way towards the jaws of the underground car park. The weather wasn't even that warm yet. The sea would be freezing, but that wouldn't stop them wading right in there, pasty bodies peppered in goosebumps. Morgan gave what Kate called his crusty old codger head shake and typed his next chapter heading.

It didn't matter that he was working on a Sunday because Kate was working, too, legs up on the sofa, laptop perched on a cushion and a slurry of case notes on the table beside her. She was sucking the end of a biro and typing with one hand. She had to have a pen in her hand at all times while she worked, otherwise she couldn't think properly, she said. Every so often, Morgan would turn and glance at her and she would look up and smile, a little distractedly, before returning to her work.

Morgan couldn't concentrate. He had hoped that seeing Layla again would cast into oblivion that show-stopping moment when he'd first laid eyes on her – a moment that felt like a beginning – and he would see it for what it was, a rush of pure, meaningless sexual attraction that could happen anywhere, at any time, with anyone. In fact, he had fully expected this to be so, until she was there in front of him. And then he'd known with mind-shattering certainty that there had been a lot more to it than that.

The strength of feeling he'd experienced was nothing short of astonishing. Even more astonishing was that she had felt it, too. He had seen it in her eyes, in the way she avoided looking at him directly as they'd sat on the rug in the boathouse, and in the set of her shoulders as she'd walked down the steps and away, holding the umbrella aloft. And then, the moment she was out of sight, he'd begun to worry he would never see her again, even though the alternative reeked of impossibility.

He had lain awake for most of last night. Then this morning, as the first light seeped into the sky and tentative squawks came from the gulls, he had reached out for Kate, intent on waking her so that he could tell her about the girl he'd met on the boat and how stupid he'd been. He needed her to understand that he was human, with every human failing ever invented, but that he loved her and would never do anything to hurt her. In Morgan's imagination, Kate would put her finger to his lips and stop his confession in its tracks. She would tell him that no one could be perfect all the time, that she knew in her heart he loved only her, and he would never let her down.

But that wasn't the reality. He'd managed to pull himself together sufficiently to turn his waking touch into a casual stroke of her bare midriff, and Kate, misinterpreting his movements, had turned round and pulled him on top of her. Afterwards, Morgan had felt doubly guilty and somehow unclean.

'I'll make lunch then, shall I?' he said now, giving up all pretence of adding to his word count.

'What?'

Kate glanced up from her laptop, giving the impression that

she'd been so deeply engrossed in her work she resented the interruption. Morgan saw at once that this wasn't so, and that her mind had been as far out of the moment as his had been. The realisation gave him a jolt of anxiety.

'Lunch. Do you want some?'

'There's no need to snap.' Kate sniffed. 'We've not long had breakfast.'

Morgan had been half turned towards her. Now he swivelled back to face the screen and, beyond it, the inky line of the horizon sketched above the rooftops of the seafront. He felt irritated, with himself and with Kate, and he didn't trust his reactions. He took a composing breath and tried again.

'Good point,' he said lightly, tapping at the keyboard. 'How about we work through and go out later for something to eat?'

'Yeah, okay.' Kate sounded placated. Her voice came softly to him across the expanse of the room, seemingly coming out from out of the shadows. 'We could go to our Chinese, if you like.'

This time Morgan turned round properly, and Kate smiled at him in a way that suggested it was costing her some effort.

'Chinese, yes,' he said cheerfully. 'We'll do that, then.'

But Kate had gone, back to her work. Or to wherever it was she had been.

Over the next few days, Morgan hammered away at the keyboard, forgetting to be uninspired by his surroundings as Poodle Chafferty began to hike off along all sorts of interesting plot paths, too many to put into one book. A sequel suggested itself, possibly a whole series of Chafferty books. He decided that this exciting higher level of creativity was his reward for knuckling down and keeping Layla out of his head.

When he finally relented and allowed her to enter his thoughts, he replayed the scene in the boathouse, then rewound it and played it again to make sure he hadn't imagined the whole thing. And yet nothing had ever felt so real before.

Was she thinking the same? Or did she just think he was weird, with his childish notes, his boathouse den and his soldier biscuit tin, like a throwback from an Enid Blyton story? Was she even thinking about him at all, or had she airbrushed him from her mind the moment she'd gone down those steps carrying that musty old umbrella and walked along the towpath, back to her real life? It suddenly seemed extremely important that he knew the answers to these questions, yet he had no way of finding out.

He'd been fooling himself, of course, thinking of her simply as a friend. And, by default, he had been fooling her, too. The truth was, he had fallen in love with her. Instantly, completely, unconditionally. He had no idea what he was supposed to do about it.

<h1 style="text-align:center">THIRTEEN</h1>

Morgan drove up to Maybridge on Friday, having sounded out Kate on the subject and deducing, with a pang of sadness, that she didn't seem to care that much. In fact, she'd been acting strangely all week. She'd accepted more than her usual number of extra shifts. When she wasn't at the hospital, she worked in the flat until late in the evening on some vaguely-referred-to backlog of case notes. Then, suddenly, she would stop what she was doing and rush up to him, arms outstretched, as if she were a toddler in need of a cuddle. It was as if she needed him to comfort her without telling him why.

At these moments he would rock her in his arms, his chin resting on top of her head, feeling the tension rising from her like a fish caught on a line while his own guilt pressed down on him like a ton weight. At one of these times, wanting to lighten the mood, he had held her away from him and gathered up her hair into two cartoonish bunches on top of her head, as he used to do in the early days, when they'd play-acted all the time. Perhaps he'd wanted to remind her of the way they were. Or remind himself.

She had twisted out of his grasp and shaken her hair free.

'Don't,' she'd said.

Just that. *Don't.*

As he entered the boathouse, he let out a long, deep sigh, as if he'd been holding his breath all week. It was a relief to find that he'd tidied everything away before he'd left last Saturday. The rug was back in the cupboard, the biscuit tin put away, the mugs washed out. It seemed easiest that way.

Holding his confused thoughts at bay, he settled down to work, letting his writing take over and block out everything else. He didn't stop until two hours later, when the door swung open and Connor stood there, his hands clasped tightly together in front of him. Ted had taken a fall, Morgan heard. When the old man hadn't shown up at the yard, Connor had gone to his cottage and found him sitting on the kitchen floor, dazed, but otherwise protesting loudly that he was as right as rain and he'd be down in a brace of shakes, if only Connor would stop flapping about like an old woman and disturbing the dust.

'It wasn't just a fall, I'm sure of it,' Connor said, coming into the boathouse. 'He must have zonked out for some reason. Bloody old fool wouldn't let me call the doctor out so I'm going to have to drag him to the surgery later.'

There was no one to run the riverside kiosk this afternoon. Maureen, who worked all year round, dividing her time between the café and the kiosk, had gone to her granddaughter's school concert, and no way was Connor going to let Ted anywhere near...

'No, no, of course not. Leave it to me,' Morgan said.

By two o'clock, Morgan had sold eighteen tickets for *Lady Tabitha*'s next trip, several cans of fizzy drink, a fistful of chocolate bars, and by some fluke managed to squeeze half a dozen swirls of ice cream out of the temperamental machine and into cones without getting it all over himself and his customers.

The kiosk was steadily busy all afternoon. At five o'clock, when the shutters came down, he wiped out the drinks fridge and swabbed down the countertops. He felt tired, but in a nice, fuzzy sort of way. While he waited for Connor to come and collect the takings, he went outside and propped himself against the sun-warmed wooden slats of the little hut, watching the flashes of light breaking the surface of the river. It was at times like this that he almost wished he smoked.

He thought about the boathouse and how, once you were inside, it felt as if you were miles from anywhere and anyone, even though the boatyard was just around the curve in the river. Kate had never been to the boathouse. The realisation hit him with a flash of guilt; guilt because Layla had been there and not Kate. But Kate had never asked to come. Perhaps she'd been waiting for him to invite her. He should redress that, and soon.

He took out his phone to check if she'd sent him a message. Nothing. His old anxiety came flooding back. What was she hiding from him? There was something; he'd seen it in her eyes. He'd tried to ignore the feeling, and been partially successful. Now it came hurtling back, ten times more powerful than before, letting him know that he could no longer delay the inevitable. He must talk to her, tonight, have the conversation he didn't want and ask her the questions he'd been afraid to ask because he hadn't wanted to know the answers: Did Kate still love him? Did she still want to be with him?

A stiff breeze arose out of nowhere, dousing his face with cold air and breaking his mood. He peeled himself away from the wall and stood, hands in pockets, on the scrappy bit of grass in front of it. As usual, he was getting this all wrong, misreading the signals. She was worried about something to do with work, that was all. Kate loved him and he loved her. They were fine. And this thing with Layla? It meant nothing. He wasn't in love with her. How could he be? It was his stupid imagination playing tricks and he'd gone and muddied the waters by spending an afternoon with her. A mistake, not to be repeated. He must make sure of that. There would be no opportunity, anyway; he was totally convinced now that she hadn't given him another moment's thought.

He had a sudden impulse to find a bit of chalk and scrawl *Morgan loves Kate* in schoolboyish letters, with a heart and arrow, on the wall of the kiosk. The idea made him laugh out loud. He must remember to tell Kate. She'd find it funny, too; she'd always maintained he was regressing.

Connor was loping along the riverbank towards him, his hand already raised in greeting. Morgan raised an answering hand and, as he watched his friend's approach, he let go of the image of the smart, funny, beautiful girl with the big brown eyes and the fishtail plait.

And this time it was for good.

On the way home, the traffic heading south was frustratingly slow-moving. Morgan spent a good ten minutes stuck behind a swaying horse box, the bulging grey backside of its occupant seeming to mock all his attempts at passing. Eventually, he reached the exit and joined the Haverstone road, only to find himself in another queue five minutes later. Sweat broke out on his forehead as he cursed out loud the cars in front of him. His shoulders were locked in a furious mass of muscle as he tightened his grip on the wheel. It seemed imperative that he get home as quickly as possible. He needed to be with Kate.

By the time he had parked and was standing in the lift on the way up to the flat, he had the mother and father of all headaches. The first thing he noticed on entering the flat was the homely aroma of roast chicken. The second was the silence. No comforting kitchen noises, no light footsteps on the wooden floor, no radio – she liked it to be on while she cooked – and no voice calling out to him in greeting. She must have nipped out to the shops to pick up some forgotten ingredient for dinner, or a bottle of wine, perhaps. But there was wine in the fridge.

In a fit of almost-pique, Morgan hauled his sweatshirt over his head and flung it over one of the hooks in the hall. Kate wouldn't approve; if it wasn't a coat, it belonged in the bedroom. His face mapped a scowl as he hitched his rucksack untidily onto another empty hook, the one where her jacket usually lived. His laptop he left on the hall floor instead of taking it through and putting it on the desk.

'Kate?' His voice came huskily from his too dry mouth.

No reply.

He glanced towards the bedroom as he passed. One of the wardrobe doors hung open. He continued to the kitchen. No food on the worktop, no plates warming in the oven, only the roasting tin and a handful of cutlery drying off in the rack on the draining board. Opening the fridge, he traced the source of the smell. A roast chicken sat on a plate, covered loosely in tinfoil. The foil was slightly warm when he touched it. On the shelf below was a salad, bright with tomato and peppers among the greenery, in the blue pottery bowl they'd bought last year on a weekend break in Lisbon, a skin of cling film stretched across the top. Foil and cling film were invented for Kate.

Morgan let the fridge door swing shut. Its motor started up again, loud in the silent kitchen. He stood still for a moment, steepling his hands to his mouth. He went through to the living room. It seemed eerily quiet. Even the blokes upstairs weren't clodhopping around. For once he wished they were.

In the bedroom, Morgan stood in front of the open door of the wardrobe. He could see through to the wood at the back. Sweat broke out on his forehead as he surveyed the empty hangers. Some of her clothes had gone. No, not some. Most of them. He closed the door and opened her underwear drawer in the chest. Everything had gone, apart from a few bits and pieces.

He took out a blue silky vest and held it to his face, catching the faint scent of the body lotion she wore.

The muscles in the back of his neck ached. His temples throbbed as the headache tightened its grip. He couldn't breathe. He dropped the vest onto the floor and rushed from the bedroom into the living room, drew back the bolt on the glass door and stepped out onto the balcony, forcing down great lungfuls of air with a rasping sound that didn't seem to be coming from him at all.

And then he knew what he had known from the moment he'd come through the front door.

Kate had gone.

FOURTEEN

Kate sat forward in the driving seat and blinked hard to bring the road ahead into focus through her tears. That was close, really close. She had meant to be away much sooner but it had been almost five by the time she'd left. Morgan was a creature of habit. Half-five, quarter to six – six o'clock at the latest, if the traffic was bad – and he'd be home.

The chicken had been the problem. The nearest shop had run out of breast fillets but for some reason her mind kept saying 'chicken' so she'd bought a whole one without stopping to think how long it would take to cook. She'd had to turn the oven up really high and then when it was done, she'd put it away before it was properly cold. At least she'd had the sense not to get vegetables which would have had to be cut up and cooked as well. The salad was a good choice. He liked salad. And there was half a crusty loaf in the bread bin...

Oh, for fuck's sake! Why was she thinking about chicken and vegetables and salad and bread at a time like this? Shut *up*!

The sign for Haverstone General came into view up ahead. The sight of it stalled her breathing and brought a fresh bout of silent tears. She thought of Xavier, waiting for her to come to him, as they'd planned. She couldn't do it – she hadn't known she wasn't going to until now. Changing lanes, averting her eyes from the hospital sign, she set out on another route.

It was a while later before she realised where she was heading. She was going home, to Milton Keynes. The decision didn't seem to have been made by her, yet made it was. And she was glad, because it seemed the obvious thing to do. Pushing aside an image of Morgan entering the empty flat, realising she'd gone, looking round for the note she had started to write before deciding against it, Kate put her foot down.

It wasn't until she was nearly home that her mobile rang. She'd kept it on the seat beside her, knowing it would ring at some point, surprised it had taken this long for one of them to get in touch. Taking a convenient side turning, she drove on a little way and came to stop on a grass verge beside a fenced-off field. The phone had gone to voicemail. She switched off the engine and listened to the message.

'Where are you?' Xavi said. 'You're supposed to be here. Call me back, please?'

With the phone in her lap, Kate snapped down the mirror and glanced at her reflection. Her cheeks were wet. She thought she'd stopped crying ages ago. Pulling a tissue from the pack in the glove compartment, she dabbed ineffectually at her red eyes while the tears continued to stream. There seemed no way to stop them. She took in a long, faltering breath and sat, eyes closed, leaning back against the headrest for a minute, before she took up the phone and scrolled to Xavier's name.

He answered in a heartbeat. 'Thank heavens. What's happened? Where are you? I've been waiting ages. I've been so worried.'

'Yes, I know.'

Silence – she could hear him breathing – then, 'You're on the way now, though?'

'No, Xavi, I'm not, and I'm really sorry. I'm going home, to Milton Keynes.'

Another silence, brimful of confusion, disappointment, all the things she would never, ever have wished upon him.

'Wait a minute. Did you say "Milton Keynes"? Your parents' place?'

'I did, yes.' Kate felt small, almost infinitesimal.

'So, may I ask why?'

Kate could imagine his eyes, prominent and glassy, the way they went when he was upset about something.

'Because it's the best thing, for me, for both of us. I can't do it now, not right away. I thought I could, but I can't. There has to be a gap.'

'You were doing the night shift. It's all arranged. They'll have to call someone in,' he said, resorting to practicalities. 'We were both on duty. You were coming back with me in the morning. We were going to be together.'

As if she needed reminding.

'Tell them I've called in sick, will you? Please, Xavi?'

She heard his sigh. 'Yeah, of course. Don't worry about the shift. They'll get someone.'

'I'm not, but I am worrying about you. I'll see you after the weekend and we'll talk then. Will you be all right?'

'S'pose I'll have to be.'

'Don't be like that...'

'Well, how would you like me to be?'

A shade of snappiness now, but the hurt was there, plainest of all.

Kate swallowed, gathering up all her strength, before she spoke again.

'I know. Please try and understand. This is how it has to be, for now.'

'Okay. Drive safely.' Then, 'I love you, Kate. I love you so much.'

'Love you, too.'

Kate threw the phone onto the seat, started up the engine and manoeuvred the car back onto the road. So now she'd hurt both of them, Morgan and Xavi. What kind of a person did that make her? She fought back the tears. Enough of the crying. It was helping no one, least of all her.

A little further down the road, she stopped for petrol then pulled over to the side of the station forecourt and sent a text to Morgan:

> I'm so sorry but I had to do this. Hope you're OK. Will be for the best. Talk soon. x.

So many sorrys, so many okays. As if those two little words could make everything come right again.

She made another call. 'Suzanne, it's me. I've left Haverstone and... I've left Morgan. I'm on my way home.'

'You've done *what*?'

'I can't go into it now. I'll tell you all about it when I get there.'

'Here? You're coming home?' Her sister sounded quite put out.

'Don't worry, it's only for the weekend. Look, do me a favour, would you? Tell Mum. Tell her I'm on my way and give her an advance warning.'

'Yes, if you want. You sound all funny. Are you all right?'

Kate raised her eyes. Like she'd be all right. She bit back a barbed response. 'I'll be around half an hour, and have the kettle on.'

She managed a smile down the phone as she clicked it off.

Mum would be fine about it, Dad, too, although Kate wished she didn't have to worry them with this.

. . .

They stood in a huddle, heads touching, arms around each other, in the middle of the kitchen – Mum, Suzanne and Kate. Mum and her girls in a group hug that was supposed to make everything better: dead hamsters; failed exams; boys who didn't phone. And it did work, usually. Dad hovered unhappily in the periphery and put sugar in Kate's tea. She didn't take sugar. Mum was a bit teary-eyed, which made Kate feel even sadder, and guilty for bringing her troubles home.

Someone put the telly on and they sat around, pretending to watch it. Mum remembered she'd been going to make Kate something to eat and sprung up out of her chair. Kate stopped her; she wasn't the slightest bit hungry, even though she hadn't eaten since her lunchtime sandwich.

It was a strange evening. Subdued, quiet, everyone busy with their own thoughts, even Suzanne, who clearly had a hundred questions on the tip of her tongue and was having some difficulty holding them back. Kate would talk to her tomorrow; they'd have a good old sisterly chinwag.

It seemed something of a relief all round when Kate said goodnight and went upstairs to her old bedroom with the white painted kidney-shaped dressing table and the signed photo of some bloke from *Neighbours* pinned to the wall behind the door. Her old brown teddy was propped up against the headboard of the single divan. She picked him up and sobbed quietly into his matted fur. Through the torrent of tears – would they ever stop? – she remembered something Mum had said earlier. 'You can't help who you fall in love with.'

It was to be Kate's mantra now, and in the months to come.

FIFTEEN

Reece led the way along the rutted lane, Melody and Layla following. The moon was hidden by cloud and it was almost pitch dark. The farm was only nine minutes' walk from the Drover's Arms, but with nobody speaking it felt like a route march across three counties.

What in God's name had possessed Layla to start talking about Danni, right in the middle of the meal? She'd seemed a bit preoccupied all evening; he had felt heavy with the sense of something coming towards them, as unstoppable as a ten-ton truck. His guess was that Layla was about to tell them this was her last visit, and he'd watched Melody cocooned in unawareness and felt sick.

It wasn't that at all. Instead, the girl had looked Melody right in the eye and asked her to tell the story about Danni's first riding lesson, how the horse had thrown her before they were even out of the yard and catapulted her face-first into a pile of horse muck. Apparently, they'd had a giggle about it, the two girls.

Melody had almost choked on her lamb cutlet, but she'd covered it up quickly and made a valiant attempt to relay the tale, while Reece had put down his knife and fork and sat back in his seat, feeling as if he'd been spit-roasted. If that wasn't enough, as Melody puttered to a halt, Layla had turned to him and asked if he remembered moving Danni into halls the weekend before their first term started, and having to lug half the stuff out again and back into the car because her room was too small to fit it all in.

Remember? It was branded on his brain with a red-hot poker. What the hell was Layla playing at? Didn't she know they avoided this because of what it would do to Mel?

Layla must have seen the warning look he gave her, after the fearful one he gave Melody, but she wouldn't let it drop.

'When you'd gone, Danni realised you'd repacked all her washing stuff and she had to borrow some of mine so that she could have a shower,' Layla had said.

Then she'd laughed, like this was nothing out of the ordinary. The laughter had soon died away, though, when Melody threw down her fork, burst into tears and rushed off to the ladies.

'Reece, I'm so, so sorry.' Layla had looked as if she, too, might burst into tears at any moment.

Despite the anxiety swooping around in his stomach – anxiety that she had caused – he had felt a bit sorry for her. He'd tried to be kind, but he had to make things clear to her.

'She can't take it, Layla. You of all people should know that.'

It was Layla's turn to be upset.

'No, I don't! I don't know any such thing! If I'm to keep on coming here then I need to talk about Danni and you should too, both of you. It isn't natural not to. You can't sweep her under the carpet as if she never happened.'

Seeing his face, realising what she'd done, she had apologised at once for saying such an idiotic thing – of course she knew they'd never do that, but he must know what she meant.

'Yes, well,' was all he'd managed to say.

A troubled silence had fallen then, both of them glancing across the pub, until Layla said she'd go and see. Eventually, he'd looked up and seen them coming back. They walked singly because of the narrow space between the tables, although there seemed to be an air of reconciliation about them.

It had been an unsettling sort of day altogether. Layla had arrived before lunch with a box of ginger chocolates as a gift and announced that she'd be taking them to the Drover's Arms for dinner; her treat. It wasn't a spur of the moment thing, either, because apparently she'd booked a table earlier in the week.

Lunch had been a rather stilted affair, and then nobody seemed able to decide how to spend the afternoon. After much over-polite deferring to one another, they'd settled on a walk in the grounds of Foxleigh Court, and Melody and Layla would then drive into Foxleigh to wander round the little shops which they both enjoyed, while he came home to do some work.

As they'd flogged around the lake and across the deer park in a fake family threesome, an air of preoccupation had prevailed and Reece observed each of them, himself included, disappearing inside their own thoughts.

Layla, he could understand, after the last time and the business with the cheque and everything; there was bound to be a touch of rancour there until things settled down again and it was all but forgotten. In fact, it was a wonder she hadn't decided to stay away altogether.

Melody worried him more. These days he could no more suss out what was going on in her mind than fly to the moon. He only hoped she wasn't plotting something regarding Layla that could only lead to more heartache and disappointment for her.

And then all this, tonight. What a disaster. What a bloody awful disaster. He wasn't looking forward to the rest of the weekend one bit. Actually, he wasn't looking forward to the rest of his life.

SIXTEEN

Sunday evening, and Layla was babysitting Finn, who, thankfully, was fast asleep. Layla couldn't believe it when she'd come home from work two nights ago, after a long evening shift and a bit of a drinking session with Seth and some of the others – 'unwinding', Seth called it – to find Rowan asleep on the sofa and her bed occupied by her nephew.

She'd had to go in with Mum, which was all very well if you didn't mind the smell of the lavender water Mum sprinkled on the pillows. But by that time, Layla was ready to drop and would have slept in the bath, if necessary.

It wasn't until the following morning that she'd discovered the reason for this sudden overcrowding. Rowan had left Jeff; at least, that was her immediate assumption. As it wasn't the first time, it wasn't exactly headline news, although on previous occasions, Rowan had taken Finn to stay with a friend of hers who had a large house and room to spare. Mum had closed the door of the kitchen, when it was just the two of them, and confessed with unnecessary shamefulness – as if it was her doing – that Rowan had been caught out having an affair, and Jeff had told her to go.

So here they were, her sister and her nephew. And although the affair was supposedly over, the situation with Jeff was hardly going to be resolved overnight, if at all. At least Layla had her bed back; a blow-up mattress had been turned into a bed for Finn in Mum's room, and Rowan either slept in with Mum or on the sofa, if she'd been out.

Tonight, April was down at the Maybridge Arms, giving her all to the karaoke. She'd said she wouldn't go but Layla had insisted; Mum needed a break from all this melodrama. Jadine was out with Smart Alec – or in, if his parents were out – and Rowan had gone somewhere unspecified. Layla hoped she hadn't lied and was seeing her lover, whoever he was. She wouldn't put it past her.

Whatever the truth of it all, Layla didn't much care – her own problems weighed heavily enough without taking on other people's. That wasn't the case, though, was it? Of course she cared, mainly about April. She really didn't need to be involved in her daughters' lives to that extent, and poor little Finn must wonder whether he was coming or going.

Layla nipped upstairs to check on him. He was still fast asleep, arms thrown out against the pillow, wearing a puzzled frown, as if he was in the midst of solving a difficult problem.

Back downstairs, she poured a glass of Shiraz and went outside to sit on the back doorstep. Mid-May, and the days were lengthening. The evening air had a summery feel about it. Several motorbikes roared along Warbler's Way. Disturbed by the noise, next door's chickens squawked, bringing Foxleigh and the Morlands to her mind – not that they were ever far from it.

Was it really only last weekend that she'd made such a terrible mess of everything? There were only two words to describe it: unmitigated disaster. It was all her fault – the tension; the scene in the pub; Melody's tears; Reece's exasperation; all of it. The crazy part was that she'd planned that conversation, rehearsed those questions about Danni in her head as if they were lines in a play. She'd even chosen the backdrop – the pub, away from the house. Well, she'd certainly created a drama; she'd got that bit right.

Last Saturday, she had still been awake when Melody had come to her room around midnight – how could she sleep? She'd felt afraid of what was to come, while at the same time a tiny ray of hope shone, hope that Melody was going to ask her not to come back to Foxleigh again. But it wasn't that. Instead, she'd been dry-eyed and calm, speaking to Layla in a soothing voice, like a mother comforting a child after a bad dream.

'I tried, Layla, truly I did, when you brought... her into the conversation. It was too hard and I'm so sorry,' Melody had said.

And Layla had said she was sorry, too; sorry that she'd overstepped the boundary and tried to make Melody do something she wasn't ready for.

This was true; it was how she felt. At least, she had at the time. And now? Everything had got so confused in her mind that she no longer knew what she thought, or how she felt, or where she was supposed to go from here.

Then Melody had said something else, something that turned Layla's heart inside out.

'I do talk about her, all the time. I talk about her in here,' – Melody had tapped her temple – 'and in here.' Her hand strayed to her chest. 'Just not to anyone else.'

They'd shared a hug then, and had a little cry together. Then it was over and Melody went off to bed. In the morning, everything had seemed normal – normal for them – except that Reece's jollity was a bit lacking in credibility, and Melody's 'See you soon' was weighted with unspoken appeal.

This was never going to stop. Never. She'd stuck pins into them, thinking that if she drew a little blood it would provoke some sort of allegiance between Melody and Reece, even if it meant turning them against her. Instead, they'd reacted singly, barely glancing at one another across the great divide, and she'd been left feeling worse than useless and totally out of her depth. All she'd wanted was to steer them back to one another. She wasn't in charge of the boat, though, was she?

Suddenly, she wanted to be five years old again, being rocked on April's lap, with the rhythmic scuff of her tweed skirt beneath her legs and the breath of Estée Lauder on her face. But Mum wasn't here, and even if she had been, there was nothing she could do or say that would help. Not if she hadn't been told the truth.

Rowan didn't come home all night. It was already gone 9am and April was obviously worried. She pretended otherwise and concentrated on distracting Finn, who hadn't yet asked where his mother was but surely would as soon as the penny dropped.

Jadine and Layla took it in turns to make furtive calls to Rowan's mobile. They found it switched off every time. There was no point in trying the salon because it was closed on a Monday, as was Jadine's. They left messages, but their sister's own message was only too clear. *Leave me alone.*

Layla was convinced nothing awful had happened to Rowan. They would have heard by now. Convincing her mum was another matter. April was all for calling the police until Layla reminded her that Rowan was a grown-up, supposedly, and, as such, an unlikely candidate for the missing persons list.

The phone rang at half past nine and everyone jumped. Layla picked it up. It was Nan. 'Where's Rowan? Is she there? She said she was coming round to do my hair. I've already washed it!'

'It's all right, Nan. Jadine's going to do it instead... No, no, don't get a taxi, not with wet hair. She'll come to you.' She put the phone down and turned to her sister. 'Jadine...'

'Bollocks I will.'

'Jadine, will you please just do it?' Why did her sister have to argue about the least little thing?

'Yes, go on love,' April said. 'You can't leave Nan dripping.'

Jadine put her hands on her hips. 'I am getting a lift, right?'

'Wrong,' Layla said, before Mum could offer. 'You'll walk it in ten.'

'But...'

'Go!' Layla pointed towards the door.

Jadine went. A moment later, the front door banged shut. April and Layla raised their eyes at each other, then both of them looked at Finn, who was gazing down at his jeans and trainers with a perplexed look on his face.

'Aren't I going to school then?'

April took Finn gently by his shoulders.

'No, darlin', it's half term and I'm having a half term, too, so I can look after you, remember?'

'I'll have him today, Mum,' Layla said. 'You put your feet up and stop worrying. You-know-who will be home before you know it.'

'Where's me mum? Has she gone to the shop?'

'That's right, love.'

April's voice was lazy with tiredness and stress.

'Sometimes me mum's not in bed in the night but it's all right 'cos Jeff makes me breakfast,' Finn said, giving them a bright smile.

Layla's heart squeezed. She daren't look at Mum.

'How about you and I go out somewhere, Finn?' she said.

He looked doubtfully up at Layla. 'Where?'

'Oh, I don't know. We'll think of something.'

Finn did a little skip and a jump. 'Orright.'

· · ·

They drove to the city centre and left the car in the cathedral car park. Finn liked looking in the windows of the souvenir shops, and the Spice Emporium was close by; she could pick up some bits to go with tonight's chicken.

Raj, the owner, knew Layla as one of his regulars, though not by name.

'Ah, at last!' he cried, as they entered the shop. Raising his eyes, he clutched the broad drum of his chest dramatically. 'A real cook! Professional, yes? And today you come with your assistant.'

He beamed at Finn, who looked down shyly at his shoes. Layla smiled, and began to scan the nearest shelves.

'Where you work?'

Raj knew full well the answer to this, but that never stopped him asking. Layla gave the familiar response.

'Tidehall Manor. You should try it sometime. Take your wife there for a nice dinner.'

Raj's black eyes narrowed to slits, his head rolling to one side, as he pretended to give serious consideration to this suggestion.

'I might, I might. She's very busy with the children. We have five. Did you know that?'

She did. Wandering along the aisles, she chose harissa paste, cumin seed and sun-dried tomatoes. More cosy banter as Raj placed her purchases in a brown paper carrier as reverently as if they were the Crown Jewels, and they were out in the sunshine again. The narrow streets were beginning to fill with other shoppers and tourists. Visitors to the cathedral were making their way across its grass frontage towards the ornate arched entrance. A green-and-gold painted signpost stood opposite the Emporium. Layla's eyes were irresistibly drawn to one of its fingers:

To the river.

She looked down at Finn, now jiggling impatiently beside her.

'How do you fancy a boat trip?'

'Like on my birthday?'

'Yes, like on your birthday.'

Finn thought for a moment. 'Okay,' he said.

The boat – *Lady Tabitha* again – was almost full; it was the perfect day for the river. Finn, squeezed in next to Layla on the slatted wooden seat, had his thumb in his mouth. With the other hand, he picked at a bubble in the varnish. His straw-coloured hair was pushed up into quills where his head rested against the back of the seat. He was always well-behaved with her, almost docile. Layla wished she had that effect on the rest of her family. She tilted her face to the sun, listened to the chug of the engine and the faint swish of the water and tried not to think about anything at all.

The boathouse came into view. She turned her head towards the other bank, the nearer one. Finn was pulling himself upright, pointing.

'What's that funny place?'

'A special kind of house to keep a boat in. Look over there, swans with babies!'

'I can't see no boats.'

'*Any* boats, and you won't because they're all gone now.'

Finn plugged his thumb back in and returned to his varnish bubble. Layla wished she could switch her own attention on and off so easily. The bend in the river had soon removed the boathouse from sight, but the images stayed with her of swaying branches mirrored in dark, abandoned glass, a musty picnic rug, soldiers marching round a biscuit tin, and someone who listened so closely to what she had to say that she heard her own, exact, words repeated back to her much later in the conversation.

Had he thought about contacting her – thought about her at all since that day – or had he dismissed her, the whole thing, once she was out of his sight, like an enjoyable yet instantly forgettable dinner? She rooted in her shoulder bag for her phone, scrolled through to his name. He had entered it for her and asked her to do the same for him. A social nicety, a way to end. She had his name, his number and his umbrella. He'd told her to keep the umbrella. It had a hole in it, anyway.

The phone beeped, startling her. Nervously, she opened the message and saw April's name come up.

> R home safe. She's not said where she went but never mind ours is not to reason. x.

Most of the passengers piled off the boat at the zoo, but a few remained on board for the return journey. Finn was easily coerced into staying put by the promise of ice cream as soon as they got back. He seemed tired and unnaturally quiet. The poor little guy must be worried about his mum, even though he hadn't shown any response when Layla had assured him earlier that she'd be there when they got home. *Damn Rowan.*

Her phone beeped its message signal again. Her stomach swooped. Could it be...? It was Seth, with a question about shifts. She stabbed out a quick reply. This jumpiness was her own fault. It had been a mistake, coming to the river. She should have stayed well clear, even though Monday was not, ostensibly, one of Morgan's days. Finn would have been just as happy to have gone to the model railway museum or to ride on the mini go-karts in the park. It occurred to her that, subconsciously, she might have been hoping to bump into Morgan. If so, her subconscious had a lot to answer for.

He wasn't here; all this introspection was pointless. She watched the skipper – a tall guy with shoulder-length hair – casually handling tickets as he ushered the passengers aboard, and felt numb.

The phone was still in her hand, his name showing on the screen. She must have scrolled to it, her fingers – her brain – on automatic pilot. All she had to do was press and speak to him and say hello. She wouldn't, though. It was too close to the edge, too much like a version of herself she no longer had any use for.

Layla didn't know what had happened during the journey back down river, but something had. Her sight had been fixed all the time on the back view of the guy at the helm, the calm set of his head and shoulders, the laconic movements of his hands on the wheel. By the time the prow of the boat knocked gently against the jetty, a decision had been made without her being aware of having made it.

She hung back as the crowd began to disembark, moving her phone from her pocket to her bag, taking off her sunglasses, before she took Finn's hand and tacked onto the back of the queue. When they reached the front, Finn bounded up the steps and onto dry land. Her turn. She took a deep breath, swallowed an acid-drop of fear, and as she reached the top step and the skipper dropped his polite hold on her arm, she turned round and glanced back as if she might have left something behind.

'All right?' he said.

'Yes... actually, I was wondering...' – another breath – 'is Morgan about today? Morgan Hampshire?' As if there were going to be two of them.

The skipper reeled back, just perceptibly, and appraised her openly as if he didn't know quite what to make of her. 'Morgan? You know him then?'

'Kind of.'

'No, he's not here today, sorry. Catch him at the weekend, though, most likely. Should be about then. Is there a message?'

Layla drew her gaze directly to his. 'Just tell him I said "hello", would you?'

'Who will I say...?'

But Layla was already walking away towards Finn and the ice-cream kiosk.

SEVENTEEN

Kate's eleven o'clock was late. And she'd been crying. Kate had seen her car arrive while she'd been typing up notes in the shared office. She'd closed down the computer, gone out into the magnolia-glossed hallway and stood beneath the fly-crusted strip light. It had been several minutes before her client had entered through the swing doors and nodded towards the receptionist, who didn't need to be told her name.

Kate waited until Melody Morland had chosen her seat in the consulting room then sat down opposite her, placing her appointment book on the scuffed table between them and casually sliding the box of tissues across to Melody's side.

'Shall we start?'

Melody sniffed and nodded. Kate switched on her recording machine.

'Do you know why you don't talk about your daughter?' Kate asked, when they'd been going for a while.

Melody was silent for a moment; her hands, which she'd been twisting in her lap, stilled.

'We talked about her at the beginning, all the time, while there were arrangements to be made, things to be dealt with, but it felt then as if she was still with us, still there, somehow. When that part was over, I don't know... We just stopped.' Melody thought for a moment, biting her thumbnail. 'It wasn't on purpose. At least, I don't think it was.'

'The girl who comes to visit – your daughter's friend – has she never spoken about Danni before, while she's been with you?'

'I don't know. I don't remember.' Melody's eyes cast about the room and came back to Kate. 'Maybe once, but it would have been a long time ago. That's why it was such a shock.'

'And how did you feel later, Melody, after the initial shock had passed?'

Melody thought.

'I think I felt sorry for her. Oh God, it's all so confusing! Yes, I did. I felt sorry for Layla, because she shouldn't have to deal with... all this. It isn't her fault and it isn't fair. I tried to put it right...'

'You spoke to her about it?'

'I went to her room – we'd all gone straight up when we got home – and we had a little talk.'

As Melody's voice wavered, Kate reached for her hand and clasped it between her own two hands, a virtual hug, giving her the strength to continue.

'I know what I'm doing to her,' Melody said. 'I can see it in her face every time she comes to the house, every time she leaves, but I can't stop. I don't know how to.'

'Do you want to stop?'

'Sometimes I do. Then I think she must be coming for her own sake and she needs me as much as I need her, and that's why she hasn't walked away, because I'm not stopping her, am I? How could I?'

Melody's expression opened up to let in the light as the justification took shape in her mind. In this situation it was hard to tell what was real and what was not.

'Melody, have you asked Layla directly if she wants to keep up the contact with you?'

'Oh no, I couldn't do that. She might think we don't want her and that would be terrible, wouldn't it?'

Kate released Melody's hand and sat back in her seat.

'Your husband – Reece, isn't it? Does he think it's time to stop, to let go of Layla?'

Melody's brown eyes widened in surprise.

'I really have no idea.'

Kate dropped the file into the cabinet and shut the drawer with a clang. Usually this signalled the point at which she cut away from the client. This time, though, it felt as if a piece of Melody Morland was still attached to her, like a stubborn placenta.

It was the thing about the husband, the almost-shock the woman had registered at Kate's question, as if knowing what he felt was a concept so ridiculously alien it may as well have sprouted little green antennae. Kate thought about her and Morgan, how one minute they were connected and real and reading each other's minds, and the next they were like strangers who happened to be passing through the same space at the same time. The Morlands had lost a daughter; they had a reason for inhabiting their separate worlds. She and Morgan had only themselves to blame.

Or perhaps not Morgan. Perhaps it was just her.

At times, she had looked out of the flat window at the ocean and imagined the two of them sinking deeper and deeper into the metallic blue water, their arms reaching out to one another, never quite touching. The same image inhabited her dreams at night. She was beginning to hate that view. Not that it was hers to hate; not any longer. From Tracey's spare room, which wasn't really spare at all, she saw small windows, red-tiled roofs sprouting defunct TV aerials, and merry-go-rounds of drying washing.

Even that was history now. Beneath Kate's desk crouched a large black rucksack, as heavy as a body. It contained all that she'd brought from the flat, the important stuff. Her life in a bag. Tracey had been lovely to her, unexpectedly gentle and accommodating in her attempt to make Kate feel at home. But as the week wore on it had been obvious that Kate was one complication too many in Tracey's overcrowded life; she wouldn't impose any further. Tonight she was moving into the nurses' home in the grounds of the hospital, to an end-of-corridor room which smelled of stale fried food and cigarettes. She'd lived in worse as a student. It would be fine.

Sooner or later she'd have to brave the flat and fetch the rest of her stuff. Given her pared-down living arrangements, much of it would have to be stored at Mum and Dad's. She couldn't leave it where it was; it wasn't fair on Morgan. Since she'd left they'd spoken briefly and texted, mostly about practicalities.

Morgan had rung two days afterwards. She was surprised it had taken him that long.

'I got your message,' he said. 'Why did you just go without giving us the chance to talk?' His voice had sounded flat, unemotional.

'It seemed the best way,' she'd said. 'We'll talk soon, though. We'll arrange something.'

He hadn't replied. Instead he'd asked her where she kept the passwords for the water and electricity accounts.

'I'll text them to you. There'll be a parcel arriving. A new smoke alarm thingy. The one we... you've got now wasn't working when I tested it.'

'Already come. I've put it up.'

'Right, good.'

That had been more or less the sum total of their communication since she'd left the flat. The deeper conversation, the proper one, was still to come. It would have to be faced before long. Surprisingly, Morgan hadn't pushed it. Or perhaps not so surprising; she was the one who liked things tidied up, labelled and put away.

Kate the pragmatist. Morgan the dreamer. She'd loved that about him. It had also irritated the socks off her.

Lunchtime. She wasn't hungry. She went to the window of the now empty office, in time to see Xavi crossing the gravel in front of the outpatient annexe, his fair hair gleaming golden in the sun. No dates, no shared meal breaks, and no proper talking for the time being; they'd agreed. Only work stuff, small-talk and the allowable, 'You okay?' whispered when no one was around, as if their affair wasn't the most talked about secret in the whole of Psych.

She watched the deliberate march of his feet, the frustrated hunch of his shoulders, and felt guilty for prevaricating. She had been right to do so, though, for both their sakes as well as Morgan's. They were simply on hold, she and Xavi, while she caught her breath. They weren't over.

So not over.

Straining at the window, hungry for Xavi's every move, she saw him reach his car and tap his pockets for the keys. She was so much in love with him it gave her stomach ache. She wouldn't keep him hanging on much longer, only until she'd laid matters to rest with Morgan and cleared her head a bit.

EIGHTEEN

'No, it doesn't, since you ask. It doesn't help at all to know that you walked out because you decided we weren't head-over-apex in love any more. Doesn't even come close.'

It was Sunday afternoon, one week and two days since Kate had left. Morgan had been wondering when she'd finally get around to having this conversation. Despite his misery, he wasn't going to be the one to instigate it. He still had some pride. Now, they stood facing one another on the chalky clifftop path above Haverstone. A sharp wind flung itself off the glittering sea, crashing against his face like the breakers on the rocks below and reducing his eyes to stinging liquid slits. An extra annoyance in an already annoying day. And he wasn't feeling very well, either.

'That's not what I said, Morgan.'

'No, but it's what you meant.'

Her exact words had been, 'We can't give each other what we need,' as if she'd scoured the agony columns and picked a sentence at random.

He almost wished she had someone else. Devastating though it would be, like a knife driven down the middle of their relationship, at least the cut would be clean. It was the first thing he'd asked her – the obvious thing – half an hour ago, before they'd come up here at his suggestion; being with Kate in the flat reminded him too much of what was at stake. But there was no one else, apparently, only this wishy-washy something-and-nothing.

'Nothing lasts forever,' Kate said from behind a pair of over-sized sunglasses.

Where had she pulled that one from? A fortune cookie? He took a step closer, removed the sunglasses and handed them to her. She blinked at him in the glare.

'Relationships change naturally over time, Kate. People grow used to one another. It doesn't mean the love's gone. It's a different sort of love. Not worse, or lacking in any way. Just different.'

Now he was at it, too. The whole conversation, such as it was, might have been filched straight from a magazine or the script of a telly soap. The problem was that Kate had not come to talk. All the while she'd been quiet, stoical and purposeful. Kate was a girl on a mission. She'd come to collect the rest of her stuff (tick), and say a final goodbye (not ticked, but it wouldn't be long at this rate).

He waited for her to speak again. For a long moment, it seemed she wasn't going to. She looked down at her feet, fiddling with the sunglasses in her hand and looking unsure of herself for the first time since this debacle had begun. Morgan allowed himself a dash of hope. Then she looked up.

'It hasn't been right for months. Be honest, Morgan. It hasn't, has it?'

This, too, was a repetition of what she'd said earlier. He hadn't agreed with her then and he wasn't about to now, even though, deep down, he suspected she might have a point. It wasn't irretrievable, was it? And why was she so determined to jump ahead, miss out the stage where they talked late into the night and tried to work it all through? Even if they did, in the end, go their separate ways, it should have been a joint decision. Instead, she had decided, all on her own. Kate had decided. He had not.

'Has it, Morgan?' she repeated, trying to force an admission out of him.

She took hold of his upper arm, but he shrugged her off, turned away and carried on walking along the path. To one side, the sea – endless, glaring, inescapable. To the other, an expanse of flattened grass, and beyond it, the giant bowl of the campsite, a miniature city of pastel-coloured caravans and sail-white tents. The path sloped upwards to the crown of the cliff. When he reached the top, he stopped, waiting for Kate to catch up. She was walking deliberately slowly, her footfalls heavy, showing her disapproval at his refusal to answer her question.

He watched her coming towards him and tried to look at her objectively, seeing her as others might – a pretty girl out for a walk on a brisk, sunny afternoon. Her hair was pulled back from her face at the sides and fastened with combs. It billowed out behind, spiralling amber against the blue of the sky. She was wearing a skirt. Kate never wore skirts. No, it was a dress with an ethnic pattern in greens and blues and browns, stopping short halfway up her pale thighs. Over it she wore her old denim jacket. She didn't look like a heartbreaker.

He waited until she was there in front of him before he said, 'What about the sex?'

'What about it?'

'I thought it was pretty spectacular.'

'It was just sex.'

'Well, thanks. Thanks for that, Kate.'

He wanted to say more, a lot more. The location seemed to demand it, as if they were actors in a film; the gusty clifftop, the sea battling away beneath, thundering onto the rocks. But he held back, afraid that once he'd started he would never stop and all his frustrations and wonderings of the past months would come gushing out. Kate would be upset or at least defensive and he didn't want either of those things. Besides, flinging accusations wasn't the way to win her over. Not that he had a better idea.

By tacit agreement they turned back along the path the way they'd come, Kate in the lead, striding down the slope, slithering over lumps of chalk and rabbit droppings, as if she couldn't get away from him fast enough.

Morgan watched her bouncing copper curls and thought there had to be something else, something other than these vague non-reasons. Why else would she have upped and left in such a dramatic fashion? It didn't make sense. His mind roved the possibilities, immediately discarding the one where Kate went through his phone and found Layla's name among his contacts. She would never do that, no more than he would do it to her. And even if she did, she would ask him about it outright.

But supposing he had somehow acted in a way that had aroused her suspicions? He'd been distracted by Layla, undoubtedly, although during that time he'd tried very hard not to think about her while he was with Kate. His brief moment of disloyalty remained a safely-guarded secret; he was as sure of that as he could be.

His hand closed around the phone in his jeans pocket. Her number was still on there. He hadn't thought to delete it. Why should he when he'd done nothing wrong?

Kate stopped and swung round to face him, as if she'd just remembered something. The action was so sudden that Morgan, deep in thought, had to stall his own feet in order not to cannon into her.

'Will you stay?' she said.

'How d'you mean?'

'In Haverstone, in the flat.'

'For God's sake, Kate, we haven't come to that yet, have we?'

He flung the question at her and was rewarded by a slight flinch in her body language before she sighed and folded her arms.

'I had hoped we wouldn't do this.'

'Oh right, so you thought it would all be on your terms and I'd roll over, wish you luck and send you on your merry way, is that it?'

'Morgan, please...'

Her eyes gleamed with tears, the most emotion she'd shown since she'd arrived. He wanted to hold her, brush her tears away, tell her to come home and promise her it was all going to be all right. But he couldn't, because he had no idea how to make it all right, and the more he thought about it, the more he realised he'd been burying his head in the sand.

'The flat, Morgan?'

She'd recovered herself already, all trace of emotion banished. They were back to practicalities.

'I don't know. I haven't thought. Funnily enough, the flat hasn't been high on my list of stuff to think about.'

'I'll carry on paying my half of the rent until everything's sorted out,' Kate said, as if he'd already said he wanted to stay.

He nodded, unable to trust himself to speak. She knew full well it wouldn't be easy for him to go on living in the flat alone; it wasn't cheap. She also knew how to make him feel totally inadequate.

They had reached the bottom of the slope where the rough path became a strip of tarmac leading past the backs of the beach huts towards the pay-and-display where they'd left Kate's car. Morgan began to feel panicky. He was making this far too easy for her, showing weakness at the very moment when he should be taking charge, finding a solution.

He caught up, fell into step beside her. 'Perhaps it's the flat that's the problem.'

'What?' Kate frowned.

'The flat. It's not the most romantic place in the world, is it?'

'*Romantic?*'

It did sound stupid, once she repeated it. Didn't she realise, though, that he was only trying to get her to talk, not leave him in this limbo? He tried again.

'What I meant was, supposing we move somewhere else, somewhere entirely different? It could be what we need, a way of starting afresh.'

Kate moved ahead of him again as if she wanted to shake him off. He watched her departing back with a sinking sensation, accompanied by an unexplained pain in his chest and a shallow wetness in his breathing. She spoke without turning round.

'And you think moving house would solve everything, do you?'

'Not everything, no, but it might help.'

He felt even more stupid now. She had no right to make him feel like that, she really didn't, when all he was trying to do was find out what she wanted, what it was that he, apparently, had failed to give her.

'Okay then,' he said, 'how about I give up the bookshop and get a better job, something that's more of a career?'

Kate stopped and turned. Her eyes met his. He held out his arms and she stepped into them. As he held her, he felt the weight of her sadness matching his own. Again, he allowed himself to hope but, even in her closeness and her apparent need of him, he sensed a distance, as if she wanted to hurry him along. After a moment, she broke free.

'There's nothing wrong with your job. You should do what you want to do, not what you think would impress other people. You still enjoy it, don't you? The bookshop? And the writing – that's your career, Morgan, if you want one. You're going to be an author, a famous one, remember?'

Morgan laughed, despite himself. He didn't recall fame

coming into it. Kate's answering smile was natural and genuine. It said she still believed in him. For the moment, she was back. His Kate.

'Yeah well, there's a long way to go before that's likely to happen.'

They were standing by her car now. She had the keys in her hand. Several black plastic sacks bulging with her possessions were hunkered down on the back seat. The boot was full of books and files in supermarket carrier bags. In all their time together they'd never managed to acquire any decent luggage, apart from the rucksacks that had followed them from their student days. Was that a sign that they weren't proper grown-ups?

Morgan let the random thought billow through his mind when he should have been searching for words, the right words to make Kate stay. He couldn't – wouldn't – believe that there weren't any.

'Kate...'

'Yes?' She was in the car now, reaching over to hold the passenger door open for him.

'I love you. I really do.' He raised his hands in a helpless gesture, then coughed violently.

'I love you, too, Morgan, but I'm not *in love* with you, not any more. I'm sorry.' She sat up straight in the driver's seat, leaving the door open for him. 'Get in. I'll drop you back at the flat.'

Morgan stuffed his hands in his pockets. He was beginning to feel most peculiar now. He coughed again, behind his hand.

'No, I'd rather walk.'

He didn't fancy being bumped about in the car. Neither did he want to drag this out any longer than necessary.

'If you're sure.' Kate started the engine. 'I'll be in touch. And get something for that cough.'

Morgan didn't reply. He closed the passenger door for her,

then stood and watched as she reversed, swinging round to the exit and waiting for a bus to pass before turning onto the road. Only then did he call after her.

'I love you, Kate! Don't do this!'

But he knew she couldn't hear him.

NINETEEN

A chest infection, the GP said, lowering her stethoscope, when on Wednesday he finally presented himself at the surgery. Rotating her chair to face the computer, she chugged out a prescription for a course of antibiotics. Morgan pocketed it as furtively as if he was a junkie come for his controlled fix. He felt feeble, bothering the doctor when the waiting room was packed to the gunnels with more deserving cases. But he couldn't remember ever feeling this ill before and none of the stuff he'd found in the bathroom cabinet had made the slightest impression on his condition.

Back in the flat, his weary feet took him straight to the bedroom where he'd been holed up almost constantly since Monday. One look at the mashed-up pillows and dampish furrowed sheets had him stripping off the bedding and ramming it all into the laundry bin. With no energy left to re-make the bed, he took a blanket to the sofa and set up camp there with a carton of orange juice and the TV remote. At least if he fell asleep and dribbled on the cushions, there'd be no one to tell him off.

No one. He examined the word, surprised to find a different

reaction from the one he'd expected. The flat felt hollow and subdued but no more than it had before Kate left, even with its thinned-out contents. There was, however, a low-level air of expectation about the place, as if she'd simply gone away for a while and was due back at any moment.

Up on the cliff on Sunday afternoon – was it really only three days ago? – nothing had seemed definite or final or sorted. The pendulum had swung backwards and forwards in his mind: it was over; it was not. By nightfall, when he'd given up the fight to stay upright and fallen, coughing and feverish, into bed, he'd given up trying to work it out and was too ill to care.

Raising himself up on one elbow, he swallowed down the first of his antibiotics with a slug of juice and flopped back onto his makeshift bed. Staring up at the ceiling, he purposely built an image of Kate driving away with a carful of belongings, leaving Haverstone. Leaving him. For good. The concept had no substance, no ring of truth about it.

At the time, there had been cause for reasonable doubt but, strangely, not now. If there was one thing he knew about Kate, though, it was that she wouldn't be told what to do. As much as he felt the urge to, it was no good ringing or texting or hassling her in any way. Nothing was guaranteed more to send her scampering in the opposite direction.

No, he must wait it out until she realised her mistake and came back of her own accord.

His thoughts wandered to his mother, how Kate was like her in her stubbornness and how like his father he was in the way he reacted to the same situation. Well, not exactly the same, because with Nick and Ellie – they preferred him to call them by their first names – there had been a third party involved, but it amounted to the same thing.

Morgan had just turned thirteen when his mother left. He hadn't felt sad because he'd been too angry, with her, with both of them. His father's apparent calm acceptance had frustrated him. It seemed to Morgan to be a sign of weakness. He had wanted to have it out with his dad, ask him why he wasn't fighting for her, compelling her to give up this... other person and stop being so stupid, but he possessed neither the emotional nor physical vocabulary. It took several years and a whole lot of growing up before he understood that it was strength, not weakness, which stopped his father from chasing after her.

Strength, and pride. That, and the peculiar circumstances of the situation.

Whatever battles there were – and there must have been some – were conducted in muted tones behind closed doors until eventually, without fuss, Ellie moved out of the family home and into a dinky plastic-windowed new-build on an estate full of other dinky plastic-windowed new-builds, halfway to Bury St Edmunds.

The place was totally wrong for her, Morgan thought at the time. Once his anger had cooled, his pubescent mind had focused on this almost exclusively, as if it was the most important aspect of the whole thing. He couldn't see how his mother could ever be happy there. Where would she do her paintings and practise her alternative therapy stuff, for a start? But it was where her new lover lived, so he supposed it was obvious that's where she would go.

And then it was just Morgan and Nick left to rattle around in the big old weather-boarded house, with Ellie's paintings haphazardly decorating the walls, her early attempts at pottery gathering dust on top of the cupboards, hummocks of salt-crusted thrift in the front garden, and the beach exactly twenty-eight steps from the front door.

But the real tragedy of the situation hadn't been that his parents were headed for the divorce court. He felt sad about that, it was true, and he missed his mum, especially at bedtime. She phoned him every other night, came to see him once a week and gradually his dad stopped pretending that nothing had changed and this new reality became the norm. And it was all right, kind of. Besides, there were tons of other kids at school with separated parents, three in his class alone; none of them seemed to think it was that big a deal.

No, the real tragedy – at least he'd thought so at the time – lay in the twist that Morgan had discovered quite by accident.

His mother was still living in their house at the time; she and his father keeping well away from one another, the flight paths of their days intersecting only through Morgan, like warring wasps around the same pot of honey.

It was the first day of the summer holidays. The blue-skied heat made the ground tremble if you stared at it for long enough. Morgan had been on the beach with Jamie and Glenn, two of his best mates. Not the beach directly in front of his house, but the one half a mile further along, opposite the ice-cream place, the gift shop and the minuscule apology of an amusement arcade. They'd been in for a swim and were hunkered down on towels in the semi-shade of the wooden breakwater. Morgan's towel, he remembered, had red, white and blue stripes and was so threadbare it was almost see-through. Jamie produced a KitKat from his bag and had begun to break it into sections when suddenly he stopped and nudged Morgan.

'Hey, isn't that your mum?'

'What? Where?' Morgan had shaded his eyes and peered along the beach.

'No, look. In the sea.' Jamie pointed a chocolatey finger.

It was. It was Ellie. She was chest-deep in the water, head thrown back like a sun-worshipper, making slow sweeping movements with her arms but not actually swimming. It was strange, because Morgan had seen her pack her easel and all her art stuff into the boot of her car right after breakfast, and when he'd asked her where she was going she'd ruffled his hair and said she was going to a farm to paint an old barn or something.

He'd thought that perhaps she'd changed her mind at the last minute, decided on the beach instead and her swimming stuff was already in the car. It seemed unlikely, but even more unlikely that she'd lied about where she was going; the need for subterfuge had long gone. It made no sense.

A long, cold finger of anxiety had probed Morgan's insides. He ducked his head and shrank back into the shade of the breakwater. The last thing he wanted was the embarrassment of his mother waving to him when he was with his mates or, even worse, coming over and striking up a conversation.

He drew his knees up and watched her cautiously over the top of them. She was coming out of the sea now, wading towards the shore, her long dark hair trailing like seaweed across her tanned shoulders and, oh God, she was wearing a bikini! An orange bikini. And there was precious little of it. Ellie never wore a bikini; she wore a black, all-over swimsuit which she called a costume.

As he watched, she stopped the swimming movements and turned so that she was facing out to sea. Morgan saw someone swimming towards her, another woman, powering through the water as if she couldn't get there fast enough. Ellie bent forwards and playfully scooped up water with both hands, splashing the swimmer. The woman stood up unsteadily. She was tall – a head taller than his mother – and wore a swimsuit so white it glowed against her light brown skin. Her blonde hair was tied up in a ponytail darkened by the water. She looked like a Bond girl.

The two women were close to the shore now, knee-deep in the surf, splashing each other and squealing with laughter like children. Morgan seemed to have forgotten how to breathe. He glanced at Jamie and Glenn. Their eyes, narrowed against the glare, were trained on his mother and the other woman, their mouths hanging open in lascivious wonder.

Stop it! he'd wanted to yell. *Stop looking at my mum like that!* At the same time, he tried to think whether he'd ever seen the other woman before. He decided he hadn't. Before it all went wrong, Ellie's friends used to come to the house and they'd sit round the kitchen table for hours on end, talking and laughing, drinking wine or stinky herbal tea and being in the way whenever Morgan or his dad needed to get to the fridge. Morgan knew most of them by sight, if not by name. This one, though, was a complete stranger.

'What a stormer,' Jamie said, suddenly turning to Morgan as if he'd only just remembered he was there. Then, seeing Morgan's face, 'Not your mum, you cretin. The blonde one.'

'She's more than a stormer. She's totally fucking gorgeous,' Glenn had said, still watching, stretching out the syllables in 'gorgeous' in a way that made Morgan want to hit him.

He turned to Morgan. 'Your mum's friend, is she?'

'I dunno,' Morgan muttered. 'Are we going or what?'

He pulled his T-shirt from his bag and struggled into it, working it down over his damp torso.

Then, as he was fumbling his way into his shorts with one eye on the scene in the water, something terrible had happened. Something even worse than his mother cavorting about and making a holy show of herself in front of his mates and everyone else on the beach.

It was, in fact, the most appalling thing he'd ever witnessed in his whole life.

The woman in the white swimsuit stopped splashing, reached out to his mother and took hold of both her hands. They stood in the shallows, laughing and laughing, their heads thrown back and their shiny wet bodies only as far apart as the length of their linked arms. And then the laughter stopped as suddenly as if a switch had been thrown, and they pulled one another close, so close there was no daylight left between them. And then they'd kissed. Properly. Heads tilted. Mouth-on-mouth and everything.

'Holy shit,' Jamie breathed.

Morgan couldn't move. His heart raced. Black spots tangoed in front of his eyes.

'Would you credit that?' Glenn's voice was full of delighted wonder. 'Hampshire's mum's a lezza. Would you friggin' credit it?'

'No way,' Jamie said, letting the words out on a long, slow breath, like he meant the opposite.

'No, she isn't!'

Adrenaline fired Morgan into action. Forcing his damp feet into his trainers and shoving the rest of his stuff in his bag, he stood up and half ran, half lurched his way up the beach to where his bike stood against the end of the breakwater.

'Fuck off!' he yelled at his friends, as he pedalled away. 'Fuck *off!*'

His head was beginning to throb now – short, stabbing bursts of pain, beating at a new memory as if trying to drive it out. But it wasn't ready to leave yet. The sun through the window was hurting his eyes, flooding the room with harsh, angled rays. And there was Kate, silhouetted against the light, impatiently jiggling the key in the lock then flinging the glass door wide open and stepping out onto the balcony. Their first moments in the flat, the two of them bright and shiny with love and hope.

Bright and shiny as the sea.

'Come quickly!' she'd called, as he'd worried two rucksacks and a bulging plastic bin bag through the door and into the living room. 'Look! Isn't it brilliant?'

Dropping the bags, he had gone over and stood behind her, resting his hands on her shoulders as she gazed across the single row of rooftops opposite, towards the beach and the rolling waves. Her rapturous expression had made him laugh and he'd lifted her hair and kissed the warm, soft nape of her neck.

'Brilliant, yeah,' he'd agreed, nuzzling into her neck and making her giggle.

He'd looked back at the sea and tried to rouse in himself some of Kate's excitement, but all he could see was his mother emerging from the waves like a mythical goddess, hand-in-hand with her lover. She was smiling as she came towards him. She seemed to be moving above the surface of the water rather than through it, and as she drew closer and closer to him, Morgan felt himself cowering as his inner thirteen-year-old took charge.

When Kate had finished admiring the view, she'd found him standing in the flat's empty, echoey kitchen with no idea as to how he got there.

Morgan got up and closed the blinds. Back on the sofa, he listened to his own rasping breath penetrating the silence in the room. He must have drifted off to sleep, because ten minutes later he awoke with a jump to the jangle of his mobile. Ten minutes? No, according to the time on the muted TV, he'd been asleep for two-and-a-half hours. Groping down the side of the sofa, he retrieved his phone and spluttered into it before firing a round of explosive coughs.

'You sound as rough as a bear's backside,' Connor said.

'I feel it, mate, I feel it.'

Why was Connor phoning? He never phoned. Sometimes he texted, but usually there was nothing that couldn't wait until Morgan's next trip to Maybridge. He had a thought.

'Is it Ted? Is he all right?'

'Grandad's fine, or as fine as he'll ever be. Plaguing the life out of me, as it happens. Keeps saying I'm keeping him out of things, which is true as it goes. Actually, I've got a message—'

'I'll be up on Saturday,' Morgan cut in, 'if you need help with the boats or anything. I can catch up with the writing here, so it's fine.'

'No, it's not that. Listen, someone gave me a message for you, well a kind-of one. Only I thought I'd better pass it on in case it was important.'

'Wassat?' Morgan's voice struggled out through his mucus-laden throat. He was so tired, and so not in the mood for a chat, even with Connor. His brain finally caught up. 'Did you say a message? For me?'

'I did. Hang on a sec.' Morgan heard Connor shout to someone in the background. He came back to Morgan. 'Idiot driver's backed a delivery lorry right into the yard and now he can't get out again, wouldn't you know? Anyway...'

Morgan waited while Connor, obviously distracted, remembered where he'd left off.

'A girl. She got on the boat with a little boy. Didn't give her name. Said to say "hello" next time I saw you.' Connor laughed. 'I sincerely hope you're not toying with the affections of the legendary Kate.'

'Kate's... Never mind.' He didn't have the strength to go into that now. 'What did she look like, this girl?' As if he had to ask.

'Beautiful, mate. Beautiful. All eyes and long dark hair. Nice assets, too.'

'Was that it? Was that all she said?'

'Yup. "Hello." That was the sum total.'

Morgan caught the grinding rev of an engine and a series of reversing beeps.

'Sorry, I've got to go,' Connor said, and ended the call.

Layla. She'd asked after him and passed on a message. She hadn't forgotten about him. As the days had trickled by, he'd begun to doubt his version of their meeting in the boathouse. Now, the feeling returned with full-blown clarity, the feeling of something beginning.

TWENTY

Hello you! Nice surprise even at crazy o'clock. We could talk for real except my sister's asleep in the same room. Don't like that you're ill. Is it terminal? (joke!)

Crazy o'clock it may be but I've been asleep all day so now I'm totally wide awake but a bit out of it on the antibiotics. Yes it's terminal – terminally boring. No, just a chest infection. I'm coughing my g… Never mind. Did you enjoy your boat trip?

I did and so did Finn (my nephew). Your friend Connor did the business. He's not as good as you ;-) It's been a bit of a nightmare at home (families – you don't want to know!) so it was nice to get out for a while. You didn't say much about your family before – probably because you couldn't get a word in edgeways! What are they like?

OK I guess. They never interfered much while I
was growing up, so I guess that counts as OK.
My father's a retired academic but he keeps a
foot in the door of a couple of universities. He
has a humungous collection of fossils, a legful
of steel pins (result of falling off a cliff, silly
bugger), and a girlfriend called Fiona. My
mother is a reflexologist, aromatherapist and
artist, and has a girlfriend called Judy. I call
them Nick and Ellie, not Mum and Dad. So all
pretty standard stuff ;-).

Your mum has a girlfriend? Are you cool with
that?

I am now. I wasn't at the start but it was a long
time ago and everyone's friends again, even
Nick and Ellie and their respectives. You said I
wouldn't want to know about your family. Well I
do. I want to know everything about you
including what you had for breakfast. Sorry,
that's the medication talking. Don't answer if
you don't want to.

Cold leftover pizza if you must know. Moving
swiftly on, Dad died when I was 15. Mum's a
domestic goddess by day and karaoke queen
by night. It's how she lets off steam and believe
me there's a lot to let off. My younger sister
Jadine has just discovered Sex with a capital S.
Rowan (Finn's mum) thinks she's a woman of
the world but runs home at the first sign of
trouble, which is where she is now. More of that
another time, if you can stand it. Not sure I can

Interesting sisters! You must tell all. Sorry about
your Dad, though. That's sad.

Thanks. Yes, it was a sad time. Mum copes
pretty well. It's what she does.

How about we meet up again in Maybridge?
We could actually have that coffee this time. I
know I've got a nerve even asking considering
my spectacular failure to keep in touch.
Pressing send while I still have the courage.

Yes, let's do it.

TWENTY-ONE

'I don't feel as bad as I look,' Morgan said hurriedly, correctly interpreting Layla's expression.

Her first thought was that he wasn't being truthful; her second that he was either used to being around women with stereotypical nurturing tendencies or those who were phobic about catching germs. She wondered which category Kate fell into.

She had felt guilty from the moment the café door opened and she'd seen him striding towards her in crumpled jeans and a blue T-shirt, a black leather jacket slung over his shoulder. He looked in no fit state to be out and about. His face had the cheesy pallor she associated with really old men, his eyes peering over-brightly from it like an animal peering out of a hedge. Dark stubble outlined his chin – not unattractively – and he'd lost so much weight that his cheeks had a sunken appearance and his midriff was almost concave.

'Yes, well, you probably shouldn't have come out in the rain,' she said, then laughed. 'I'm turning into my mother.'

'As long as you're not turning into mine.' Morgan winked.

Layla was puzzled for a moment, until she remembered.

She gave a little embarrassed laugh, felt herself blushing a bit. Morgan laughed, too, until it degenerated into a coughing fit, and after that everything felt easy and natural, as it had in the boathouse.

They walked along the riverbank in the opposite direction from the boathouse, past the road bridge and the backs of the high street shops, to where a clipped expanse of grass gave onto the site of the old priory ruins.

The rain had stopped and the great slabs of flint stood out against the brightening sky like broken teeth. As they left the towpath and crossed the grass, Morgan took her hand and held it, glancing at her as he did, smiling a question, checking that she didn't mind. She smiled back and hoped he hadn't noticed the tightening of the muscles in her shoulders, the momentary break in her stride.

Inside the airy arena created by the ruined walls and arches, a bunch of foreign language students wearing identical backpacks jostled one another in a high-pitched frenzy of chatter. Maybridge was full of them at this time of year. One of the boys – fair-haired, the tallest of the group – held his arms high above his head, flexing his muscles. He looked like a younger version of Harvey.

The lightness of the day shrank away, leaving something dull and heavy in its place. Layla was wondering how to detach herself from Morgan without it seeming like a pointed gesture when he said something that brought her up short.

'Kate and I aren't together any more. We've split. She's moved out of the flat.'

Startled, she let go of his hand. 'Oh. Well, that's... I'm so sorry.'

'It's all right.' Morgan rubbed the top of his head. 'It was bound to happen, in the end.'

They were standing close to the tallest, most intact, of the priory walls, where ivy scrambled over the flints and waved mocking tendrils through the gaps where the windows used to be. Morgan leaned his back against the wall and turned his face up to the sky, as if that was the end of the conversation, and yet Layla didn't feel as if he was blocking her out. She thought about trying to draw him out, to get him to talk about Kate, in case it helped. No, bad idea; she hardly knew him. If he wanted to confide in her about the state of his relationship, then he would.

Again she felt a heaviness descend. The clouds came back, smothering the remaining sun. The air was humid. The students had trailed away towards the gate leading to the city centre, leaving the two of them alone in the green space.

Morgan ceased his inspection of the sky. 'It's going to rain again. Shall we go back inside?' He indicated the direction of the café with a nod. 'Or we could go to the boathouse?'

Layla thought about the picnic rug spread out on the wooden floor, the chuckle of the kettle, the tang of linseed oil, the river slinking by, and knew that the boathouse was where she wanted to be more than anywhere else in the world. With Morgan. Which was precisely why they couldn't go there.

'No, I don't think so. Not today. I have to get going soon, anyway.'

'Look, Layla...' Morgan stepped out in front of her so that she had to stop. 'I'm not here with you because Kate's gone. It's not like that at all. I'm not that kind of bloke, although I wouldn't blame you for thinking otherwise. And I never meant to deceive you, yet I seem to have done just that. After the afternoon we spent together I was thinking we could get together again, just as friends.' He slapped a hand to his forehead. 'I was kidding myself. I'm an expert at that, got a natural talent for it.'

'Okay,' she said, drawing the word out.

'And now,' Morgan continued, 'I'm probably about to make a complete prat of myself, but I'll have to chance that.'

Layla waited.

'I've wanted to kiss you ever since I walked into the café – no, ever since you walked onto that boat – and I don't think it's going to go away, the wanting, I mean.' He shrugged, gave a self-effacing smile. 'So there it is.'

Layla glanced across at the river, then looked back at Morgan, daringly, right into his eyes. Her heart performed a drum-roll.

'Well, if that's what you want...'

She smiled.

It was the sweetest kiss, the sweetest ever. While it lasted, Layla lived in the moment, let all that had gone before slip away and almost forgot to be afraid.

TWENTY-TWO

Morgan's previous qualms over Kate chipping in the lion's share of their living expenses were nothing compared to the way he felt about it now. 'Kept man' might have been a phrase from the dark ages but it partly summed up his feelings. *Partly?* Okay, it wasn't even close. He'd expected any day to receive a message from her, saying that the payments into what used to be their shared bank account – and still was in name only – would shortly cease. But no, there it was again, the figure Kate had come up with, showing efficiently on the credit side of the account.

Without further thought, he transferred the amount right back where it belonged, into Kate's own account, before closing the lid of the laptop with an efficient snap.

He supposed he should let her know, although she'd find out soon enough. He used to rib her about her constant, rigorous checking of the account's activities and she would retaliate by jokily accusing him of living under a stone. He didn't imagine she'd changed her habits that much.

The next step would be to pull apart the account, with Kate's authorisation – an important step in separating their names from each other for eternity. Important, but not final, because there was still the flat. He hadn't been putting it off on purpose, not exactly. It was just that there'd been no need to travel down that potentially rocky road until now. Now being the point at which Morgan silently acknowledged – to himself, to the seagull which seconds ago had landed on the balcony and deposited a large dropping onto the concrete, and to the world at large – that Kate wasn't coming back. And, more to the point, neither did he want her to.

This last crumb of truth had been hard to swallow. It smacked of weakness, of giving up too easily and admitting that Kate was right; they had fallen out of love. He'd got there in the end; sooner than expected, if he was honest. After all, he could hardly carry on deluding himself that he was broken-hearted over Kate while he was so desperately, headily, uncompromisingly, in love with somebody else.

So, the flat. He picked up the laptop from the desk, took it across to the sofa and sat down, but a sudden violent coughing fit had him up again and heading to the kitchen for a swig of the foul-tasting cough linctus he'd bought from the chemist. Back again, wheezing slightly, he gazed around the room which had felt as vast and empty as a prairie immediately after Kate's departure. Now it was simply a place to be, the proverbial roof over his head. He wouldn't miss the flat. In fact, it would be a relief to be shot of it. But where to live instead?

He smiled as the wild fantasy of him and Layla moving in together entered his head, building their own forever little love nest. The fantasy stretched further, to the boathouse which, miraculously, had acquired such luxuries as running water, cooking and washing facilities and heating. He indulged his daydream a little longer, then pushed it aside, opened the laptop and began to search the property websites.

The results were depressing. Once again, he'd been deluding himself. He'd imagined a light and airy studio flat with space to swing more than the legendary feline, either here in Haverstone or in the nearby town where the bookshop was. But the rents for such places, even those which fell way below par, were beyond ridiculous. How could people afford them? He certainly couldn't, not on his present income, and he wasn't going cap in hand to his father either. He'd never done that before and he wasn't going to start now.

Something about the bookshop had changed, even in the week since he was last there. He had returned to work once the worst of his illness was over. Then the annoying chest infection had flared up again, and after a grim morning spent coughing over the stock and the customers, he'd been packed off home for the rest of the week. Now it was Friday, a writing day rather than a bookshop day, but he couldn't settle down to write with the threat of imminent homelessness hanging over him. Clearly, he'd have to take action.

As soon as he entered the shop, he noticed a desultory air about the place. The three-for-two paperbacks were jumbled on their table and nobody had bothered to pick up the books that had fallen to the floor. Another table held stationery, greetings cards and children's toys, all with red, marked-down stickers, in carelessly raked piles with no attempt at demarcation. A young male assistant Morgan didn't recognise was listlessly shuffling the top twenty hardbacks about on the display stand in a futile attempt to disguise the gaps in the chart. He knew the girl on the cash point – she'd worked there almost as long as he had. Her head was bent over her mobile phone. She barely glanced up as he passed.

Continuing up the four flights of stairs, he raised his hand in greeting at several of his colleagues as he went, but didn't stop to chat. He needed to get this over with. On the café floor, the coffee machine stood silently behind the unmanned counter and a forest of chair legs pointed ceilingwards above the empty tables. The tightness in Morgan's chest wasn't entirely viral in its origins as eventually he reached the half-landing which served as the manager's office.

Neil, the manager, sat at an ink-graffitied desk, the pale dome of his head framed by the grimy window behind him. As Morgan approached, he looked up, completely unsurprised, as if he'd been there all the time. Morgan lifted out the wooden chair in front of the desk with one finger and sat down without waiting to be invited.

'I'd like to come back full-time. Work the Fridays as before, and the Saturdays. All of them, if you like.'

There was no point in prevaricating. No point in even saying it at all – he'd known that as soon as he walked in – but he was here now.

'Sorry, son, no can do.' Neil shook his head and took a mouthful of coffee from a thick white mug depicting the chain's logo, before putting it down with a grimace of disgust. 'It's all gone arse-upwards. They're closing branches down right across the country. This is one of them. Don't you read the papers?'

Morgan allowed himself precisely thirty minutes to feel sorry for himself. During that time, he'd pushed into Starbucks and bought a hot chocolate, trudged back to the car, crushing the empty drink cup in one hand as he reached it, and driven as far as the road sign that signalled his return to Haverstone. Then it was over; time to get a grip.

Reaching the flats, he left the car in the car park but, instead of going straight upstairs, he set out along the road and down the main street to the seafront. Immediately the salt air made his chest felt looser, his breathing easier. He stayed on the oppo-site side of the road to the beach, walking purposefully to create the illusion for himself that he had to be somewhere by a certain time. The activity helped his thought processes along, much as his walks along the riverbank helped to keep the plot of his novel flowing. He needed a plan. By the time he reached the end of this stretch of pavement, where the road turned inwards, curving away from the seafront, he would have one.

Lit by a shaft of sunlight, the gold lettering embossed on the glass revolving doors of Haverstone's largest hotel crackled against his pupils as he passed the entrance. Seconds later, he stopped and doubled back.

Morgan walked back to the flat with a bounce in his step. He had a job. Part one of the plan had been achieved. It was only kitchen portering but he was lucky, the duty manager had told him, that they weren't already fully staffed, considering the number of Europeans seeking summer jobs along the coast. He didn't care how menial it was, nor that he'd be working long hours for the minimum wage. Meals would be provided while he was on duty, and the job came with the option to live in.

So, part two of the plan was also taken care of. Morgan congratulated himself and cracked open a beer from the fridge. There were two weeks left at the bookshop, then he'd start at the hotel. Meanwhile, he would give notice on the flat.

Buoyed up by the progress he'd made this afternoon, he fired up the laptop and worked on his out-of-date CV. By the time he was satisfied he'd done his best with it, tiredness overcame him and the tightness in his chest set him off coughing again. Part three of the plan, the part where he searched for a decent job with career prospects – something in the psychology field, or maybe journalism or publishing, both of which appealed – would wait for another time.

. . .

The next day, Saturday, Morgan drove up to Maybridge with a lightness about him that he hadn't felt for a long time. Even Kate's snappy text message last night had not brought down his mood, a message in which she'd reminded him — rather accusingly, he felt — that she had paid twenty per cent more towards the deposit on the flat than he had. He had genuinely forgotten that when he'd repaid her exactly half. His reply had been short and businesslike, apologising for the oversight and assuring her that her share of the refund would be adjusted accordingly.

After he'd sent his reply, he read her message again, word by word, and tried to work out what was behind it. There was something, he could tell. Kate's previous generosity over money didn't fit with this nit-picking.

For some reason she had felt the need to attack him, which pointed to one thing: Kate was unhappy. Well, if that was the case he was genuinely sorry, but there wasn't a damn thing he could do about it. He wouldn't go so far as to say that Kate was no longer his problem — his heart could never harden to that extent — but neither was he going to ask her what was wrong and invite her confidence, when that was the last thing he needed. There was such a thing as self-preservation, and pride.

Any niggling doubts he had about Kate's well-being faded away as soon as he unlocked the door of the boathouse and stepped inside the warm, woody cavern. Dust motes spun in the disturbed air as he crossed to the sun-flooded trestle table and set out the laptop and his writing notebooks. The old office chair creaked as he sat down.

His mind flew to Layla. It was only a week since she was here. In one way, it seemed like a lifetime had passed in between; in another, it seemed as if she'd never left. He spun round on the chair as if he expected to see her standing there, waiting. She wasn't, of course. He wouldn't be seeing her today. She was taking her mother out for lunch; she'd told him when she'd rung him the night before last. He'd tried not to mind, but already he was missing her.

He turned back to the table and opened the laptop. His gaze strayed to the scene beyond the window where spring-bright branches cast stippled patterns on the fast-moving water. Last Saturday, she had asked him about Kate – straight out, no messing about. She had wanted to know if he still had feelings for her. What would happen if Kate suddenly changed her mind, or he changed *his* mind...?

It had been quite a speech, as if a dam had been breached. It had cost her something, spilling it all out. He'd waited quietly until she'd finished speaking, then waited some more in case she hadn't. Satisfied she was done, he'd taken both her hands in his – they'd been standing right here, beside the trestle table at the time – and told her, with equal sincerity and, he hoped, clarity – the whole story of Kate and the break-up and how their relationship had foundered long ago, only he'd been too blinkered to realise it.

Layla's hair had fallen across her face as she turned her head away from him. It was only a moment, and when she looked back at him, the honesty between them was so palpable that he'd smiled with relief and pure happiness. It would have been the perfect moment for a kiss. Instead, still holding hands, they had drawn close and leaned their foreheads together in a shared moment of such intimacy and tenderness that no kiss could have rivalled it.

Morgan smiled, remembering. He reached for his phone to send her a text. Stopping himself in time, he put the phone back in his pocket. *I want to take this slowly.* That was something else she'd said last week when, eager to kiss her again, he'd taken her into his arms and felt almost mortified when she pulled away. She'd brushed her mouth against his as she was leaving, but that was all. She wasn't playing games with him. He'd seen something in her eyes, a secret she wasn't ready to share with him, perhaps never would. But he wanted to be with this girl, on any terms. He could wait for whatever was to come.

Opening his notebook, Morgan read through the research notes he'd made during the week, then turned his attention to the screen. He was hardly aware of time passing as he hammered out three thousand words almost without hesitation. A rap sounded on the door. Morgan turned round, flexing his shoulder muscles, to see Connor standing in the doorway.

'Sorry to barge in,' he said, letting the door swing shut behind him as he came towards Morgan. 'I can see you're busy.'

'It's cool, I could do with a break. You want me to take a boat out? Great day for it.'

'No ta, we're covered. I've taken on a couple of blokes for the summer season. One's a student who was here last year. He's a good worker, reliable. The other's a bit of an unknown quantity. Please God he knows one end of a boat from the other and his tattooed head doesn't scare off the punters.' He gave a half laugh before the serious expression returned. 'As it happens, I've bigger problems than the boats.'

'Oh?' Morgan got up and filled the kettle from the water container. 'Got time for a coffee? It'll have to be black. I forgot to bring any milk.'

Connor passed a hand distractedly over his head and glanced at his watch. 'Go on then.'

Morgan made the drinks. He sat in the office chair while Connor sank down onto the floor, his back against the cupboard.

'Grandad's in hospital. Had another funny turn right outside the kiosk yesterday. Maureen called the ambulance, so he didn't have much choice.'

Connor's problems concerned much more than the daily running of the riverside business. He'd spoken to the doctor and it seemed that Ted had suffered a minor stroke.

'He'll be okay for now, according to the doc, but he has to

stop work,' Connor said. 'Altogether, not just cut down. How the hell am I meant to persuade him to do that? He's seventy-eight but he's always had so much energy I've tended to forget how old he is. It's not only the physical stuff, the actual graft. He keeps on top of the accounts, the health and safety, all the boring, essential crud that keeps the place afloat.'

Morgan grinned at the pun. Connor hadn't noticed he'd made one.

'You know all that stuff, though. You know how to do it,' Morgan said.

'I do, but I can't do it all. I can't be in the office, run the boat trips, manage the café, the gift shop and the kiosk, and sort out the staff. Staff management's one hell of a job on its own – you wouldn't believe the hoops you have to jump through... Okay, I'm coming to the point.' Connor put his coffee mug down on the floor beside him and looked directly at Morgan. 'I need someone I can rely on, someone who's around all the time, at least for the rest of the season, and I thought... No, forget it. You've already got a job.'

'As it happens, I haven't. Not the one I had, anyway.'

He told Connor about the bookshop closing, the stop-gap hotel job he had lined up. He even told him about Kate, the whole story – he'd only hinted briefly at it before. It felt cathartic, a release, to talk about it; he hadn't realised how much he needed to do that.

The hopeful look on Connor's face was hard to miss, although he was obviously trying to disguise it as he sympathised over Morgan's plight.

'Look, mate,' he said, 'I gotta be honest here. I've seen her, that girl with the long dark hair, the one who asked me to say hello for her. I've seen her coming here, and I've seen the pair of you on the riverbank with no room for a fag paper between you.'

Morgan suppressed a smile. 'We've not exactly been hiding. Anyway, what's that got to do with anything?'

'She lives here, in Maybridge, right? So in my twisted mind, I thought if you did happen to be planning a move up here and a change of scene, well...'

'What about Ted? Won't he think he's being edged out?'

'Grandad won't take much persuading to stand down if he knows it's you and not some stranger. You could still do your writing in the boathouse, in the quiet times.' Connor shrugged. 'Forget it. It was worth a long shot, though.'

'Okay.'

'You'll do it? Oh, mate, are you sure?' A beam broke out on Connor's face.

Morgan grinned back. 'Yep. Why not?'

Why not indeed? There was nothing stopping him, was there? The manager of the hotel would soon find someone else. He loved it here, the river and everything, and he could write in the evenings. The idea of a clean break from Haverstone appealed, too. If Connor didn't need him after the summer season was over, he could find something else to do up here, if he hadn't made plans by then to move on somewhere else.

And, as Connor had unsubtly pointed out, there was Layla. They'd be able to see one another all the time instead of just at weekends, and perhaps, if things worked out, eventually they'd be able to get a place together.

Morgan thrust the idea away. He was getting ahead of himself, way ahead. Slowly, she'd said. The excitement he'd allowed himself to feel faded fast as he wondered how she would take the news that he was moving to Maybridge. Would she think he was crowding her, pushing things too far?

But she would understand that his decision wasn't about her. Layla held other people's feelings in high regard. She would know it was better for him to leave Haverstone and make a fresh start in a place that already felt like home. It all made perfect sense.

TWENTY-THREE

Kate stripped off her uniform and threw it onto the bed. Reaching beneath the grubby venetian blind, she lifted the casement to open the lower half of the window and let in some air. The slats of the blind were tilted half open, allowing her to see out while nobody could see in. At least, she didn't think they could as the room was on the second floor of the nurses' home and there were no other windows directly opposite. Not that she cared. If anyone caught an eyeful, good luck to them.

Peeling off her underwear, she stood naked by the window, gazing between the slats of the blind at the dense blue sky pierced by tall chimney pots that topped the buildings of the older part of the hospital. She smoothed her hands slowly down and across her body, feeling it begin to cool as it came into contact with the air. It had been a bit of a nightmare today. Two emergency admissions last night had filled to capacity the ward she was working on, and the nurse manager had taken herself off to some meeting or other, leaving Kate and an agency nurse to answer the ever-ringing phone as well as deal with the patients.

She was so hot and so tired. For two pins she could have

thrown herself onto the bed and slept until morning, but it was only six o'clock. She'd jump in the shower and sluice away the pungent remains of a hard day on the ward – not that it ever went away entirely. Then she'd go over to the cafeteria for comfort food and a chat with whoever happened to be there.

As long as it wasn't Xavi.

She'd deliberately avoided looking up his shifts, difficult though it was, so she had no idea where he was unless they were on duty together. Except on clinic days, of course, when they bumped into one another – physically – at least six times a day because of the narrowness of the corridors and the meagre staff space. And then she had to endure that look, the lost look in his eyes, the silent appeal which the smiles he gave her had no hope of disguising.

It scared her to think it had come to this; that she could have fallen so completely out of love with him as completely as she had fallen in. It hadn't been love, of course. She knew that now. She'd been flattered and comforted by his attentions, and physically attracted to him, but that was all. Xavi was decent and kind, but she was never in love with him. And to think she'd given up Morgan, the flat – her whole life, apart from her job – in order to be with him. Only she hadn't, in the end. It hadn't taken her long to realise that prevaricating over moving in with Xavi hadn't been about slowing everything down. It had been about her, what she really wanted, and about swerving the biggest mistake of her life. One of them, anyway.

She'd made another mistake on Saturday night. She'd jumped into bed with a junior doctor she hardly knew, in his room after a party. It hadn't meant anything, the sex; like scratching an itch. At least they'd been *compos mentis* enough to use a condom. Not a mistake of mammoth proportions, then, but a mistake nonetheless. She didn't believe in casual sex, yet she'd betrayed that belief willingly and without a smidgeon of guilt, until the following morning.

She no longer trusted her own judgement. It was almost laughable, considering how she'd railed against Morgan for the way he drifted through life. She'd seen that side of him first as an endearing trait, then as an annoyance, and finally as a weakness. Until that Sunday afternoon on the clifftop, when she'd suddenly seen, with a clarity as brilliant as the sea, that just because Morgan followed the flow and refused to fight her over the little things she'd thought were so important at the time, it didn't mean that he wasn't as focused and determined as she was. Or she had been.

Morgan had loved her. For all she knew, he had never stopped loving her, even throughout her protests that there was nothing left between them. Perhaps she should have been honest enough to tell him there was someone else. It might have helped him to accept the situation. She'd wanted to save his pride and protect him from more pain, but what difference would it have made if she'd already broken his heart? Had she broken two hearts in as many months?

The rapidly cooling sweat on her skin sent shivers through her body. She picked up her towelling robe from the bed and wrapped it round herself but she didn't move from the window. Instead, she stood and thought about Morgan until the sun began to melt over the rooftops.

TWENTY-FOUR

'It doesn't matter, Mel. There's plenty of bread. If we do happen to run out, I'll go and get some more.' Reece edged himself between Melody and the kitchen counter where the enamel bread bin gaped, its lid cast aside. Placing his hands on her shoulders, he turned her to face him. 'It's fine. Stop worrying.'

Melody sighed, her tired eyes searching his face as if she didn't quite trust what she saw there.

'I just want everything to be perfect, that's all. We're having the mussels tonight. She likes those. They serve them with brown bread and butter in the hotel, she said. I got a small brown loaf, but supposing she wants brown toast in the morning...?'

Melody spoke more to herself than to him, her gaze already returned to the bread bin.

'Mel.' Reece gave her shoulders a little squeeze, then let her go and replaced the lid on the bin with a firm clang.

'Yes, you're right.' Melody raised a forefinger. 'Oh, I know, we'll have chips with the mussels. Mussels and chips! That's a classic, isn't it? Yes!'

At once she was brighter, energised by her own solution to the problem which hadn't existed in the first place. Her eyes glittered with new purpose. Reece couldn't decide whether this was better or worse. The tablets she was on were meant to calm her, help her stay on an even keel. If that was the case, they were worse than useless and did little to prevent the tidal thrust of Melody's moods from one pole to the other.

Perhaps they were placebos. He supposed he should find out but he didn't have the heart for it. He was losing heart slowly, day by day. Soon there'd be nothing left, then what would become of them?

'She's here!' Melody was out of the door at once, flying across the gravel so that Layla had to brake sharply to avoid hitting her.

Reece stood in the doorway, watching the two of them walking towards the house: Melody, her arm round Layla's shoulders, her high, exaggerated steps almost a bounce; Layla's stride purposeful yet resigned. She was laughing at something Melody had said, and when she saw Reece she gave him a bright, open smile that quietened his churning gut.

Layla had brought flowers for Melody – a cheerful posy of sweet-scented freesias – and a bottle of Merlot for him. He accepted his gift with a grateful smile and stood the bottle on the counter. They'd long ago tried to stop her bringing presents each time, but still they came – a tribute to her upbringing as well as her generous nature, he always thought.

Melody began fussing about the shelves, searching for the perfect container for the flowers, until Layla jokily edged her aside and laid her hands on a blue-and-white jug.

'This is what we want,' she said, holding it aloft.

'Yes! So it is! That's exactly what we want.' Melody beamed. 'Clever girl.'

Happily, she ran water into the jug, dropped in the freesias and carried it through to the hall table. 'There. Now I shall see them every time I go in and out.'

The empty mussel shells lay abandoned in pools of buttery juice at the bottoms of the bowls. Reece stared at them over the top of his wine glass. They stared back, poking their sharp black tongues at him. He should have felt reassured by the relaxed dinner-table talk. Instead, he'd felt trapped, poised on the edge of the deepest chasm, unable to move.

The mussels had been greeted with relish by Layla, and no, she wouldn't rather have had the bread because Melody made the best chips *ever*, which happened to be true. Layla had been amusing them with the continuing saga about her family and the overcrowded house, and how she longed for her sister and her young son either to move back to their own house or move on somewhere else. But out, definitely *out*. She'd made it a funny story, exaggerating the humorous bits for effect, and they'd all laughed together.

If Melody still disapproved of Layla's family, she showed no sign of it. She seemed composed; serene, even. The two glasses of Chablis she'd drunk had helped, of course. Reece wasn't sure she should be drinking if her medication was the real McCoy, but this wasn't the time to raise the subject.

The only slight dip came in the form of Melody's startled frown when Layla had asked if they wouldn't mind her leaving tomorrow evening instead of staying over until Sunday. But Melody had rallied immediately, concurred with Layla's plan as, almost visibly, she reshuffled Saturday's meals in her head, and it had all been fine.

Tonight – *this* – wasn't a problem. No, the problem was that behind all the bonhomie was a bloody great arrow pointing towards impending disaster. Layla couldn't carry on coming here for ever, a permanent fixture in their lives. She obviously knew it and so did he, but did Melody? Sooner or later, it would end, gradually rather than suddenly. Although, he thought ruefully, suddenly might be better all round.

Later, as he and Layla tipped the shells into the bin and loaded the dishwasher, Melody having been sent away to sit down, Reece saw his chance to have a private chat. He thought he might be able to ascertain Layla's intentions regarding Melody and the weekend visits. Instead, she seemed to have something she wanted to say to him, as she leaned conspiratorially towards him while they stood at the sink together. At first he thought she'd pre-empted him, and his stomach tightened. Then he saw her expression – the soft, new brightness of her eyes which he realised now had been there all along, only he hadn't taken it in properly.

'What?' he said, smiling at her, equally conspiratorially.

'I've met someone. Kind of.'

She blushed a bit. He didn't think he'd ever seen her blush before.

'Ah.' He gave a knowing little nod. 'And would this by any chance be a special kind of someone?'

'Might be. It depends.'

'What does it depend on?' Reece asked quietly.

She shrugged. 'Oh, you know. How it turns out. Stuff.'

She turned away, picked up the tea towel and began to dry a wine glass. Although she wasn't looking at him she was smiling. He felt privileged to be the recipient of her secret – it was a secret, he could tell. Maybe she thought of him as a sort of father figure and that was why she was confiding in him. Although this was about her love life, so maybe not.

'Have you told...?' He glanced pointedly at the half-closed kitchen door.

'No, I haven't told Melody. Not that there's much to tell. Would you mind not saying anything to her, not yet, anyway? Sorry, I've got no right to ask. Forget it.'

'No, no, I think you're right. It's for the best,' Reece said, nodding.

He took the glass from Layla's hand and put it in the cupboard. He knew exactly what she meant. Melody would make a major issue of it, insist on knowing what this 'special person' was like and all about him, before Layla was ready to tell. She might even – Reece paled at the idea – ask Layla to bring him to the farm so that they could meet him. It would be all too much.

Besides, he knew Layla well enough to understand that she was being extra sensitive to Melody's feelings by not including her in this mini-revelation. She knew it would only trigger another reminder of all that had been lost along with Danni. Clearly, by confiding in him, Layla thought he was made of sterner stuff. He wished it were true.

He swallowed tightly, his earlier misgivings returning tenfold. But the moment had passed to quiz the girl about her intentions; her mind was elsewhere, yet not, he thought, entirely happily.

'So, is there a problem?' he ventured.

'When is there not?' Layla spoke sharply, not how he'd expected her to react at all. She folded the tea towel and hung it on the rail, squaring it up so the sides were exactly equal before she turned back to him. 'I just mean... oh, that I'm properly out of practice. I haven't been out with anyone in a long while, not on dates and stuff. I haven't been able to. It hasn't seemed right, somehow.'

Reece looked at Layla, the way her eyes were searching his face, willing him to understand without her having to spell it out.

'Not since Danni went?'

He couldn't bring himself to say 'died', not now, not in front of Layla. She nodded, looking down at the floor. She seemed almost ashamed.

They stood in silence for a moment – Layla awkwardly, like a child who'd confessed to some misdemeanour; Reece struck dumb by this new revelation. The tally had risen; one more life put on hold since that tragic night. He didn't want that for Layla. He and Mel, well, they would find their own way, in time. But Layla...

'No, sweetheart.' He touched her shoulder. 'That's not right. Danni wouldn't have wanted that. You have your life, Layla, and you must live it, otherwise you're doing her a disservice as well as yourself. This boy, the special one, don't send him away. Give it a go, have some fun and see what happens, and if he turns out to be a complete doughnut, then so what? You won't know until you try.'

Layla's shoulders shook, her head still bowed. For a moment he thought she was crying, and then he realised she was laughing.

'What are you like?' She looked up at him, shaking her head slowly.

'*Me?*' Reece tapped a finger at his chest, his face straight, pretending he didn't know what she meant.

'Doughnut?' She shook her head again. 'There are worse things than going out with a doughnut, I suppose.' She giggled. 'I promise I'll let you know at the first doughnut alert.'

'Well, see that you do.'

Ducking his head, he kissed her on the cheek. She seemed a little taken aback by his impulsive show of affection, her face colouring slightly. Immediately regretting the gesture, Reece picked up the sponge and began mopping up the water splashes from the draining board, keeping his face averted until he heard Layla leave the kitchen.

Layla left just after seven on Saturday evening. It was a cheerful goodbye, with cheek-pecks all round and no attempt on

Melody's part to pressgang the girl into giving a date for her next visit – assuming there was to be one. It was so easy, in fact, that Reece found himself holding his breath as the sound of the car's engine faded into the distance, and Melody returned to the kitchen to handwash the best tea plates and put the remains of the chocolate cake away in the tin.

She turned to smile at Reece as he followed her into the kitchen.

'Such a lovely girl. She seemed really happy. Do you think she's happy, Reece?'

And the way she spoke, with her shoulders in the right place and her forehead smoothly untroubled, caused him to exhale with relief.

'Yep, I'd say she's happy,' he said, giving Melody the firm answer she needed. 'Would you mind if I went and did some marking?'

'Of course not. I'll finish clearing up, then I might pop outside. It's such a gorgeous evening.'

Leaving Melody standing dreamily at the sink, Reece went through to his study. A pile of coursework scripts lay on the desk. He favoured them with no more than a glance before sitting down in the shabby old chair to gaze out of the window. Mel was right; it was a beautiful evening. The sun slanted across the yard, glowing rosily on the brickwork and turning the feathers on the solitary chicken within sight to a rich red-gold.

His eyes lifted to the horizon, where the trees stood dark and still against a cloudless sweep of cerulean sky.

Layla would be well on her way home by now. He pictured her in her sleeveless pink shift dress, brown arms extended to the wheel, the lower portion of her thighs exposing themselves as she operated the pedals. And here again came that feeling, rushing upwards from his feet to take his breath away, the same impossible feeling he'd had earlier when they were in the kitchen together. His mind went into overdrive as he fought to suppress his body's natural reactions. His daughter's friend, for goodness' sake! What was he, some kind of perv?

The logical part of his brain flagged up the likely reasons: grief, stress, worry, an imagined moment of intimacy after too much wine. All that, yes. All that. Reece nodded as if there was an audience he needed to convince as well as himself.

But it wasn't that straightforward. Another part of his brain was conveying a different message. Wanting something he could never have was a game, an enjoyable, harmless fantasy, so why shouldn't he indulge it? Christ knows, he'd suffered enough, and it wasn't as if he intended to do anything about it in reality. In a way, it made life easier for him as far as Mel was concerned. There'd be less pressure on him to wean her away from Layla if he, too, wanted the girl to keep coming here. And when, eventually, the visits stopped, he would deal with it then, not before.

Reece sighed with something approaching real pleasure. Then, shunning the work piled on the desk, he left the study and went to find Melody in the garden.

TWENTY-FIVE

'Oh, heavens, Layla, I'm so sorry. Whatever must you think of me, crying off at the last minute?' Melody used both hands to sweep her hair back – a gesture of exasperation, revealing threads of grey around her hairline and highlighting an alarming pallor to her skin tone. 'And you're only here for the one night!'

Was that a dig? Whatever, Layla decided to ignore it. She'd worked until late last night, Friday, on a seven-course bash for the mayor of Maybridge and assorted dignitaries, then driven over to Foxleigh this morning, which had been some sort of feat considering how knackered she was. She wasn't in the mood for Melody's nonsense.

Of course, it was her own fault she'd come here today, not Melody's. It was only three weeks since her last visit to Foxleigh. She could have said no to this weekend, to all weekends to come. But she hadn't, and she wouldn't. Despite the fragile promises she'd made to herself, she still couldn't see the way out. It was like crawling miles through a tunnel towards the light at the end, only to find that the further she crawled, the further the light receded. The whole thing smacked of utter defeat.

She went across to the sofa, where Melody was sitting with her feet up.

'No, it's fine, really. The last thing you need is to be watching Shakespeare in the night air with a migraine. Why don't you go upstairs and have a lie down? Reece and I can do supper. We'll leave yours ready in case you fancy it later.'

Layla looked at Reece for assent. He said nothing, and continued to stand loosely in the sitting room doorway as if he had no idea how he came to be there.

Melody got to her feet. 'Yes, I think I will. Thank you, Layla. You're such a kind girl.'

Layla waited until Melody was on her way upstairs, then, sliding past Reece, who seemed both struck dumb and rooted to the spot, she went to the kitchen. Everything had been laid out, ready for their meal. Layla arranged slices of cold roast chicken on two plates with the salads, then put the pan of Jersey potatoes on to boil.

'Busman's holiday,' Reece said, appearing beside her.

He didn't smile, and neither did Layla. She shrugged.

'There's hardly anything to do. She'll be better after a rest. You could go up and see if she'd like a cup of tea, or some water.'

Reece seemed as if he needed instructing. Besides, without knowing why, Layla wanted him away from her; the air between them felt laden with an oppressive, invisible mist. But he only moved as far as the dresser drawer to fetch out the mats and cutlery.

The night was clear and still, and unusually warm for early summer; perfect for being outdoors. Layla sat in one of the fold-up canvas chairs they'd brought with them, with a soft blue rug draped over her knees that Reece had insisted on, although with her jeans and white chunky cotton jumper, she didn't need it. She looked up at the deepening cobalt sky arching above the circle of woods that surrounded them. Shafts of light radiated from the makeshift stage, threading silver ribbons through the motionless trees and lifting the branches into sharp relief, as if they'd been sketched in black ink.

'Did you do this one at school?'

'What?' For a moment Layla had almost forgotten Reece was there. 'Oh yes, we did it in the first form. *A Midsummer Night's Dream* was about all the Shakespeare we could handle at that stage, and even then I remember getting the characters muddled up in the exam because of those stupid disguises.'

Reece chuckled. He'd seemed more himself, once they were in the car. Perhaps it was relief at being out of the house, away from Melody. She didn't like to think it, but it couldn't be easy for him.

'Danni studied it, too.' Reece drew invisible inverted commas around 'studied'. 'We took her to see a performance, hoping it would help, but they were very much amateurs and once the ass's head had fallen off twice she couldn't stop giggling and we had to take her out.'

Layla almost started at the mention of Danni's name. She covered it with a laugh.

'Well, if it happens tonight you might have to do the same with me.'

A silence fell between them. Reece looked down at his lap, then around the amphitheatre and, finally, up at the sky. Anywhere other than at her. Layla watched him surreptitiously, trying to work him out. Something was different about him, had been since she arrived at Foxleigh earlier. But what?

The lights dimmed and the play began. Reece seemed to gather himself. He smiled at Layla, then turned his attention towards the stage.

Neither of them spoke until the first short break between

acts, when Reece asked her what she thought of the performance so far. She told him, truthfully, that she thought it was excellent. She was about to say how magical it was, watching Shakespeare on a perfect summer's night in the middle of a wood, but she didn't want to sound childish.

Reece seemed to be studying her face, examining every part of it, as if he'd never seen it before. His attention made her feel slightly uncomfortable.

She wanted to look away but found she couldn't. His eyes shone in the semi-darkness. He seemed closer to her, although she hadn't noticed him move. He raised his arm, as if he was going to put it around her shoulders, then lowered it again, clasping his hands on his lap and staring down at them.

Layla dropped her gaze to her own hands above the rug. They were luminous pale, the colour of moonshine, and seemed detached from the rest of her, as if they belonged to someone else. She could hear Reece's breathing. Or perhaps she was imagining that, and it was only the expectant murmur of the audience around them as the actors arrived back on stage.

Even so, there was something not quite right about tonight, about being here with Reece, without Melody, that she couldn't pinpoint. She only knew she didn't want to think about it too deeply.

'Thanks for bringing me,' Layla said as the play ended and they joined in the applause. 'I really enjoyed that.'

'Did you?' Reece seemed surprised. 'Well, that's good then. And you're very welcome. If we can't treat our girl occasionally, then...' He shrugged, a little embarrassed.

Our girl. A vision of the birthday card with 'daughter' on it rose before Layla's eyes. The words were out before she could stop them.

'Reece, I wanted to say... well, I might not be able to keep up the visits to Foxleigh, in the future. Work's really busy, with the summer season, the weddings and everything. And then there's

Mum, having to cope with my sisters and Finn while she holds down a job. I don't spend nearly enough time at home as it is.'

Reece was visibly shaken. She hadn't expected that from him. Melody, yes, but he was the stronger one, the more resilient; the one more likely to understand and accept. Yet looking at him now, a deep frown furrowing his forehead, his shoulders sagging, it seemed she might have misjudged him. Unless it was Melody he was thinking about, not himself. Yes, that must be it.

When, eventually, he spoke, it was in a half whisper so that she had to strain to hear amid the surrounding chatter. 'You must do whatever you think best, Layla.'

A second's awkward silence, then he sat bolt upright and slapped both hands down on his knees. 'Come on then, let's get home.'

Melody was still up when they got back, curled up on the sofa in her dressing gown. Her face was scrubbed clean of make-up but the colour had returned and she looked almost back to normal. Layla was glad to see it. She felt a rush of warmth towards her and gave her a kiss on the cheek. Melody smiled.

'You were right. A lie down was all I needed, and I took a tablet. The milk's in the pan for hot chocolate. I thought you might need warming up. Unless you'd rather have a glass of wine?'

There was nothing Layla would have liked more than a glass of wine, a very large glass. However, Reece was already halfway to the kitchen, rubbing his hands together as if they'd come in from a very cold night.

'Ah, hot chocolate, yes. I'll put the milk on.'

Layla wanted to follow him. She felt she needed to keep watch in case she missed something important, something which would confirm or refute the sensation she'd had all the way home, that Reece was engaged in some kind of internal battle, and that it involved her. In the car they'd chatted on and off about the play, ostensibly ordinary chat. The silences, when they came, had billowed into the confined space like steam seeking an escape route.

Layla excused herself after she'd finished her drink, and went up to the attic room. She stood at the window, watching the moon glow behind the trees, and thought about the last time she was here. Had she imagined it, or had there been something extra – a kind of edge – to Reece's jocular encouragement when she'd told him about Morgan? Imagined or not, she hadn't felt she should mention Morgan this weekend, and Reece hadn't asked.

When they'd been out this evening, he'd seemed at a loss as to how to behave, how to *be*, with her. His relief when they'd arrived back here had been palpable; relief coupled with something else – disappointment, perhaps?

She was over-thinking this, obviously. She was tired and a bit stressed, not only from being back here again but from the strangeness of the evening. Even so, if she'd been looking for signs as to what was going on with Reece, they were there for the taking. He had developed a crush on her. She was eighty per cent sure she was right. And eighty per cent was enough. She couldn't come back to Foxleigh again.

'*Stop*, Mel. That's enough now.'

Reece gently extricated Melody's mobile phone from her hand before she hit 'call' again and slid it into his own pocket. He tried to hold her. She stepped back on the path, eyes accusing, on the brink of tears.

'She might pick up if I try again. If I explain about the anniversary, she might change her mind about coming on Saturday. Oh God, I'm so stupid! I should have mentioned it when I texted her.'

'That's the last thing you should have done. Of course she knows what day it is. She could hardly forget, could she?'

'So why isn't she coming, then?'

Melody flung the question at him as if it was somehow his fault, which it possibly was. Reece ran his hand across his head.

'She told you when she replied. She's working. And besides, she might not want to come, knowing what day it is. Have you thought about that?'

'I just need to speak to her.' Melody stooped down, tugged a sprig of groundsel out of the soil and put it in the pocket of her cardigan.

'We've talked about this, Mel,' Reece said. 'We agreed we mustn't put any pressure on her. If – *when* – she comes again, it has to be of her own free will, not out of any sense of duty.'

Melody tossed her head.

'I don't remember that conversation.'

No, you wouldn't, thought Reece. Because it had never taken place.

Melody wandered further along the brick path that threaded through the rose garden.

'Look,' she said, brightening in that sudden way of hers that gave Reece more anxiety than hope. 'Danni's roses – they're almost perfect. What wonderful timing! I shall cut some and put them in the silver vase, on the day.'

June 24th. A week today. One year on from the day their daughter died. He'd been trying to shut it out, but that was never going to work. How on earth were they going to get through it? Reece felt as if somebody had prised his heart out of his chest and trampled it into the earth of the rose beds.

'We should do something, go out,' he said, matching Melody's metal-edged brightness with his own. 'Somewhere Danni used to like. What about the seaside?'

Melody looked doubtful. 'I don't know. I think I'd rather we were in our own home. Oh, I *would* like Layla to be here. She will come, if I ask her properly. I know she will.'

And wouldn't I like that, too? Reece thought, as the battle within him gathered force again.

He hadn't acted naturally with Layla, the last time she was here. His manner had appalled him, as if he was observing it as an outsider, yet he'd felt powerless to stop. She must have noticed, wondered what was wrong with him. Was that why she was staying away? He knew Melody had suggested other week-ends than this coming one; she hadn't told him that, but he'd seen the texts. He'd got into the habit of checking them when he suspected that contact was more frequent than Melody made out. It was underhand, yes, but the need to keep a watch on the situation – for Mel's sake as well as Layla's – excused his actions.

According to Layla's replies, she was working every weekend for the foreseeable. She had warned him of that, when they were at the Shakespeare play. And she had a boyfriend now; she'd want to spend her free time with him, wouldn't she? Presumably she was still seeing him – she hadn't said, and Reece hadn't wanted to ask – but Melody, of course, knew nothing about that. Even so, Reece couldn't help feeling that Layla's absence was partly due to his own wacky behaviour.

She had become his shining light; his spot of warmth in a cold climate; his harmless fantasy. Harmless as long as she knew nothing about it, which, please God, she didn't. However, far from enjoying his little secret, now it threatened to eat him up. He missed her. Irrational though it was, he missed Layla, every second she wasn't here. He felt like a sixteen-year-old boy caught up in the misery of unrequited love. Grief manifested itself in the strangest ways. Knowing that didn't make his feelings any less real.

Melody was coming back along the path towards him. He

took her phone out of his pocket and handed it to her with a resigned sigh. She thanked him with a half smile, acknowledging the unspoken message: *Okay, do what you want.* If Layla was upset by Melody's constant demands, it was regrettable, but he was powerless to stop it happening. He needed all his strength to control what was happening inside him. There was nothing left for anyone else.

TWENTY-SIX

Layla had worked until three on Saturday, covering breakfast and lunch. Her next shift was Sunday afternoon. She was glad she hadn't been forced to tell Melody a direct lie about having to work to get out of the weekend. It troubled her conscience a little that she hadn't been completely truthful, either, but she refused to feel guilty about it.

The anniversary of Danni's death had been uppermost in her mind for weeks now – how could it not be? The invitation to go to Foxleigh this weekend was therefore no surprise. Melody's texts and voicemail messages had sounded increasingly desperate, but Layla had hardened her heart and refused to call her back. She knew exactly what would have happened if she had. She would have caved in and, setting aside her misgivings about Reece, swapped her Sunday shift and driven up to Foxleigh this afternoon. She would then have spent a miserable time haunted by memories, while trying to bring some small comfort to the Morlands, when what she really needed was to party hard and forget about it.

Which was where Morgan came in.

He'd been so sweet about breaking the news to her that he

was moving to Maybridge. It had taken her ages to convince him that she didn't feel rushed or pressurised into anything she wasn't ready for, and that he mustn't even think of turning down Connor's offer for her sake. The fact that he would have done, had she said the word, alarmed and delighted her in equal measures.

The river and the boathouse had become an irresistible draw these past few weeks. They had been to pubs, the cinema and for drives around Maybridge and its environs so that Morgan could get to know the area. But mostly they walked along the riverbank, holding hands, not saying very much because it didn't seem necessary to keep up an endless conversation. Then, likely as not, they'd end up at the boathouse, which was where Layla was heading now.

It was her favourite time of day along the river, with the sun dipping below the trees and the silent water flowing coolly by, inky and mysterious in the fading light. A heron stood among the reeds on the opposite bank, as still as a statue. She stopped to watch it for a moment, unhooking the heavy backpack and setting it down on the path. The delicate grace of the bird reminded her of Danni. Fighting back the familiar sudden rush of sadness before it overcame her completely, she heaved up the backpack and hurried on.

Layla seemed to be taking an age to get up the steps. When Morgan opened the door to her, he saw she was weighed down by a bulging backpack which turned out to contain a bottle of vodka, a bottle of lemonade, two clear plastic tumblers and a family-sized bag of salt-and-vinegar crisps.

'What's all this, then?' he said, laughing as she unloaded it all onto the top of the cupboard next to the kettle.

'I want to get drunk with you, and then,' – she tapped him on the chest – 'I'll see who you really are.'

The look in her eye was mischievous, challenging.

'Oh yeah?' Morgan grinned. 'You think this is going to do it, do you?'

She shrugged. '*In vino veritas*, and all that.'

'For all you know,' Morgan said, 'I might be a hardened drinker. This might not even scratch the surface.' He nodded towards the vodka.

'That's a chance I'll have to take.'

'Seriously, though...' he began.

'We're not going to do serious, not tonight, are we?'

She fetched the rug and cushions from the cupboard, tossed them onto the floor and sat down. Morgan joined her.

'No, but tell me you're okay, only this is kind of a first, isn't it?'

Layla sighed, and Morgan immediately felt guilty for having burst her bubble. She'd worried him, though. If there was something wrong, he wanted to know.

'I'm not okay, exactly. It's a year ago today since my friend Danni died.'

'Oh dear, I'm sorry. Of course you'll be sad. It's only natural.'

'I don't want to be sad, not tonight. I want to forget about it.'

She made it sound like a plea rather than a statement.

'Okay,' Morgan said.

He remembered her telling him she'd had a friend who'd died suddenly during their last year at university. She hadn't given him any more information than that, and he hadn't asked. They'd hardly begun seeing each other by then, but he'd learned enough to know when she didn't want to talk about something.

She reached for the vodka and beamed a smile at him.

'Right then, get stuck into this, shall we?'

. . .

An hour later – surprisingly, Morgan noted as he stole a glance at his watch – the level of vodka had moved a fair way down the bottle, while the level of lemonade had hardly changed because they kept forgetting to put it in. Propped on a cushion in front of them was the laptop. They were taking it in turns to read out bits of his book. If Poodle Chafferty was squirming under the spotlight of all this unprecedented attention, he wasn't letting on, Morgan thought wildly, as Layla elbowed him aside to get at the keyboard.

'My go.'

She paged up and down, and back again. The laptop tilted sideways on the cushion, like a ship in a storm. Rather than straightening it, she leaned sideways to read out the words on the screen. *Chafferty crawled slowly towards the cliff edge, sliding through the wet grass like an anaconda after its prey. The dog lay down beside him, panting in Chafferty's ear. Chafferty put out a hand, restraining the dog from going too close to the edge. Voices rose through the darkness. Two voices, indistinct. He knew at once who they belonged to. Chafferty shrank back. He doubted they could see him in the half-dark should they chance to look up, but he couldn't risk it. The dog put his head down between his paws and whined faintly.*

Layla stopped reading. 'Can a dog whine faintly?'

Her eyes were all bright and sparkly. There was a flake of salt-and-vinegar crisp at the corner of her mouth. He wanted to kiss her so badly that his mind refused to focus on anything else.

'Of course it can.'

'All right, don't go all huffy,' Layla said, misinterpreting the shortness in his reply.

'I'm not.'

Her bare arm was against his. Its velvety warmth made his insides feel like a tightly coiled spring, while his spine seemed to be made of plasticine. He tried to sit up straight but the most he achieved was a slight lean to the left. Immediately, Layla fell into the space and filled it with the lazy liquidity of her body.

'What colour's the dog?'

He had to think about that.

'Dark brown,' he said eventually.

'Has it got a proper poodle cut? Like with stand-uppy bits on its legs and head and everything?'

'Ish a working dog, not a fucking entrant for Crufts.'

Layla giggled and leaned further into him, her head resting on his shoulder. He ducked his own head so that it rested on hers, as his arm found its natural way around her.

'It's funny, your book,' she said lazily.

'Good. It's meant to be.' He snapped the laptop lid down. 'So, what have you found out?'

He held her a little closer, breathing in the flowery, slightly medicated scent of her hair.

'Found out? About what?'

'Me. You said if we got pissed, you'd find out who I really am.'

She twisted round, her beautiful eyes gazing at him in surprise. 'Did I say that?'

'You did.'

'Yes, I did, didn't I? Ah, well, in that case I may have to ask you some questions, like, what's your favourite colour?'

'You could, and I would say blue but really I've got no idea. Or, we could just do this...'

He kissed her.

She wanted this. She wanted *him*. So much. They'd kissed before, lots of times, but never like this. Their lips hardened against one another as the intensity of their kisses increased, building to such a height that her whole body sang with pleasure and longing. The picnic rug had crept from beneath them and they were half lying on the dusty floorboards.

They paused for breath. Moving a little apart from him, she tilted her head back. The upside-down view through the window brought on a wave of dizziness. She struggled into a sitting position.

'Wassa matter?'

Morgan's eyes narrowed in concern. A protective arm went around her shoulders. The vodka bottle with its depleted contents stood on the floor on his other side, glinting in a shaft of pinkish light from the window.

Layla stared at it, couldn't tear her eyes away. That night, the party – still so uncompromisingly fresh, its images etched deep into her brain. And Danni downing vodka before she went off and did... what she did. She'd been a fool to think she could erase those pictures from her mind, by whatever means. Perhaps the vodka had been a subconscious choice, a message from that part of her brain where the narrative never went away...

No.

She fought the unwelcome emotion. 'I'm okay. A bit spinny, that's all.'

'Spinny?' he laughed, then stopped, knowing it wasn't the right time for laughter.

'Up here.' She tapped her temple.

'Shall I get you some water?'

'No. No thanks.' Her words collided head-on with his. She needed him to stay close to her. If he moved away for even a second, she would fall into the abyss.

'Better now?' he asked, after a moment.

She smiled. 'Yes.'

The dizziness had passed; the rest of it had not. Perhaps if she just... Moving closer to Morgan, she linked her arms around his neck, finding his mouth again with new urgency.

'My beautiful girl,' Morgan whispered, as briefly they broke apart.

His voice reached her through a mist of unspent kisses. She pressed her lips to the base of his neck, brushing his skin with feather kisses, while her hands moved under his T-shirt and over the hard smoothness of his back. Pulling away, he tugged his T-shirt over his head in one impatient movement, then removed her top and flung it aside. He ran his hands over her shoulders, down her back, his fingers hooking beneath her bra straps, sliding them down.

Another moment and they were back on the floor, kissing feverishly. Her plait had come loose, or he had pulled it loose – she wasn't sure which – and his hands were in her hair, raking it back in long, sensuous movements which arched her back and sent her mouth in search of his. As she raised her head, his fingers lost their grip. Between them, they misjudged the movement so that her head fell back and hit the floor, not hard enough to hurt but enough to cause a jolt of surprise.

He began to apologise. But the voice Layla heard wasn't Morgan's. It was Harvey's, apologising if their lovemaking had become a bit too rough and he'd unintentionally hurt her, when she'd hardly noticed because her passion for him blotted out the entire world.

And now she was in danger of losing herself again, drowning in Morgan, his kisses, their shared passion.

Her heart raced, her chest contracted, wringing the breath out of her. She began to shake uncontrollably. Morgan was watching her, his expression anxious. He was talking to her; she could see his lips moving but could hear nothing except her own pounding pulse. She was on her feet, groping for her top, pulling it on. Morgan was standing, too, moving towards her. She held out her hands, the palms facing him, warning him off.

And then, without knowing how she got there, she was on the towpath, and running.

TWENTY-SEVEN

Layla paid off the taxi with half the money that was supposed to last her the rest of the week, and hurried across the silent quadrangle. Around its perimeter rose the faceless blocks of the first-year halls of residence. Filtered light shimmied its way through the frosted glass of the stairwells and shone from a few curtainless windows high up. Otherwise, all was in darkness, apart from a row of streetlamps spinning nests of blond light at intervals along the tarmac path.

Harvey had given her a key pass; one he'd obtained at small cost from a student who was leaving. It had only worked for a couple of weeks before it had been deactivated by the university authorities. With too much at stake for a halls' occupant to be caught letting in a night-time visitor, there was only one option remaining. Dodging round the side of the building, Layla waggled open the high metal gate that had a faulty lock and a steady flow of illicit traffic as a result. At least Harvey had a ground floor room; it would have been mission impossible otherwise. Her heels sank into the grass as she felt her way along the back of the building in almost total darkness, counting the windows as she went. All this for love!

'What's so funny?' Harvey steadied her as she swung her legs over the windowsill and landed in a giggling heap at his feet. 'Keep the noise down! You'll get us both shot.' He helped her up. 'Are you pissed?'

'Not much. It's worn off now. Anyway, they can't shoot me, I'm graduating in a few weeks. That makes me immune. You, on the other hand...' – she grabbed him, pulling his head towards hers and kissing him hungrily, running her hands over the naked top half of his body – 'you...'

'Me what?'

'Don't know. I forgot.'

'I love you.'

'I know.'

'Say it back.'

'No.'

'Say it.'

Layla's hair was gathered up and yanked back from her face, stopping just short of painful.

'Okay, okay! *I love you.*'

Nestled into the crook of Harvey's arm in the tousled single bed, soothed by the steady rise and fall of his huggable rugby-player's chest, Layla was almost asleep. And then, from some-where in the shadowy room, music began to play – a soft, repeti-tive tune that she half recognised. Oh yes, her phone. With effort, she opened her eyes and saw its flashing light on Harvey's desk where she'd dropped it. She should answer it. It was two o'clock in the morning; it might be important. On the other hand, it was probably a wrong number. Or a nutter.

Yes, that, definitely.

After all, it was the early hours of the morning.

And then she must have fallen asleep properly, because the next thing she heard was Harvey whispering in her ear, whispering silly, wonderful love-gibberish, as his hands slid over her body.

'You didn't think I'd finished with you yet, did you, Miss Mackenzie?'

Layla turned in his arms, breathed in his scent that mingled inextricably with her own. In Harvey's bed, in his embrace, she was in heaven. Nothing, nowhere, could be better than this. Not ever. She found his mouth with hers.

Over on the desk, her phone rang again, stopped, beeped a message, then another.

It was twenty-five minutes before she read it.

'Harv! Wake up! Something's happened. I have to go.'

'What?' Harvey rolled over and lay with his hands behind his head, watching as she retrieved her clothes from the floor, stubbing her toe painfully on the corner of the bed as she threw them on. Her shoes – where were they? She switched on the overhead light to find them. Harvey screwed up his eyes.

'Christ, d'you have to?'

Layla threw him her phone. 'Read it.'

'Read it to me.' He pulled the duvet over his head.

'Haven't got time.' Layla reached over her shoulders to fasten the top button on her dress. That would have to do. 'It's a message from Danni's phone but it's not from her. It's from Helen, one of our friends. Everyone's really worried about her. I've got to get back there, now. Do you want to come with me?'

Harvey emerged from the duvet and half sat up. 'Must I?'

'Not if it's going to take you ages to get dressed, no.'

He lay down again, glad to be let off the hook. 'You're panicking for nothing. I bet it's someone winding you up.'

'No, it's not. I've got a bad feeling about this. You don't have any money, do you?'

'Try my pockets.'

His voice was muffled by the pillow now. Layla raided the pockets of his jeans and came up with a ten-pound note.

'This'll do. I'll ring you later, let you know if anything's happened.'

'Which it won't have. Switch the light off on your way out, babe.'

Once she was out in the quadrangle, Layla forced herself to stop for a moment and take slow, deep breaths. Perhaps Harvey was right and she was panicking for nothing. But Helen, the girl who'd rung her using Danni's phone, was someone they both knew well, a responsible type. She wouldn't mess about.

At least she'd been able to leave the building by the front door. Getting out wasn't as problematic as getting in. She'd have to take a chance on the CCTV. As she rounded the corner into the street, she began to hurry again, her heels click-clacking loudly on the pavement. There were sometimes taxis along here, outside the all-night kebab place... Ah, here was one now, coming along the street. She hailed it.

As the taxi skeltered through the deserted streets, the driver having picked up that there was no time to waste, Layla sent a text to Danni's phone in case Helen saw it:

> On my way. Be there in 2.

But the feeling was already returning that this was a fool's errand after all. Helen must have been genuinely concerned about Danni's behaviour at the time, but maybe she'd overreacted, and whatever had been going on was all over by now. Danni would be tethered in a passionate embrace with that awful Art character – Layla pushed the image from her mind – or dancing with her mates. She might even have pulled herself together and gone home. Another little crisis averted.

Disappointingly, it wasn't the case. Once she was back in the house, Layla didn't have to look far for Danni, only as far as the first flight of stairs. Danni sat, or rather lolled, against the wall, legs outstretched, while others using the staircase pressed against the banisters to get past her. The straps of her dress had slipped down past her shoulders, the neckline now precariously low.

Layla went up to her. 'Time to go home. Come on.'

She extended a hand towards Danni. Danni brushed it aside, almost burning Layla's hand on the butt end of a spliff lodged between her fingers.

'Lay! Where'd you get to? Here, have a puff.' Danni let out a laugh that was almost a cackle as she thrust the spliff towards Layla.

Layla recoiled, and looked at Danni's face. This was worse than she'd imagined.

Helen appeared at the bottom of the stairs. 'She was all over the place, and all over that bloke she was with earlier. Anything could have happened. We were dead worried.' Helen's face was full of concern. 'It's not like Danni, is it? She's usually quiet. Well, quiet*ish*...'

Layla turned, holding on to the banister rail. 'I know. I don't know what's going on with her. I shouldn't have left her. Thanks for phoning.'

'We thought it best,' Helen said. 'Just in case. Do you want a hand?'

Danni reared up at this, pulling herself up off the stair. 'You're another busybody,' she said, jabbing a finger towards Helen. 'I'm absolutely fine. There's no need for all this drama...' Her words fell over one another and melted into a slurry nothingness.

'We'll be okay. I'll get a cab in a minute,' Layla said to Helen.

'Well, if you're sure. I'll leave you to it.'

Layla turned to Danni, who had dropped back onto the stair. 'Right, I'm taking you home, now. And no arguments because I'm just not in the mood. Got that? Come on, get up.'

Danni scowled, but rose to a kind of standing position. Layla thought she was going to follow her down the stairs. But Danni had other ideas and began walking up them instead.

'*Danni!*'

Danni spun round and nearly pitched herself, and Layla, backwards. 'This is the finals party, right? Our last one *ever!* You're such a spoil... sp...'

'Spoilsport, yes, that's me. Whatever.'

Layla made a grab for Danni's arm but found only air as Danni began to make her way up the stairs at surprising speed, considering the state she was in. Layla caught up with her at the top. She stopped, and turned round.

'Why are you following me? I'm going to get another little drink while there's still some left. Come and have a drink with me. Please?'

Layla shook her head. 'No, Danni.' There was no point in mentioning that the drinks were downstairs, not up here. 'And you don't need any more either. If you won't let me take you home, at least let's go outside and get some air.'

'*Air?* What for? I want vodka, not air!' Danni's eyes blazed, dark in her white face. 'You're not my mother. You *don't* get to tell me what to do!' A pause. 'Neither does she, though she won't have it. She doesn't understand. This is *my* life.'

She? Was Danni talking about Melody now? Where did Danni's mother come into this? Confused, Layla sunk back against the landing wall, only to watch Danni treading purposefully up the next flight of stairs. Desperate as Layla was to leave right now, get herself home and fall into bed, she couldn't leave Danni. She'd never forgive herself if Danni hurt herself in some way, or that Art bloke found her and took advantage. Him, or anyone, come to that. It wasn't a wild party, not as wild as some they'd attended over the years, but fuelled by drink, and the rest, nothing was impossible.

The top floor was almost in complete darkness, with only an arrow of light coming from one of the doors and the faint glow of a streetlamp – or was it the moon? – showing through a tiny window. Layla felt disorientated, and so very, very tired. She couldn't be sure, but a flicker in her peripheral vision told her there was someone leaning in the corner of the landing, someone wearing white. Male or female? She couldn't be sure; she couldn't be sure about anything any more.

Danni stood facing Layla, gripping the top banister rail to steady herself. The fire seemed to have gone out of her. She looked at Layla almost appealingly. Seeing her chance, Layla pushed open the door of the room that faced the front of the house. It was a bedroom, as she'd expected, thankfully unoccupied. In fact it didn't look as if it was in use at all. Through the yellowing half-light coming through the open curtains, she discerned a cupboard with its doors open, and nothing inside. But there was a bed, not made up but with some kind of blanket thrown across the bare mattress. This would have to do.

Miraculously, Danni had followed her into the room. Her knees were buckling, but at least she was more or less upright, and quiet. Manhandling her friend as much as she dared without using any force, Layla managed to manoeuvre Danni onto the bed. Once she was sitting, Layla lifted her legs up, and tucked the blanket around her.

'There you go,' she said softly. 'You have a nice nap and then we'll go home.'

Danni reached up, clasping Danni awkwardly round her neck.

'You're my bestest friend, Lay. Bestest in all the world.'

'Yeah, and you're mine, you daft mare.' Layla extricated herself from Danni's grasp.

'No, really truly,' murmured Danni, 'I do love you. I *do*.'

'I know, sweetheart. Night night.'

'Lay?'

'What?'

'It's ever so hot in here. I really need some air.'

Air. Right. Now she wanted air. Danni was right, though; the room was stifling. Layla crossed to the window, one of those old-fashioned push-up types. At first she thought it wasn't going to budge but, using the little strength she had left, she grabbed the metal handles and heaved. The window groaned, trembled in its frame, then shot upwards. A waft of warm air drifted in.

The effort of opening the window made Layla's head spin. She gave herself a little shake, stole out of the room and closed the door behind her. If she let Danni sleep it off for half an hour or so, she'd hopefully be in a fit state to be taken home. As it was, no taxi driver would have let her anywhere near his upholstery.

She stood outside the bedroom door, listening for signs of movement. There were none. One of the other doors, the one where the light had shown through, had one of those rubber wedge things stuck under it. Carefully, Layla tugged it free. Back at Danni's door, she forced it into the crack between the hinged edge of the door and the wall, so that it was hardly visible. That should stop anyone opening the door, from either side.

Satisfied that she'd done the best she could to keep Danni safe, Layla went down two flights of stairs and slipped out into the night.

TWENTY-EIGHT

Three weeks. Three whole weeks and nothing, apart from one text message, received in eventual – and probably exasperated – response to the three he'd sent her. If it wasn't for that, Morgan might have believed Layla was entirely his own invention, like the imaginary friend he'd had when he was seven. Her name was Honey-Belle, and she'd had blonde hair so long she could sit on it. He used to spend hours in the tumbledown garden shed, arranging old chairs and upturned crates and crayoning pictures which he fixed to the walls with drawing pins; making a home for her.

He was going to marry her, too.

He didn't need to read the message any more. He knew it by heart.

> I can't be with you. I can't be with anyone. I thought I could but I can't. I will explain, one day. I'm so sorry. I'm all right so please don't worry about me any more. L. xxx

How could he not worry? She'd flown out of the boathouse like a tormented spirit, her eyes wide and darkened by... what?

Fear, it looked like. Had he frightened her away by loving her, wanting to make love to her? And yet she'd wanted that, too. He wasn't such a dummy around women that he could have misread her. And she had brought the vodka, which led him to another question – did she have to be drunk in order to have sex with him? Was he really that unappealing?

In his second text – the first had been a hurried one-liner asking if she was all right – he'd apologised if he'd upset her in any way, but asked if she would please come back so that they could talk. The third, sent after a chequered hour of anger and misery, simply demanded:

> Tell me you're all right and I'll leave you alone.

Morgan rolled over onto his back. The sofa-bed springs twanged. He opened his eyes, then squeezed them shut again as the light hit him with a retina-splitting dazzle. It struck not only through the corrugated plastic roof above but from all sides – he hadn't pulled down the window blinds last night.

Once unfolded, the sofa-bed filled most of the space in the lean-to conservatory which doubled as a guest bedroom; the room, which in a former life had been the bungalow's second bedroom, had been converted to an art studio. Gina, Connor's partner, taught art to various groups and displayed her paintings at the riverside gallery housed in the old rope factory.

Connor and Gina had been generous in inviting him to move in with them. Under the circumstances, it was the least they could do, Connor had insisted. He'd been made very welcome, but he couldn't hang around cluttering up the place for too long. Besides, last night as he'd passed their bedroom door on his way to the bathroom, he'd heard them making love. It had made him feel lonely.

Even if he only stayed in Maybridge for the rest of the summer season, he would need somewhere of his own.

However, a preliminary internet search had revealed that, like anywhere else halfway desirable, Maybridge wasn't exactly overflowing with affordable accommodation. Layla had promised to listen out for any likely leads. But that was before. Twenty-seven and still living like a student, or a dosser. Shameful, when you thought about it.

Not only did the lack of blinds let in the glare, it also left Morgan on full display to anyone who happened to be using the right-of-way that ran alongside the bungalow. Two heads – one male, one female, both grey-haired – now appeared above the fence, moving slowly along it like plaster heads in a funfair game. Morgan freed his arms from the blanket and took potshots at them from an invisible rifle, making pow sounds. At that moment, they both turned in his direction and had the effrontery to look offended at the sight of him, as if he was the voyeur. The heads swivelled round and hurried on.

The right-of-way passed between the backs of the houses, skirted the school playing fields and the park, emerging eventually onto the riverbank, not far from the road bridge. Morgan usually went that way to work. It was a longish walk, but it cleared his head in preparation for the day and he preferred it to taking the car. Connor drove in earlier, often at the crack of dawn. He didn't expect Morgan until around eight thirty.

There was a slight feeling of wrongness about being paid for doing something so enjoyable. Every day was different, every part of the day as varied as the weather. He could be tucked away in the office, working on invoices or publicity material, taking a cruiser out with its load of optimistic trippers, hiring out rowing boats, or assembling cream teas in the café. All in the space of six hours. Wherever Connor needed him, Morgan went, and happily.

Not so happily now. Being busy all day helped a little, but if Layla wasn't in the forefront of his mind, she waited in the shadows for his attention to refocus fully. And then the same questions tormented him in a never-ending circuit. What had he done wrong? How could he put it right if she wouldn't talk to him? What was he supposed to do?

When, eventually, the questions puttered to a useless standstill, his thoughts turned to their pathetically stunted history; the walks, the talking, the dead-of-night texts – and the kisses. At such times, he would stand on the bank and stare at the deepest, blackest parts of the river, imagining himself slowly sinking as the water closed over his head. Love should never feel like this.

Ten to eight. He'd heard the front door close earlier, as Connor left. Rolling off the sofa bed, he removed his bedding, stashing it in a tidy pile in the corner and restoring the sofa-bed to its sitting position – a dosser he might be, but he wouldn't be a slob as well. Pulling on his jeans, he padded through the hallway and tapped on the door of the studio.

'All right to use the bathroom?'

Gina came to the door and opened it a fraction, wiping the paintbrush on her purple smock. Below the smock she wore a pair of equally paint-spattered jeans, which frayed out over her bare brown feet. Behind her, Morgan caught a glimpse of a large canvas containing a nude female figure, the paint glistening in the rays from the skylight.

'Sure. You don't have to ask.' She gave him a wide, generous smile. 'I bought Cheerios yesterday. You said they were your favourite. They're in the cupboard next to the sink.'

Morgan nodded his thanks. His own smile was bleak. Kindness was hard to take, now that Layla had gone. He padded away.

TWENTY-NINE

It was Monday – a relatively quiet day on the river after the weekend tourist buzz. Morgan spent the morning in the office, testing out his ideas for revamping the website, and he planned to contact a couple of boating and fishing magazines to see if they would run a feature. Since Ted's health had begun to fail, Connor had had no time for anything apart from the essentials.

As a header on one of the website pages, Morgan had used a photo he'd taken himself, of the willows arching over the light-dappled water and, just in shot, the boathouse. As he stared at the picture on the screen, he sensed a neglected air about the place, as if it knew she had gone.

He had thought about abandoning the boathouse and working on his novel in the bungalow instead, where at least there was internet access, or in Maybridge library. But he functioned well in his wooden eyrie; his writing brain seemed to respond to the steady flow of the river and the rustling trees. He'd even added some items for atmosphere, picked up at Maybridge flea market: a framed theatrical poster for a long-ago Agatha Christie play; a kitsch, plastic model of a poodle; and a little old Remington typewriter with yellowing keys, much like the one in his father's study when he was growing up. It smelled nostalgically of ink, although the ribbon had long since perished.

No, he wasn't ready to give up on the boathouse. He planned to spend an hour or so there this afternoon, if Connor didn't need him.

It was around four when Morgan set off along the towpath towards the boathouse. Already he felt dispirited, and not in the least like cracking jokes on behalf of Poodle Chafferty, his fictional detective. The episode with Layla had drained the joy out of his writing – out of everything.

His feet dragged on the trodden-down earth, his body felt hollow, as if some major functioning part of him was missing. He stopped, and pulled out his phone. There were several backed-up messages and emails – one from his father which he'd read later, others not important or from unknown numbers and addresses. Nothing from her. He began to feel angry and resentful. Why did everything have to be spoilt when it could have been so perfect?

He couldn't get over the way she'd rushed off, leaving him with nothing. An argument would have been better than that; at least then he'd have had something to fight against, to measure the strength of his feelings with. She hadn't even given him that. He'd even moved up to Maybridge to be closer to her – no, okay, that wasn't strictly true. But knowing she'd be here had made it into something special.

He kicked out at some branches sprouting low from a tree root. They gave way with a dry crackle, almost pitching him headlong into the undergrowth. 'Shit!' he muttered, through clenched teeth. Stuffing the redundant mobile back into his pocket, he stomped on.

He felt no calmer when he reached the boathouse. The

creaky wooden steps fired miniature gunshots as his feet assaulted the treads. Turning the key in the lock, flinging the door open, he marched across to the desk and the cowering laptop. He hesitated, his hand on the shiny black lid. Why waste the next hour when he already knew it would be unproductive and pointless?

His eye was drawn to the spiral-bound notebook, open where he'd left it, the pages on view filled with his scrawl – the next chapter, roughly planned, the ideas still viable. He may as well get down a sentence or two while he was here, if he could bear it. Dragging out the chair, he sat down.

Forty minutes later, he was still sitting, his fingers having barely stilled. The writing on the screen was a stream of consciousness affair, devoid of corrections and punctuation. Already he saw that it was working. Sometimes it happened that way. Surprising that it should happen today, though, when he was feeling so angry. Actually, he felt better now; his mood had levelled out.

Allowing himself a respite, Morgan flexed his fingers, sat back in the chair and gazed out of the open window. The trees were statue-still, their leafy patterns silhouetted against the dazzling blue sky. One of the hired rowing boats slipped along the sparkling surface of the water, its occupant a lone man, wielding the oars as indolently as the flow of the river, his face turned upwards to catch the sun.

Morgan put his hands behind his head, closed his eyes and listened to the slip-slap of the oars as it grew fainter, then died away, leaving birdsong the only sound. And then he heard something else; the tapping of feet on the wooden steps. Not Connor's confident tread, but lighter, with a note of uncertainty. A rap sounded on the door – two swift knocks, as if whoever it was might at any second change their mind.

Morgan's heart leapt. An involuntary smile spread across

his face as he rose out of his seat and bounded to the door. He
opened it. The smile vanished.

'Kate!'

'I thought if I let you know I was coming, you'd try and stop
me,' she said, as if they were already mid-conversation.

What the hell was she doing here?

'How did you know where to find me?' he said, after a
moment's awkward silence.

She shrugged. 'Lucky guess. Besides, there's only one
boathouse that fits the description, as far as I could see.'

'Yes, but...'

'Actually, I phoned the office on Saturday. I wanted to find
out if you still came here. I was going to ask for you, then put
the phone down before they fetched you. The number's on the
website. The woman said she didn't know where you were right
then and to try again on Monday. That's when I decided to take
the bull by the horns and come up.' She looked up at him, but
couldn't quite meet his eye. Her hands were twisted together in
an anxious knot. 'I messaged you a couple of times, but you
didn't answer. You wouldn't have recognised the number,
though. It's changed.'

Morgan stood uselessly, still holding the doorknob. His
brain wasn't functioning.

Kate peered past him. 'Are you going to let me in then?'

He held the door wider, stepping aside to admit her, then
closed the door after her. At the same time, he tried to marshal
his thoughts. The woman she'd spoken to on the phone must
have been Maureen, or one of the other café assistants; the
phone was put through there when the office was empty.

Kate walked across to the desk, then turned to face him.
The sunlight caught her hair, backlighting her with a fiery red
halo. She seemed thinner – a little too thin, perhaps. It gave her
a waif-like appeal that was hard to ignore. She was wearing a
short, sky-blue dress, nothing like the ethnic styles she usually

favoured, and low-heeled sandals. A brown leather bag with a gold clasp was slung from one shoulder. It came to him that she had dressed up for his benefit. He felt nervy and annoyed, yet stupidly flattered at the same time.

'You didn't let me know where you'd moved to, after you left the flat.'

Her gaze was more confident now, more like the old Kate. There was a touch of accusation in her tone; he recognised that, too.

There'd been no reason to let her know his new address. Then again, there'd been no reason not to. He told her he was living in Maybridge, and how it had come about. Then, as she seemed to want more, he tore a page out of the notebook, wrote down the address of the bungalow and handed it to her. She took the piece of paper and, without glancing at it, folded it carefully and put it away in her bag.

'Thank you.' For the first time, she looked around. 'I can see why you write here. It's the perfect retreat. People pay fortunes for places like this.'

Morgan gave a dry laugh. 'There's nothing here, apart from some dodgy wiring and a bit of wet rot.'

'It's lovely, though. A real hideaway. You're very lucky.' Then, when he looked surprised, she added, 'I mean the whole thing, the writing, the river job and everything. It's you, isn't it?'

'Is it?'

He frowned, knowing he was being deliberately obtuse. She had walked out on him, cleared out of the flat and gone, without a word. She couldn't claim to know him any more. It wasn't for her to tell him what he should or shouldn't be doing; she'd forfeited that right months ago.

'I think you'd better tell me why you're here.'

She gathered her hair up at the back with both hands, then shook it free again. 'It's so damned hot...'

'Do you want to go outside?'

'No, it's all right here. I like it. Okay if I...?' she pointed at the swivel chair.

'Of course.'

She sat down. The chair swung round in a jovial way. She stopped it with her foot. Morgan's eyes strayed to the cushions wedged into the corner by the wardrobe, the picnic rug poking out from underneath. Kate was looking, too. And wondering, probably. Well, she could go on wondering.

He went over and propped himself against the cupboard where the tea things were, crossed his arms and waited.

Her nervousness was back. She fiddled with the strap of her bag.

'I thought it would hurt us both less if I made it a clean break.' She gave a little humourless laugh. 'Turns out there's no such thing.'

Morgan said nothing; he had no intention of helping her out.

Kate continued. 'I thought it was what we needed, a fresh start. I thought we'd gone on too long, that we knew each other too well for there to be any surprises left.'

'So you decided to give me one big surprise. A roast chicken and an empty wardrobe.' He couldn't resist the jibe.

'I know, and I'm sorry for the way it ended...'

'The way *you* ended it.'

'Yes, that's what I meant. I'm sorry.'

'Look, if you've tracked me down to apologise, then you've wasted your time. What's done is done. You can't change the past. You of all people should know that.'

She nodded. Russet curls bounced. 'That's not all I came to say. This isn't easy for me, Morgan. I don't often admit I'm wrong – well, you know that – but leaving you was the worst, the stupidest, thing I've ever done in my entire life.'

'Look, Kate,' Morgan said, 'I don't know where you're going with this, but I really don't want to have this conversation. It's pointless. You've got your life now and I've got mine. I refuse to rake over old ground. Yes, I was hurt when we split up, probably more than you ever imagined, but I dealt with it. And, quite honestly, I don't think about it any more.'

From the dismay on her face, she took this to mean that he didn't think about her any more. He had sort of meant that, and it was near enough the truth. For a long time he'd believed his whole future lay with this girl; it was only natural to find her in his thoughts occasionally. And now, so soon, he was facing a new, more intense, heartbreak. It left no room for anything, or anyone, else. He wished she would go. He wished she'd never come.

She had got up from the chair and was standing in the middle of the room, a few feet away from him.

'Why didn't you try harder to win me back?'

The accusing tone was back. He wasn't going to rise to the bait; the last thing he wanted was an argument.

'I did try, if you remember. That afternoon on the clifftop,' he said, deliberately keeping his voice even. 'But you were very determined, and I didn't try again because, deep down, I knew you were right. We had a great time, a brilliant relationship, but we'd run our course. We weren't meant to last, Kate. It took me a while to accept that – pride, I suppose. And stubbornness.'

The more he said, the more fuel he was adding to the fire. But he couldn't seem to stop himself.

'I want you back, Morgan. I love you. I've always loved you. Anything else was a blip, a smudge, a moment of madness...'

Her arms were outstretched, the palms uppermost. She was placing herself in his hands, offering herself up for whatever was to come next. He couldn't stand it.

'No.' He shook his head.

'No? Just that?'

'Just that. I'm sorry. It's too late. Perhaps it always was.'

She looked down, struggling, he suspected, to keep the tears at bay. When she raised her head, he saw that she hadn't quite succeeded. Deep inside, he was moved by her distress. On the surface, he had to keep control.

'Kate, you put me through hell, I don't deny that. You don't love me any more, and I don't love you. Not in that way.' He spoke gently, taking a step closer to her. 'You should go soon. Look, why don't I make us both a cup of tea? Then I'll walk you to your car, wherever it is. Did you manage to bag a space at the boatyard?'

Stick to practicalities, that was the answer. She sniffed, then suddenly spun away from him, her shoes slipping on the wooden floor.

'Okay, I may as well tell you. I lied. There was somebody else, at the time. You must have suspected, surely?'

What? She was making it up, she must be. Kate, strong, independent Kate, who always got what she wanted, had not got what she came for today, so she was lashing out, sticking the boot in. If she wanted to play games with him, he would play along with her.

He shrugged. 'So you had somebody else. Why tell me now? Kate, it doesn't matter now. I don't care. Can't you see that?'

'I had an affair, Morgan, with somebody at work. Doesn't that mean anything to you?' She stood, hands on hips, her chin jutting defiantly.

'No, it doesn't, not now. I'm over it. Over you. I'm sorry if that sounds harsh, but there it is.'

Harsh, but not entirely truthful. Her words stung. The knowledge that Kate had cheated brought a painful mix of emotions with it. But he couldn't let her see that, not now.

Kate crumpled. The defiant pose gone, the tears fell properly, turning her green eyes to dark emerald, glossing the freckles on her cheeks. He began to regret his straight-talking –

he didn't like seeing her upset – but anything else would have left room for doubt.

'Come here.' He held out his arms and she walked into his embrace. 'Kate, don't do this to yourself.' He held her, pressing his mouth briefly to the crown of her head. Then he let her go and moved her, gently but firmly, away from him.

'I'm still in love with you,' she said, into his eyes.

He returned her gaze for a moment. 'No, you're not. You may not see that now but you will, and I'm sorry if things haven't worked out for you. You're strong. You'll be okay.'

Few words were exchanged after that. Kate gathered herself and rustled a tissue out of her bag to dab away the remains of her regretful tears. She didn't want tea, she said.

Morgan unplugged the laptop, put it under his arm, and walked with her along the riverbank, past the yard, and through to the road that ran parallel with the river, where her car was parked.

They said an unemotional goodbye, like casual friends. Kate drove off without a backward glance and Morgan began a despondent trek back to the bungalow.

THIRTY

Melody closed the lid of the laptop with a satisfied click and called out to Reece. She could see him through the open door of his study, sitting at his desk but not, apparently, actually doing anything.

'We're full, right up until the middle of October. I've taken the last booking for Willow, the week that couple cancelled because he's having a heart valve replaced. That's good, isn't it?'

Reece stared back at Melody, across the hall that separated the study from the living room. He seemed surprised to see her there, although she was exactly where he'd left her an hour ago, sitting in the upright armchair with the laptop, her books and pens on the side table.

'Yes, I suppose so, if it'll give him a few more years.'

'Not the heart valve, the bookings. Honestly, Reece, sometimes I might not be here at all, for all the notice you take.'

That wasn't fair; Melody tempered her sharpness with an indulgent smile and a lifting of her eyes. Not that Reece was watching. He'd already turned away from her, taking up his pen but not attempting to mark any of the exam scripts piled in front of him.

Melody sighed, out of mild exasperation, nothing more. Their moods never tallied now. They were like the couple in the weather house – one out and one in, all the time. Was that how all marriages became, or was theirs different because of the tragedy? They never socialised these days, didn't mix with couples of a similar age – all that had fallen by the wayside once they'd become awkward, and reluctant, company – which meant that the benchmark had been rubbed out.

It was three weeks since the anniversary. They'd spent the morning cleaning out the chicken coop and catching up with other outdoor chores. Later, they'd gone for a walk along the lanes around the village, had supper in a quiet pub, then watched a film on TV in pensive but companionable silence.

Apart from Danni's pale pink roses filling the silver vase on the hearth, they hadn't marked the day. There was no memorial to visit; Danni's ashes had been scattered on the secluded beach at Norman's Bay, her favourite place to build sandcastles when she was small. They hadn't wanted plaques or carved stones, or anything to suggest that their daughter was anywhere other than here at home, where she belonged.

Oddly enough, as the anniversary approached, Melody had felt a peculiar sense of calm descend on her over Layla's defection; peculiar, because 'calm' wasn't an emotion easily conjured up where Layla was concerned. It was a relief to feel that way. Once Reece had let her have her phone back – its confiscation being a hollow gesture in the first place, since she could easily have used the landline – she'd found she didn't need to call Layla again.

Reece was right; it may have been too upsetting for her to come here on the anniversary. Melody had no doubt that the occasion hadn't passed Layla by, and that she'd marked it privately, in her own way. Knowing that was a comfort in itself. Perhaps they would talk about it when Layla came again. Perhaps they wouldn't. Again, either was fine by her.

Melody wished she could explain this subtle change inside her to Reece – it wasn't as if they didn't talk about Danni now, albeit in a low-key, almost embarrassed sort of way, as if their daughter was a forbidden subject – but it never seemed to be the right time. Reece seemed set on closing all the gaps, as if he was perpetually plugging a leaking dam. He'd become almost frenzied about work, leaving for the university early in the morning, often without breakfast, and arriving home, exhausted. He would politely eat whatever meal Melody had made for him before retreating to the study to mark coursework and exam scripts, wrestle with timetables for the next academic year, or deal with his work emails. The end of the university year was relentless, and Reece had the extra responsibilities that came with being head of the mathematics division. Even so, surely he could let up a little once in a while? Melody thought this but didn't say it.

Weekends were the same. If Reece wasn't doing his university work, he'd be outside, banging nails into things, creosoting fences, or wielding ropes and a chainsaw to chop lumps off the trees that overhung the lane behind the holiday lets. Engaged in this activity, he had a manic look in his eye which prompted Melody, more than once, to urge him to be careful.

At night, when it should have been possible to re-establish a connection, he seemed anxious to be asleep as soon as possible. When she had instigated love-making the night before last, his response had cheered her. But as soon as it was over, he'd drifted back to a world that she knew nothing about.

Leaving Reece to whatever he was doing – or not doing – in the study, Melody stepped outside into the ochre sunlight. The day had been humid and oppressive. Now, infused with the scent of the roses, mingled with lavender and herbs from other parts of the garden, the air felt as refreshing as a cool bath.

She wandered along the path, past the rose garden and the beds of delphiniums, lupins and stocks. The roses – all the summer flowers – were at the height of perfection now, but their beauty didn't end there. The fading and crinkling of petals and leaves at the end of the season brought its own kind of ravaged beauty. A little sad, but unstoppable. *The natural order of things.*

Melody's thoughts moved on before she could stop them. A child dying before its parents was so against the natural order that it was a wonder the whole world didn't implode at the sheer preposterousness of it. She had fully expected that it would, that they'd wake up one morning to nothing but smoke and devastation and emptiness.

Oh, the guilt she felt over Danni's death! She felt it every day, every moment, like being run through with a sword. What if they hadn't argued that weekend Danni came home – the weekend that turned out to be the last ever? What if she hadn't rung Danni the moment she'd got back to her student house and tried again to enforce her side – hers and Reece's side – of the argument, only succeeding in making things worse? Would Danni have gone to that party in such a rebellious, destructive mood?

The coroner's inquest had been remarkably short, the verdict clear: accidental death. It had seemed too simplistic. Melody had wanted to jump up and shout that there was nothing accidental about it, and it was all her fault. But, of course, in the end she'd walked silently out of the courtroom, holding Reece's hand. The facts had been stated and recorded; legal duty had been done. The other matter was nobody's business but theirs and Danni's. Keeping her secret was the last thing they could do for their daughter.

This... thinking, this remembering of the last, heated, conversation with Danni, the aftermath of the party, and the court hearing when her death was pronounced as accidental, was new. Not the actual thoughts, but the way she was approaching them – with sorrow, yes, and her old companion, guilt, yet with composure and rationality. She wasn't crying, either. That was a surprise. It had been a year, only a year, and her grief would go on forever – she had long accepted that. With this new way of thinking, however, came hope, or at least, the seeds of hope.

Melody smiled – actually smiled – and headed back towards the house. She should be with Reece. She needed him; they needed each other. She wouldn't let him push her away.

And Layla. She was still a part of this, too. She loved that girl, not in the same way she'd loved Danni, of course, but she loved her, and she was fairly sure that Reece did, too. The three of them were united through Danni; nothing would ever destroy that. Layla would come back, when she had the time, when she was ready. However long it took, Melody could wait.

THIRTY-ONE

'I don't know why you two don't get together and have done with it.'

Nan, in her stockinged feet, padded up to the table where Layla and Seth had their heads bent over the laptop. They were poring over fine-dining menus from exclusive New York restaurants.

'You've got a point there, Mary. We'd make beautiful children,' Seth said, his face straight.

'Don't encourage her, for Pete's sake.' Layla nudged Seth in the ribs. 'Your hair looks lovely, Nan. Rowan's done a good job. I like the colour.'

Nan sniffed. 'I look like the ginger tom next door.'

'It's not ginger, it's Autumn Glow.' Rowan came into the room, flung herself onto the sofa and started to file her nails. 'Better than pepper-and-salt.'

'It's too curly. You roll it up too tight.'

'You can always do it yourself if you don't like it.'

'Don't snap at her, Row,' Layla said.

Nan hadn't heard. She was back in front of *Tipping Point*,

the wispy crown of her head showing above the back of the armchair. It *was* a bit on the gingery side, but she wasn't going to mention that to Rowan; her sister was as tightly strung as a tennis racquet as it was.

On the floor in front of Nan's chair, Finn sat, steadily posting cheese-and-onion crisps into his mouth while his eyes never left the screen. Every time the counters clattered down from the ledge, he broke off from his open-mouthed crunching to make a soft little 'Yay!' sound.

He must miss Jeff, Layla thought. He hadn't mentioned him, at least not in her hearing, but he must be wondering where all this was going to end. Or perhaps not. Perhaps with Finn, what you saw was what you got, and he was simply getting on with it. Whatever, he was a very special little boy. Layla felt like going over right now and giving him a hug, but he looked happy enough. Best to leave him.

The gush of running water was heard from overhead: Jadine, using Mum's en suite again, instead of the bathroom downstairs. She seemed to spend half her time in the shower, or the bath, which Layla put down to her semi-permanent state of being either pre-Alec or post-Alec. April, a firm believer in reincarnation, maintained that Jadine must have been a porpoise in a former life, or a stickleback. When Jadine had asked what she would come back as next time, Mum said she didn't know but she hoped it would be something dry and quiet.

Mum was busy, roasting a leg of lamb she'd got on staff discount from the supermarket. The smell wafted deliciously from the kitchen. They had a full house tonight, which was exactly how April liked it – it had taken Layla a while to realise that. As the weeks had turned into months and Rowan showed no sign of taking her son and moving elsewhere, a kind of shaking down had taken place, with everyone settling into their allotted space like ball-bearings rattling down the holes in a pinball machine. It was hard to remember what it had been like before, with just the three of them.

After dinner, Seth and Layla took Nan home in Seth's car. Arriving back in Warbler's Way, Layla didn't immediately jump out. Instead, without knowing she was going to, she described to Seth what had happened at the boathouse, and the shameful way she'd treated Morgan. The words tumbled out with barely any space between them.

'Wow,' Seth said. Layla frowned. 'Wow, as in, you certainly know how to make a bloke feel good.'

'You don't need to tell me. I'm not exactly proud of it. But, don't you see, I had no choice? I can't go there again, not with Morgan, not with anyone.'

'I wasn't being serious. Don't get upset.'

'I'm not. I'm trying to explain how it is for me.'

She wished she hadn't said anything now; she wasn't looking for sympathy or comfort. There was nothing that Seth, or anyone else, could do or say that would make a crumb of difference to any of it. Falling in love with Harvey, obsessing over him, allowing him to possess her, body and soul, had set off a chain reaction. A chain of titanium links, solid, unbreakable, everlasting. Before Harvey, she'd known exactly who she was and what she was about. The old Layla would never have let herself be dominated by a man, certainly never let him break her loyalty to her best friend. *Where was that girl now?*

'Layla, is there something you're not telling me about the Harvey bloke? Did he scare you, stalk you, or something? He wasn't violent, was he?'

'No. God, no. Nothing like that. I was crazy about him. We split up. It happens, I know that, but I don't need that kind of disruption in my life.'

Guilt brought heat to her face. Not telling Seth the whole story – the truth – was a kind of betrayal. More damage, more fallout. But it had to be this way, for now.

'There's no reason to suppose a relationship with Morgan would end the same way as it did with Harvey,' Seth said. 'They're different people. You're older and wiser.'

'Wiser, yes. That's my point.'

A Cabbage White butterfly fluttered in through the car window on Seth's side. Seth went to bat it away.

'No, leave it. Let it find its own way out.'

Seth raised his eyes. Layla wound the window fully on her side. The insect buffeted about on the inside of the car, its wing movements ever more frantic, until finally it found the current of air and flew out through Layla's window. An easy escape, in the end.

She'd been an idiot to think she'd escaped from the Morlands, just because she'd detected – or totally imagined, which was more like it – a subtle change in Reece's behaviour which may, or may not, have had something to do with her. It wasn't enough. That was just an excuse, not a reason; it was nothing she couldn't handle. She'd felt the lack of conviction in her mind even as she'd told herself she wasn't going to Foxleigh again.

Melody – possibly Reece, too – saw her as part of the healing process. There was no magic cure, no permanent healing, but eventually Melody would find a way of carrying on, a way of living with the loss of her daughter. If she, Layla, was helping the process in any way, then perhaps her strength lay in staying the course, not looking for a way out.

But what about her own life? This could take years. She hadn't destroyed the birthday card with its shocking words: *To a dear daughter.* She'd taken it to the hotel and stood over the shredder in the office with it in her hand, but it had seemed disrespectful to destroy it. Disrespectful to Melody and her all-consuming desire to have her daughter back. She'd taken the card back home, and tucked it in the box with the special birthday cards she'd kept over the years.

Layla had sat at their breakfast table that morning and not been able to utter one word of comfort, nothing that would help. She hadn't even accepted their gift with good grace. Seth had said she should return the cheque, and that it was a case of being cruel to be kind. Now she could see he was right, only she'd left it too late.

She hadn't been kind to Melody and Reece that day. And she hadn't been kind to Morgan, either. Her dear, lovely Morgan. Ignoring his messages, refusing to hear the distress in their tone. How could she have treated him like that? She'd never stopped thinking about him, not for one minute. He would never know that now.

Danni's parents and Morgan, woven together in her mind. The warp and the weft, neither existing without the other. They'd all be better off without her. It wasn't a gloomy thought, or a sad one. It sparkled with hope. She smiled.

'Have to get going in a minute,' Seth said kindly. 'When you're ready.'

The butterfly had come back. It wasn't inside the car; it danced crazily in front of the windscreen in a flurry of creamy wings. *I'm free*, it said. *I did it.*

'I have to go,' Layla said suddenly.

'Me too.'

'No, I mean leave Maybridge and move to New York. It was what I'd always planned. I can share Candy's apartment, and I'll take the job in the flash restaurant, learn how to cook the menus we were looking at. And then... and then, who knows?'

A soft breeze passed across her face from the open windows. She felt it as the butterfly had, pointing the way out. She laughed.

Seth looked at her, amused. 'You're really going?'

'Ha,' Layla pointed a finger at his chest. 'You didn't think I had the bottle, did you? Shows how much you know about me.'

'Yes I did. I just didn't think, with everything you've got going on...'

'Which is why I have to do it.' She opened the car door. 'See you tomorrow.'

THIRTY-TWO

'When you said you were coming, I rang your mother to ask her to dinner, but she's in Cambridge on a hypnotherapy course.' Nick laughed. 'No doubt she'll be looking for likely candidates to practise on.'

'Bloody hell,' Morgan said. 'You want to give that a wide berth.'

'Don't worry, I shall.' Nick picked up a large grey pebble and threw it, with a wide, overarm swing, into the sea.

On the one hand, it was a shame not to have seen Ellie, and also that Fiona, Nick's partner, was away visiting her sister. On the other, a peaceful few days at home in Suffolk with only his father was more in line with what he needed.

Connor had been fine about him taking time off at short notice. It was mid-week, slightly less busy than the weekend. Even so, he was grateful. He was grateful, too, that his friend hadn't asked him any questions. Not that he wouldn't tell him about Layla, eventually, but at that moment it was all too painfully fresh in his mind. Wimpish though it seemed, he'd just wanted to go home.

Fiona had made some changes about the house since he was

last here. Nothing drastic; a little orderliness imposed and a bit of subtle smartening up. A retired solicitor, Fiona was an orderly type of person who, until she'd met his father, had lived alone in a pristine, pink-painted cottage in Southwold. It must have driven her crazy, moving into a house where you daren't put anything down in case you never found it again. As she was also a sensitive woman, she had lived in this state for some while before she'd been brave enough to tackle the chaos. But knowing Nick, he probably hadn't even noticed the changes.

One of Fiona's attempts at order had been to take down some of Ellie's early paintings – now carefully stored in the loft – and re-hang the rest properly. Morgan admired the way the beach scenes and seascapes now followed one another up the stairs, culminating at the top with a large, vibrant oil painting of fishing boats in a storm.

He remembered that day. The storm had struck without warning, peaking around midday with the sky so dark they'd had to turn the lights on. The ferocity of the wind had loosened some of the roof slates, but living virtually on the beach as they did, this was nothing new. And in the days following, the slates had slid further down the roof to lodge in the guttering, which was where they remained.

Ellie had been in her studio under the eaves, her easel set up before the window, swishing away with the brush to capture the violent waves and the boiling purple clouds. In reality, there weren't any boats, but it was art, and she could paint what she liked; that's what she'd said when, with an eight-year-old's logic, Morgan had queried the absence of real-life boats out at sea.

He had felt extraordinarily pleased to see the tall figure of his father waiting on the station platform yesterday evening, hands behind his back in his usual stance, grey head turning this way and that as he waited for Morgan to appear. And then the familiar lit-up smile. The twenty-minute drive was conducted in friendly near-silence, and by the time they were jolting along the unmade road leading to the house, for the first time since Layla's defection, Morgan found he could say her name inside his head without the clawing sensation in the pit of his stomach.

An enormous pot of fish stew had been waiting on the stove.

'I even remembered to buy bread.' Nick had said, producing a stone-baked loaf from the enamel bread bin with a magician's flourish.

After they'd eaten, Nick brought out a bottle of whisky and they had sat on the veranda in the ancient deckchairs, watching the darkening sea shimmering beneath a netting of reflected stars. They'd spoken little – father and son had always been at ease in each other's company, without the need for constant talk. The conversation they did make was easy and inconsequential.

Scarcely able to keep his eyes open, he'd gone to bed before ten and fallen into a deep, dreamless sleep, leaving his father to migrate to his study, where he would remain until the small hours, content among his papers and books and fossils and lumps of quartz.

This morning, Morgan had been woken sharply by the screech of seagulls, and for one confused moment had imagined himself back at the flat in Haverstone. Waking fully, he'd climbed over the bed and looked out of the window to see Nick standing alone on the beach. His head was thrown back and his arms outstretched, as if he could capture the sea and the sky and the wind. Morgan had thrown on some clothes and hurried down to the beach to join his father.

They'd walked a little way, then Morgan said, 'It's a funny thing, but when I lived in Haverstone, in the flat, I hated that it had a view of the sea. For some reason, it made me feel anxious and I couldn't wait to get away from it. Yet here, now, it's kind of okay.'

'Why wouldn't it be?'

'Because of Ellie, because of what I saw, that day, when she was with her lover...'

'Ah, yes. But that wasn't her fault. She didn't mean you to find out like that. You shouldn't go on punishing her.'

'Is that what I'm doing? By having a phobia about the sea, I'm subconsciously showing how upset I was?'

'What do you think?' Nick spoke gently, his eyes kind.

Morgan thought for a moment. 'Yes, I guess it could be that. I'm not angry with Mum, though. I got over that a long time ago.'

'These things have a habit of sticking around without you realising it. Especially things that happen when you're young and impressionable.'

'Why didn't you fight for her?'

The question had slipped out unintentionally. Nick didn't seem thrown by it, but he thought for a moment before answering.

'I believe I did. It's a long time ago now. Why do you ask?'

'I don't know. I was angry at the time because you'd let her go so easily. That was how it seemed to me. Sometimes, I still remember that feeling and it raises the question.'

They'd reached the wooden breakwater separating them from the next beach along. Nick swung easily across it, despite his stiff leg, the one with the steel pins. Morgan followed.

'You were happy, though, you and Ellie, before all that? We always seemed like a happy family.'

'Yes, of course,' Nick said, 'and we were.'

A small crab lay at Morgan's feet, thrown up by the tide. Its claws flailed wildly as it tried to regain the water. Stooping to pick it up, he deposited it carefully where the surf licked the sand. He watched as the next wave swept it into the sea.

'So how did she get to change so completely? How could you accept that?'

'You mean, how could I accept her leaving me for another

woman rather than a man? It's a fair question.' He slid his hands into the pockets of his jeans. 'You can't help who you fall in love with. The potential is there, all the time, and often it's the person you least expect. If the person who triggers that response happens to be of the same sex, it doesn't have to be an issue. Granted, it might be for some people – repressed people, mainly – but Ellie was never going to be bound by convention, was she?'

Morgan laughed. 'No, I don't suppose she was.'

Not for the first time, he marvelled at how simple it had all become: his father settled with somebody new; his mother and her lesbian lover coming to dinner, bringing chocolates and wine like old friends or occasionally-seen relatives. The whole thing could have turned into a mishmash of bitterness and affronted silences. Instead, they'd made it seem normal, and ordinary.

Morgan glanced at his father as they crunched along the pebble-strewn sand. He felt slightly embarrassed by their conversation. They didn't usually talk about the deep stuff. Even after his mother had left and the two of them had banded together, united by drama, the talk had been about homework, snapped bike chains, and what to have for tea.

They walked on. It was still only 7:30 but they no longer had the beach to themselves. A woman threw a ball to a small brown terrier. It dashed in and out of the shallow surf, eager to play. A young couple wandered, hand-in-hand, along the strip of sand where the tide was starting to turn, sandals dangling from their fingertips.

'So now you have the river. I must come and see it one day.'

'You should,' Morgan said. 'She came to the boathouse. Kate. Turned up out of the blue and asked me to take her back.'

'Ah, Kate, yes. I liked her. Wonderful hair.'

'I said no, of course.'

'Of course?'

'She's lonely, and that's sad. But she doesn't really want to be with me. She only thinks she does.'

'Do you think she'll try again?'

'I don't think so. Anyway, I've got other problems.'

'Which is why you're here.'

'Yep. More or less.'

'Do you want to talk about it?'

Did he? What use was talking? He'd done all the talking he had words for, not with anyone else but here, inside his head. And a fat lot of difference it had made. He thought about what his father had said, about there being more than one person – any number of people – you could fall in love with. He was right, but you had to meet them first. And he had met Layla. She hadn't even given him a chance. She'd left him as stranded as that crab, with nothing to cling onto, no way back and no way forward.

He thought about Kate's revelation that there'd been somebody else. He hadn't believed her at the time. Then later, thinking about the way she'd acted in the weeks leading up to her departure, he'd decided it was probably true. It had hurt, at first; he had loved her for so long, after all. So why lie to him in the first place? At least if he'd known that, he would have had something to fight against. But his thoughts were dispassionate and purely theoretical. If you've fallen out of love, what happens after that is irrelevant.

With Layla, everything was relevant because in his mind she belonged to the present; he couldn't bear to consign her to the past, not yet. Every word, every look, every action, every nuance of body language; it all mattered. It all added up to something important, something momentous.

'There's not a lot to talk about,' he said. 'Unless you've got a crystal ball.'

'Ah, the great unknown. We are still talking about women, then.'

'Or not.'

'Indeed. Let's get back. Breakfast awaits.'

Morgan yawned and stretched, lifting his arms high above the back of the deckchair. The paperback he'd been reading lay face-down on the decking. They'd been out on the veranda all afternoon, reading, and watching the swimmers and the distant container ships gliding in and out of Felixstowe. He listened to the cries of the seabirds, the sighing of the waves, the clicks and creaks of the weatherboards. He'd done nothing all day except drive with Nick to the supermarket and back, and yet he'd never felt so tired.

Out on the road, a car approached. Its engine stilled; a car door closed. Nick, who'd been nodding over his geology magazine, suddenly hoisted himself upright in the deckchair, poised on full alert. The magazine slid to the floor.

Fiona appeared round the side of the house. Nick was already out of the chair, arms outstretched, his beam as bright as the sun. Fiona walked into his embrace and the two of them stood there, folded into one another as if they'd been apart for months.

'You're back! I thought you weren't coming till tomorrow.' Nick held her by the shoulders, casting his eyes over her face.

'Yes, I'm back. Unless I'm a hologram.' Fiona smiled. Her hazel eyes twinkled. She detached herself from Nick and stooped to pick up the bag she'd put down on the decking. 'There's only so much screaming you can take from one uncontrollable two-year-old.'

'Two-year-old?' Morgan said, looking up from the deckchair.

'Yes. My sister was babysitting her granddaughter. She's very sweet, but only when she's asleep and, believe me, that's not very often.' She laughed. 'Let me get this unpacked, then I'll make us some dinner.'

'No, no.' Nick took the bag from Fiona's hand and went to follow her indoors. 'This calls for a celebration. We'll go to the Lobster Pot.' He glanced back at Morgan. 'Is that all right with you, son?'

'Perfect.' Morgan slumped down in the deckchair and closed his eyes.

'Morgan Hampshire is a very good name for a writer,' Fiona said, with the careful emphasis of someone who had recently downed several glasses of champagne.

'Is it?'

'Yes.' She nodded vigorously, and flipped open the lid of the laptop.

'When I was in junior school,' Morgan said, 'I told everyone our family owned the whole county of Hampshire, and that was why Hampshire was my surname. I think I'd talked myself into believing it was true.'

'So how did you explain living in Suffolk?'

'I made up some story about my father wanting to step away from a family feud that went back centuries.'

Fiona's laugh bubbled up from the depths of her throat. 'Your story-telling skills started early, then.'

The pair of them were sitting snugly on the faded tapestry sofa. Snugly was the only option; any attempt to sit separately was thwarted by the relentless downward slope of the cushions. At the far end of the room, a rod of light showed beneath Nick's study door.

It was late, very late. Returning home from the Lobster Pot in almost total darkness, they'd picked their way along the ankle-cracking unmade road with the sea lapping in the background. The rinsed feel of the night air had invigorated them;

going straight up to bed had seemed out of the question. Nick had disappeared into his study, nightcap in hand, leaving Morgan and Fiona to continue a conversation they'd begun over dinner.

'Come on then.' Fiona held out her hand. 'Give.'

Morgan fished in his jeans pocket and brought out the memory stick. He gave it to Fiona and she posted it into the port. He'd never shown his work to anyone before, apart from Layla, and she'd been drunk as well.

As his words flooded onto the screen, he sank back into the cushions and let Fiona get on with it.

'This is good,' she said, when at last she lifted her eyes from the screen. 'Seriously good.'

'Seriously?'

'Yes. I wouldn't say so otherwise.'

Morgan was flattered, but at the same time he wondered about Fiona's credentials for making such a statement. She didn't seem to read much fiction, so where was her yardstick? Tiredness, and the beginnings of a champagne hangover, were weighing down his whole body. He sank further into the sofa cushions, at one with the shabby tapestry.

'Thank you.' He yawned. 'It's only the second draft. It needs a lot of work still.'

'Even so, I'd like to show this to a friend of mine. He's a literary agent, based in Norwich.'

Morgan was awake at once. 'Really? He's a friend of yours?'

'Yep. I haven't seen him in a while but I'm sure he'd take a look at it for you if I asked him. No promises, mind. He doesn't take on many new clients.'

'What's this?' Nick came out of his study, a journal under his arm. He switched the study light off and closed the door behind him.

Fiona told him.

'Ah,' Nick said, waving his forefinger in Morgan's general

direction. 'That's what you want, a leg up the ladder. Not that you'll need it but it does no harm to cut corners.'

Morgan and Fiona laughed.

'We are mixing our metaphors,' Fiona said, 'which means it's time for bed.'

The following morning was grey and drizzly, not a day to be setting foot on the beach. After a late breakfast, Morgan packed the few things he had brought with him. Fiona gave him a lift to the station, and he thought again how good she was for his father, how well they fitted together. It had all worked out well for Nick, and for Ellie. It gave him hope.

A rush of gratitude had him kissing Fiona on the cheek as they stopped on the station forecourt.

She laughed. 'What's that for?'

'Oh, nothing,' he'd said, and got out of the car.

The train wasn't long in arriving. He felt lighter, and a great deal calmer, than he had on the journey up. Gazing out of the train window, he watched the blurry landscape unfold. As he continued staring, he caught his own reflection staring back. He smiled in recognition. He was Morgan Hampshire, cruise boat skipper, some-time manager of a riverside enterprise, and writer. His future – his happiness – depended upon himself and what he made of it. Nobody else.

And with that, Morgan fell asleep.

THIRTY-THREE

Grief, Melody decided, was like perpetually swimming against the tide. She could see an island, a place of safety, in the distance, but each time she was about to reach it, the current dragged her away, carrying her back to where she started.

There were times, too, when she was moving along quite smoothly and then something would come at her out of the blue – a certain colour nail varnish, cereal on a supermarket shelf, a song on the radio, even the sight of her own feet, so like Danni's – and *whoosh*! A Niagara of sadness would descend, crushing the breath out of her. Triggers, Kate called them, which made Melody think of guns. It didn't help.

But alongside all of this, Melody detected the arrival of something new, something fragile, suggesting change. She was beginning to feel more centred, more like her former self. She didn't know how it had happened. Was it the result of the therapy, or simply the passing of time?

They had left Danni's room almost as it was, after she'd died – *died*, she hadn't used that word in a long time, if ever! Now, Melody went upstairs, along the landing where the floorboards creaked, towards the back of the house. She opened the door and stepped inside. The sunlight squeezing through the closed pink curtains shed a rosy glow over the pale walls. The room wasn't completely untouched; they hadn't wanted a shrine. The Glastonbury poster had gone from the back of the door, the chest of drawers cleared of everything except Danni's childhood collection of little glass animals standing on top; the wardrobe, although she couldn't see inside, was empty, its contents long gone to the animal charity shop. But the bed was made up exactly as it had been on Danni's last visit home, the pink-and-green checked bedding washed and aired and put back on.

After it happened, Melody used to come in here and lay on the bed for hours, gazing up at the ceiling, as if she was trying to fill the space that Danni had left. She hadn't done that in a while.

She went to the window and drew back the curtains. Light flooded in. Turning to the bed, she denuded the duvet of its cover and removed the sheet, mattress cover and pillowcases. The bed looked raw. Unveiled, exposed to the light, it seemed to flinch. Melody repositioned the pillows against the headboard and arranged the duvet squarely over the mattress. She folded the bedding into a neat pile, carried it along the landing and put it away in the tall linen cupboard. Coming back, she noticed she'd left Danni's bedroom door ajar. She left it as it was.

It was Monday morning. Reece was at work. The hens clucked in the yard. Feeling the sudden need for company, Melody walked down to the holiday lets to see if there was anyone about. Three sets of new arrivals had kept her busy on Saturday. Willow had an elderly but sprightly woman and her middle-aged daughter. They were a lively pair, giggling together like schoolgirls as they'd unpacked their bags from the car. Melody knew they were out; she'd seen the car bouncing through the gates earlier.

The car belonging to the occupants of Hazel was missing; a cursory glance at the windows showed no signs of life. They seemed a nice family – the couple in their forties, and a polite lad aged about ten. Reece had remarked that the man looked like a geography teacher; could spot them a mile off, he reckoned.

Larch looked unoccupied, too. A dark green convertible Mini Cooper was parked beside it, the bonnet sprinkled with leaves. Its owner may have gone for a walk, Melody thought.

A dense silence had settled over the converted stables, the yard in front and the trees behind. Disappointed, Melody was about to leave when she heard movement. The door of Larch was open and its sole occupant, a man who looked to be in his late fifties, stood outside.

'Good morning,' he called, beaming at Melody. 'Beautiful day.'

She smiled back. 'Hello. I didn't think anyone was in.'

'Did you knock? I didn't hear, sorry.'

'No, no.' Melody felt colour flood to her face, as if she'd been caught snooping. 'I popped down to check that everything was all right, that's all. I didn't mean to disturb you.'

'I'm very glad you did,' he said, coming further out towards Melody. 'I was deciding what to do today.' He laughed. 'I haven't got very far.'

His name was Gareth, she remembered from the booking. He was a smallish man, shorter than Melody – about five-foot-eight, she thought – but with a compact strength about him that made up for his lack of stature. He had slightly receding dark hair and startling blue eyes behind black-rimmed glasses.

'There's Foxleigh Court, just up the road. It's a Tudor house. The grounds are beautiful – it's a lovely day for a walk. Or there's the owl sanctuary. Or you could drive down to Rye or Hastings, if you want somewhere further afield... Ah,' – she noticed he was holding a sheaf of leaflets – 'you found those. You won't want me to do the tourist guide bit, then.'

'You know what I'd really like?'

'What's that?'

'To take Bertha over there for a bit of a spin' – he nodded towards the Mini – 'with somebody in the passenger seat. Don't happen to be free for an hour, do you?'

'I could be, I suppose...' Melody wasn't entirely sure he was being serious.

'Excellent. So, what do you think? You don't have to talk if you don't want to. Sit there and enjoy the ride.'

Melody smiled. 'Okay, why not?'

It was a long time since she'd done anything spontaneous, Melody realised, as the car, with its top down, roared round another bend, narrowly avoiding the ditch. But Gareth seemed an expert driver and she sat back and enjoyed the freeing sensation of the sun on her face and the wind in her hair.

'Why do you call her Bertha?'

They'd driven in companionable silence for the last four miles; she felt it was time she said something.

Gareth glanced at her. 'I've never had a car like this before – I'm more of a Volvo man, or I was. So I thought, why not do something even less like me and give her a name? I could see she was female, so that was a start. It's a private joke, not a very funny one. Bertha was the name of the house-mistress at boarding school. She was big and slow, and my Bertha is small and fast.'

'And is the holiday a change, too, as well as the car?' He didn't seem the type to be spending a week alone in a place as quiet as Foxleigh, and she was curious. 'Unless it's not a holiday, as such?'

He could be hiding out, running away from something, or someone... Her imagination was in full flight now. Reece had always said the stable lets would be an ideal bolt-hole for anyone wanting to lie low. Not that he would tell her if he was.

'It is a holiday, and yes, it is very different from what I'm used to but I think I shall enjoy it. I haven't had a holiday away since... well, for five years actually. Before that, it was hotels, abroad mostly.'

He didn't offer more. Although Melody wanted it, she didn't feel she could ask.

They passed fields of ripened corn, a row of tile-hung cottages and a village where ducks waddled on the grass beside a pond. As they left the village, the sign for Haverstone appeared.

An image came to Melody of the hospital and the tacked-on grey-brick clinic, with its strip lights and squeaky rubber floor. An involuntary shiver ran through her. Her appointments with Kate were less frequent now; the last was two weeks ago, the next in a week's time. She didn't want to go. Not then, not ever again. Suddenly she knew that, with absolute certainty. And to think, that clinic used to be her sanctuary, her path back to sanity. Now, she didn't even want to clap eyes on the place, with its poignant reminders of her wrecked emotions.

'Are you all right?' Gareth gave her a concerned look.

'Yes, I'm fine. Look, you might not want to go much further down this road. There are usually tailbacks the nearer to the coast it gets.'

'Of course. I mustn't keep you too long from whatever it was you were doing.'

Which wasn't very much, Melody thought.

'There's a roundabout soon,' she said. 'We could turn off there.' She didn't care where they went, as long as it wasn't anywhere near Haverstone.

Gareth completed a half circuit of the roundabout and turned onto a narrower road with folding hills on one side and gentle wooded slopes on the other. A mile or so on, he took another turn, and they were back in the village with the ducks. In the picture-postcard high street was a frilly-curtained tea shop, with hanging baskets and a sign on the pavement announcing morning tea and coffee.

'Shall we?' Gareth asked, slowing Bertha to a crawl.

Moments later, they were inside, seated opposite one another at a gingham-clothed table in the window.

He asked her about Foxleigh and how long they'd lived there. Melody's answers were vague, as if she couldn't remember. She didn't want small-talk and, if she was reading him correctly, neither did Gareth. He was only being polite.

'The old farmhouse is beautiful,' he said, eventually. 'A sizeable place, for two people.'

'Yes.'

Melody sipped her coffee, holding the cup with both hands, as if she was cold. It was quiet in the tea shop. Murmured conversations went on at other tables, the tinkle of china, the steady tick of the grandmother clock in the corner.

'My daughter died,' she said.

Her companion nodded briefly, eyes narrowing behind their screens. 'I thought there might be something.' Another pause, and then, 'How long?'

'A year. Just a year.' Melody gazed through the window towards the row of half-timbered cottages on the opposite side of the street. She looked back at Gareth. 'Danni died in an accident in her last year at university.'

'My daughter died, too. It's almost five years now. Her horse threw her. He was spooked by a lorry and she ended up under its wheels. She was twenty-seven.'

'Oh. Oh dear,' Melody said.

A wave of shock passed through her, distressingly familiar. She wondered where his wife was, if he had one.

'Unfortunately, Sally, my wife, also died. Two years ago. Cancer.'

'Oh no.' Melody put down her cup and steepled her hands to her mouth. 'How dreadful.'

'She never got over losing Hannah – well, of course she didn't. We were beginning to pick up our lives, and then she... Well, there you are.' A pause, and then he smiled. There was no trace of self-pity in it. 'It's all wrong, isn't it? Children are supposed to stick around, give you grandchildren, and be there to look after you in your dotage. That's how it's meant to work.'

The sudden mention of grandchildren sent Melody's nerves skittering. She concentrated hard on a loose thread in the table-cloth, willing the sensation to pass.

'I think,' she said eventually, picking at the thread with her fingernail, 'that after the bad part – the very, very bad part – it's the guilt that's the worst thing.'

'Yep,' Gareth said. 'That's the one. Would it have happened if you'd done this instead of that? Been here and not there? The things left unsaid... Pointless, of course, but it doesn't stop you beating yourself up.'

We're strangers, thought Melody, and yet we have this in common. How tragic, yet almost comforting in a strange sort of way.

A man and woman got up from the corner table and left. Steam hissed fitfully in the kitchen. The grandmother clock ticked on.

'What are you meant to do?' Melody said. 'How do you go on?'

'You try to see in front as well as behind. You look round the next corner, and the next, and you do your damnedest not to be afraid. Other than that, I haven't the faintest idea.'

As they drove back, Melody's mind turned once again to the clinic, although not in terms of her treatment. Now that she'd decided she wasn't going back any more, she thought about Kate – not Kate the therapist, but Kate the young woman with hopes and dreams and insecurities. She wondered about the girl's parents, her family, her loves, her heartbreaks.

Kate had never been anything less than professional in the way she dealt with Melody, but Melody saw past that, to the girl with the crazy red curls and the green eyes full of sadness. It was a one-way street, the faux-intimate relationship between patient and therapist. But Melody felt that the many hours she and Kate had spent closeted together in that impersonal cell of a room had allowed something of Kate to seep back towards her, as if a drain clogged with leaves had overflowed. On her last visit, Melody had been tempted to turn the tables and say to Kate: *That's enough about me. Tell me about you. What's happened to make you so sad?* She hadn't, of course.

She would miss Kate. Even though Melody had at times become angry and frustrated at her own inability to express herself, or at Kate's supposed nonchalance over Melody's distress, she would miss her. But it couldn't be helped. She hoped – oh, how she hoped – that Kate's life would turn out the way she wanted it to. Melody felt sure that, right now, she had a way to go with that.

They were entering Foxleigh now. She made a sudden decision.

'Would you drop me here, in the village, please? I need a few things.'

'Of course.' Gareth smiled. He had a lovely smile. 'I'll park up and wait for you.'

'No, honestly. I'd rather walk back from here,' Melody said. She was in no hurry to get home. The house felt so empty.

Moments later, she stood on the pavement outside the bakery and watched the Mini swoop away, Gareth raising an arm and tooting merrily as he went. Melody smiled into the sunshine. For the first time in ages, she didn't feel quite so alone.

THIRTY-FOUR

Reece sat in his office overlooking the quadrangle formed by four honey-stoned buildings. Students trooped to and fro beneath the arch in the far corner, heading for the library, the refectory, or a last game of pool in the student union bar. Most had gone home now. Those that were left had retakes, or were waiting for flights to lift them out of the country. Others had no real reason to hang around the campus; they just did. He knew how they felt.

He'd put in a full week last week, and done some work over the weekend. There was no real need for him to be here today – he could have fielded his messages from home – but home had a different meaning these days. Most of the time he couldn't work out whether Melody wanted him around or not. When he was close by, he felt the irritation flying off her, attaching itself to him like iron filings to a magnet. Yet when he was elsewhere in the house, or outside, it wouldn't be long before she came to seek him out, as if she needed to make sure he hadn't vanished into thin air.

Rejected and claustrophobic by turns; that was how he felt at home. He didn't blame Melody any more than he blamed himself. They were different people now; they hadn't yet worked out how to be, either alone or with each other.

His confusion and guilt over his feelings towards Layla showed no signs of abating. Melody, although outwardly she'd relaxed considerably over the whole thing, still spoke about Layla in a way that suggested she knew they'd be seeing her soon. Reece wasn't at all sure that they would. All he knew was that he still missed her, and she occupied his thoughts in the most dangerous way possible.

The other night, he'd dreamt about her. It wasn't unusual, but this time it was different, more intense, and disturbing. Her beautiful face, the scent of her skin, the timbre of her voice – inside his dream, he'd been drowning in her. At first light, he'd found himself reaching out for Melody. She'd tensed momentarily, and then she'd responded to his touch and they'd had slow, sleepy sex. He'd been only half awake; the woman he'd made love to was only half Melody.

Reece nudged the computer mouse and the screensaver swept aside, revealing emails from the Dean's office, the head of department, and lecturers from his division. He responded to them all in turn, making notes in his diary of the various upcoming meetings as he went, and then his hand strayed to the middle drawer of his desk and reached for the packet of chocolate biscuits. He took one out and bit into it. It was gone in an instant; he'd barely tasted it. He'd been doing far too much of this recently, comfort eating. It wasn't healthy; it would have to stop. He went to shut the drawer but instead took out another biscuit and crammed it into his mouth. It was only a bloody biscuit. What the hell did it matter?

Later, on the way to the pigeonholes to see if he had any mail, he ran into a colleague, Paul, in the corridor. Paul punched him lightly on the shoulder, almost letting the pile of exam scripts slip from his grasp.

'The Dark Horse, about five?'

The real name of the pub, a convenient three-minute walk away from the campus, was the Black Horse; it had earned its nickname from the constant clandestine visits made by university staff and students who were meant to be somewhere else at the time.

'Don't think so. I should get home,' Reece said.

Paul hoisted up the scripts. 'End of term, mate. You deserve a break. See you there.' He marched off down the corridor.

End of term 'breaks', spent mainly in the Dark Horse, hadn't been exactly thin on the ground these past few weeks. Reece had forgone most of them, but perhaps a pint and a laugh was precisely what he needed. His phone was in his hand, ready to text Melody, by the time he was back at his desk.

Reece squeezed into a space at a table by the window already occupied by half a dozen maths lecturers. At other tables, and standing around the bar, were the familiar faces of colleagues from various departments, including a handful of social science bods who seemed to have taken up permanent residence in the place. Along the far side of the long bar, several students were arranged on stools, elbows resting on the bar. They looked as if they'd been there for some time, as did most of the clientele. Clearly, he had some catching up to do, which wasn't a problem as two pints had already appeared at his elbow.

In between the banter, the jokes, and bouts of disproportionate hilarity, holidays became the main topic of conversation, complaints about husbands, wives and partners featuring strongly.

'Separate holidays, that's the answer,' Paul declared,

smacking his empty glass down. 'They do their thing, you do yours. Job done.'

A holiday, Reece thought. Should we be doing that? He hadn't even thought. It seemed too frivolous to be even considering it; he was sure Melody felt the same. Not that she'd want to go anywhere with him, not as things stood. Gloomily, he lifted his glass.

'Well, I'm all for that!' Jemma, a computer science lecturer, yelled, six inches from Reece's ear. 'All mine wants to do is fry himself on the fucking beach for a fortnight!'

He flinched. He had a headache, he realised. He also realised it was his round, probably had been an hour ago. Struggling up from the chair, he circled an enquiring finger in the air, over the tops of the depleted glasses. Reaching the bar, the orders already fading from his brain, he happened to glance up at the clock. It was ten past nine. Bloody hell. He'd been drinking almost solidly for four hours. He'd told Mel he'd be home by seven at the latest. But the barman was lining up the glasses on the bar. He'd see this round out, then make his way home. Quite how he was going to get there was beyond his brainpower to decipher at this precise moment.

He wove his way back to the table, making several journeys to deliver the drinks, then sat down again. Dusk had fallen and the wall-lights had come on, sending a glare straight through his skull. He felt okay, though; pleasantly woozy, in fact. The alcohol had stunned his ability to feel much pain. Leaning back in his seat, he let the increasingly raucous laughter go on around him and gazed at a new crowd of people gathering at the far end of the pub.

As Reece stared, without realising he was doing so, a dark head appeared across his vision, and big brown eyes, a wide, sensuous mouth. Layla! He was half out of his seat before he realised that the girl he was looking at was nothing like her. Sinking back down in his seat, he saw the same girl again, her face swimming in and out of his vision like the face of a ghost, and then the face was replaced with another, fairer one. Reece blinked. The face retreated, then swam forward again. Danni's face. His daughter! Again, Reece lifted himself off the seat.

And then he remembered.

'I have to go... get home,' he said, to nobody in particular.

The table rocked, setting several glasses teetering, as he edged his way out. He stumbled to the double doors and pushed them open, taking a long, deep breath of cool air to steady himself.

No time seemed to pass at all between his leaving the pub and finding himself enfolded into the luxurious passenger seat of a BMW.

'It's all right. I've been on lime and soda since six.' Jemma grinned at him from the driver's seat. 'I'd never leave this little baby in the uni car park overnight. Now, where do you live?'

Melody smiled as she opened the front door to let him in. At least, he thought she was smiling, only he couldn't seem to see too well.

'I kept you some dinner. I could warm it up,' he heard her say, as his eyes and ears began to function. 'Or perhaps not,' she added, looking him up and down.

And then, of course, he began to apologise, lots of times, until she stopped him.

'Reece, it's fine. I understand. You needed to let off some steam, take time out. You'll have one hell of a head in the morning, though.'

'Why are you being so nice to me?' he heard himself say.

Melody just laughed.

Again, a swathe of time vanished, during which Reece had no idea what he'd done. Except he'd had a shower. Yes, he remembered that. And then he found himself in bed, wearing his pyjama bottoms and T-shirt, with a plate of toast on the bedside table along with a jug of water and a glass.

'No crumbs in the bed, please,' Melody said, lifting her shirt over her head and getting in beside him.

'No, matron.'

He started to laugh, a sudden rising of mirth, bordering on hysteria. And then, just as suddenly, the laughter died inside him, taking the bonhomie of the evening, the alcohol-fuelled sensation of well-being, and everything that was good in the world, with it.

Slowly, he turned towards Melody. She was lying on her side, her head propped up on her elbow, watching him.

'She's not coming back, is she?' His voice was small, hardly there.

Melody stroked his forehead with her fingertip. 'No, my love, she isn't.'

THIRTY-FIVE

For once in her life, Kate hadn't the faintest idea what to do next. No plan, no focus, no fervent wish to do something or be somewhere. Nothing. Even work had lost its shine. The psych wards were quiet. It was like that sometimes, usually after a spell of admissions taking place at a dizzying rate. All or nothing. Kate preferred to be busy, even though she sometimes felt as if she was asleep on her feet. The slower pace gave too much room for thought, too much scope for the whys and what-ifs.

What if she hadn't got involved with Xavi? Would she and Morgan still be together? Sadly, no matter how many times the question asked itself, the answer was always 'no'. So why had she gone chasing after him, ditched her pride and asked – no begged, almost – for another chance? It was exactly the sort of needy behaviour she deplored in others, the kind of thing she heard all too often in her clinic sessions. Her patients had an excuse; their minds weren't fully functioning. As their therapist, she should be the one with vision, the one able to see a clear path ahead. She hadn't been that person for a long time, and it was shameful, it really was.

Her own counsellor – the therapists all had counselling

sessions of their own – had disagreed, told her she was being unkind to herself, then praised her for her commitment. But praise was no comfort when you knew, deep down, you were rubbish.

At least she no longer had to run the gauntlet when Xavi was about. He'd left to go and work in a private hospital. It wasn't because she'd let him down so badly – he'd taken great pains to explain that to her, and she believed him – but she couldn't help feeling guilty over the way it ended. And it had ended, properly – she'd owed him that. She couldn't let him carry on living in hope. It was unfair of her, and cruel.

One evening after clinic, when she'd been feeling braver than usual, she'd waited for him in the car park. They'd gone for a coffee and she'd spoken honestly about her feelings. Xavi had been quietly accepting. It hadn't come as a surprise. He'd seemed sad, but relieved, and thanked her for telling him. Which, of course, made Kate feel even worse but it was no less than she deserved.

And then something happened which changed things for the better, not dramatically but enough to give her fresh hope. Arriving for her day in the clinic, she found a message asking her to phone Melody Morland. She was puzzled – Melody's appointment wasn't until next week and if she needed to rearrange, she would normally do that through the receptionist. Patients couldn't phone therapists directly – their numbers were all protected.

Sitting down in the almost empty office, she made the call. Melody answered immediately, as if she'd been waiting. Kate heard apologies first, lots of them, as if Melody felt she was letting Kate down for ending the sessions so suddenly.

'I feel,' Melody said, once she'd finished apologising, 'that I need to do this on my own now. Whatever's to come, I have to face up to it and deal with it, and I'm ready to do that now.' A breathy sigh, then, 'Oh, Kate, you've been so marvellous,' –

Kate cringed – 'I don't think I'd even be here if it wasn't for you.'

Kate said nothing. Melody was over-dramatising; she wasn't to be taken literally. There had never been any danger of that sort; she was as certain about that as it was possible to be.

'Also,' Melody said, saying what had probably been the main thing on her mind all along, 'there's only so much talking and sharing you can do, and what there is left I need to do with Reece, with my husband. I won't let our daughter's death drive a wedge between us. I won't.'

Kate smiled. Melody's new determination was a gift.

'You're ready, Melody. That's the important thing. Remember, the door is always open if ever you need us.'

'Yes,' Melody said. 'Thank you.'

Silence. Kate waited a moment. Melody must have gone. She was about to put the phone down when Melody spoke again. 'And you, Kate, are you okay?'

Kate didn't reply. This wasn't the kind of conversation you could let happen.

'Sorry,' Melody said, laughing lightly. 'It's the mother in me. I am a mother, still.'

'Yes,' Kate said. 'You are.'

Another silence, and this time Melody really had gone.

Usually, when a patient finished treatment, Kate closed them off in her mind, but something of Melody Morland lingered, like a waft of perfume after the wearer had left the room. Strangely, every time she thought about Melody, she thought about Morgan, and vice versa, as if in some unseen way the two were connected, although she couldn't imagine how.

But there it was. She wouldn't have to think about either of them any longer. Except that she would, of course. Especially Morgan.

One evening, she sat by the window in the sunlit, high-ceilinged flat she now shared with two other female nurses. The flat was in a converted Edwardian house. It had no view of the sea. Instead, it overlooked Haverstone Park and was only five minutes by bike to the hospital. Taking her phone, she scrolled through and deleted Xavi's name from her list of contacts, then Morgan's. And then she deleted the number of the old flat – goodness knows why she'd kept it. Finally, she fetched her bag, took out the still unfolded piece of paper on which Morgan had written his new address, tore it up into little pieces and dropped them into the waste bin.

There was still the boathouse. She would never forget how it looked and smelt, and the inspiring beauty of the riverside setting. And that was fine, because it was Morgan's special place; she'd seen straight away how he belonged there. She hoped he would continue to enjoy it. She hoped he would be happy.

For the rest of the week, her steps along the hospital corridors were lighter, her sleep less troubled, her laughter more frequent. But she needed something else. Melody's last words to her played themselves back. 'I am a mother, still.'

On Friday, Kate packed her weekend bag and went home to Milton Keynes.

THIRTY-SIX

'Where did you go, when you stayed out all night?'

Rowan looked up suddenly, surprised by the question Layla had no idea she was going to ask. They'd been talking about Mum and Jadine and Finn, having a giggle over this and that, like they used to do. Layla realised how much she'd missed that.

It was Monday, Rowan's day off. Layla was on a late shift. Finn had broken up from school and had gone to play at a friend's house. This morning, Layla had noticed that her sister's face had a kind of lost look about it, which prompted her suggestion of an outing, just the two of them.

They were in the cathedral café, where leafy plants rose from giant pots; people trod carefully on the stone floor to avoid unnecessary noise. Even the clatter of china seemed muted.

Rowan gathered up a handful of blonde hair as if she was going to make a ponytail, before letting it fall again. 'Nowhere, really.'

'You must have gone somewhere. Don't tell me if you don't want to.'

'It's not a secret. I went to a hotel, the big one on the motorway. Alone, in case you were wondering. I needed to have a proper think, without... Well, you know what home's like.'

Only too well, Layla thought. 'Did it work?'

Rowan shrugged. 'Sort of. It cleared my head a bit, anyway.'

'I'm sorry, Row,' Layla said.

'What for?'

'I haven't exactly been the perfect sister. I thought you and Jeff would work it out, like always, and then when Mum told me... Well, to be honest I didn't have the strength to get involved in all that. Which is stupid, I know, but it's the truth.'

'I know. It's cool. I had a mad moment, fell for somebody I shouldn't have – or I thought I'd fallen for him. Boredom, bloody-mindedness, whatever. Until I realised he wasn't that great, not very nice at all, as it goes, and I ended it. You couldn't have talked me out of it, though. No one could.'

'But I could have been there to listen, if you'd wanted to talk.'

Rowan smiled. 'Don't be daft. You're off the hook.'

'How d'you mean?'

'There was no way I was going to burden you with my problems, nor was Mum, or any of us, except Jadine cos she hasn't got a clue. You've had a horrible time, losing your best friend. It must still hurt a lot.'

Layla sat back, biting her lip, as realisation dawned. Her family had been tiptoeing round her, shielding her from any unnecessary worries, because they knew she was still grieving for Danni. Did they suspect there was more to it than that? If so, all credit to them that they hadn't pushed her into talking about it. She felt a rush of affection for Rowan. It brought a single tear. She wiped it away, but not before her sister had noticed.

'Don't be soft.' She giggled.

Layla joined in. She hadn't felt this close to Rowan for ages. The clock seemed to have wound itself back, set them to where they were before.

'Why d'you keep looking at that phone? Expecting a message, are we?'

Rowan pushed the mobile aside. 'Might be.'

'Come on, then. Who is he?'

Rowan couldn't stop the smile. 'It's Jeff. We've been dating.'

'*Jeff?* Dating?'

'Yes. As in, going out on dates? It was his idea. And no, before you ask, we aren't sleeping together. He's taken me to some cool places for dinner. We even went to your hotel. That's not cool, though. Just freakin' expensive.'

'You went to Tidehall and you didn't tell me? Was it any good?'

'You're the chef and you don't know?' More laughter.

'Fair point. Are you getting back together, then?'

'Might do. We're taking it steady, not rushing into anything.'

Layla smiled. This was a change from Rowan's usual method of charging ahead and damn the consequences. Perhaps the two of them were more alike than she'd realised.

The lost look Layla had seen this morning reappeared on Rowan's face.

'I wish,' she said, glancing out of the window, 'that Jeff was Finn's real dad. Finn's one reason I want us to get back together. He worships Jeff.'

'Finn's not the only reason, though?'

'No. Jeff's the one for me. I only hope he sees me the same way.'

'I'm going to miss you, when I go to New York.'

'So I should hope,' Rowan said.

Layla put down the pan she was holding and glanced across at Big Barry, who was coming out of the cold store. She felt a bit guilty about Barry; she hadn't told anyone at the hotel she was leaving, other than Seth. There was still time before she had to hand in her notice – her visa hadn't even come through yet. Once she went public, she'd have to talk about it, and she couldn't do that without her voice catching.

Danni had wanted to be a journalist; she'd planned to look for an internship in New York. They were supposed to have embarked on the big adventure together. She should be here. It was so unfair that she wasn't.

'Coffee break?' Seth broke into her thoughts.

'What? Yes, in a minute.'

'No, now.'

They sat on the wall at the back of the service area.

'I wanted a word, sunshine,' Seth said.

'That sounds serious. Oh, go on then, if you must.'

Seth put a hand on her shoulder. 'Look over there.'

'Where?'

He was pointing across the flower-edged lawns towards the wide gravel drive, the tall, wrought iron gates between soaring stone pillars.

'Right. Imagine the Hampshire guy is walking in through those gates now. What do you do? Quick. No thinking time. Gut reaction.'

'I run away and hide, and I don't come out until he's gone.'

Layla sensed the tension in Seth as he worked his way up to the next stage in the game. She froze him with a look. His eyes searched her face for a moment, then he relaxed his shoulders.

'Okay. Just testing.' Then, after a beat of silence, 'I'll miss you, you know.'

'Will you?'

'Well, I might a bit. Would you miss me, if I was the one buggering off to the other side of the world?'

'Stop fishing. You won't be here, anyway.'

Seth himself would be leaving Tidehall Manor, and Maybridge, at the end of the year. The next stage of his training would be conducted in a London hotel, under the keen eye of his father, in person rather than from a distance. Seth was pretending to dread it, but it was all an act, a transparent one at that. Time to move on, and up. For both of them.

'It's hardly the same thing. London.'

'No, but still...'

Seth was right. It wasn't the same thing at all. She gazed unseeingly across the expanse of lawn. If New York hadn't felt real before, it did now. All this talk about missing people was chipping away at her confidence. A lifetime's ambition it might be, or one of them, but the whole thing had an unmistakable flavour of running away.

First, there was Morgan. She'd already run away from him, literally, and only succeeded in narrowing the metaphorical distance between them. Even Seth could see that.

And the Morlands. Had she spent more than half a year trying to break away from Danni's parents, only to discover that she needed them more than they needed her? Because she craved their forgiveness?

Who, then, was she running away from? Herself? She was defined by that night, by her unspeakable act of selfishness. However far she ran, there was no escape from that.

She glanced at Seth. He had his head down, scrolling through his phone with his thumb, his eyes narrowed in concentration. Suddenly, she longed to pour it all out to him, the real story of the night Danni died, not the expurgated version she'd fed him and everyone else. She half opened her mouth to speak, but the thought of Seth's shock, his distaste, hijacked the words before they formed. He would protest that he didn't think any less of her, but deep down he would surely wonder what kind of a person she really was, and he'd have every right. She couldn't bear that. Not on top of everything else.

A shudder ran through her. Noticing, Seth shuffled along the wall a bit so that they were shoulder-to-shoulder, but didn't look up from his phone. He was looking up cheap flights to New York. Chatting on about coming out to visit her.

Enough.

Layla slid down off the wall, retrieved her coffee cup and walked quickly back to the kitchen.

At home that evening, when everyone else was occupied, Layla retreated to her thinking place, the back doorstep. It wasn't quite dark yet. The trees were etched like charcoal drawings against the fading glow of the sky. The air was soft and still. Still as death.

She rested her elbows on her knees, steepling her hands to her mouth. It was some minutes before she realised she was crying. She didn't try to stop the tears. Instead, she let them flow, wetting her fingers. It didn't matter that she was crying because she was alone out here; there was no one to see. After a while, she sat up and rubbed her eyes with the shredded remains of a tissue she'd found in her pocket.

There was movement at the end of the garden – a fox. It turned its head towards her, fixing her briefly with its orange gaze, its ears on full alert, before it slid away as silently as it had arrived. In that split second, when Layla's eyes met the animal's stare, something stirred inside her. A voice came out of the darkness, out of her head. Her own voice.

They deserve the truth. Tell them, before it's too late.

THIRTY-SEVEN

Layla vaguely recalled seeing an all-night café as they'd made their way to the party. She found it easily enough, two streets away. The place was packed, mostly with taxi drivers, but she found a seat at a tiny table in the corner. The coffee was strong enough to stand a spoon up in, but it was hot, and just what she needed. The fug that had built up inside the café from the deep fat fryer and the steam from the coffee machine was actually quite comforting.

She stirred her coffee slowly while the low buzz of tired conversation went on around her, her gaze fixed on the window where beads of condensation caught and held the light from passing cars and the houses opposite. She narrowed her eyes, and the globules of light blurred and meshed into a multi-coloured shimmering curtain.

What the hell had got into Danni tonight? Something must have happened to pitch her into such a frenzy of craziness far beyond her comfort zone. Danni liked a good time as much as anyone, but tonight she'd been on mission of self-destruction Layla would not have believed, had she not witnessed it for herself. It couldn't have been entirely down to the mysterious falling-out with her mother, nor her heartbreak over Nathan – whom, after all Danni had said, had been summarily dismissed without a backward glance.

No, there must be something else, something she hadn't been able to share with her best friend. Layla couldn't help feeling a bit put out about that, as if Danni hadn't trusted her enough to take her into her confidence.

She sipped her coffee, hands clasped around the thick white china mug. The sounds of the city at night shouldered in, then retreated, as the café door opened and closed: the swish of traffic from the ring road, the throaty revving of taxi engines, the scream of sirens. One of the younger taxi drivers caught her eye and flashed a smile. She gave him a fleeting smile back, then diverted her gaze to her phone but the battery had died. Probably just as well; she could do without any more bad news tonight.

At her best guess, it was around forty-five minutes before Layla roused herself, left the café and set off back to the party house to collect Danni. She hadn't intended to leave it that long, but she was so tired, from all the stress as much as the late hour – or early, whichever way you looked at it. Her feet dragged on the pavement as she flogged through the streets.

Reaching the road she wanted, she stopped, and rubbed her eyes. All had been in darkness before. Now, beams of yellowish light strobed across the tarmac and lit up the brickwork of the houses. And blue lights. Pulsating, bright blue lights. Police cars angled across the street.

Oh God.

Layla broke into a run.

. . .

The front door of the house stood open, emitting a bright square of light. The atmosphere seemed highly charged, unnatural. She tried to make the steps but her way was barred, deliberately – Helen, the girl who had called her earlier, had her hand firmly on Layla's arm. This had to be to do with Danni. Had to, otherwise why was she being stopped?

Shrugging off Helen, she tried to push her way towards the house. Once again, she was restrained.

'Don't, Layla. Stay back,' somebody said.

'Where's Danni? What's happened?'

Sirens wailed, drawing near. An ambulance, waved through by a police officer in a high-viz jacket, pulled up close to the house.

Layla pressed forward but was ushered firmly aside by the same officer. 'Let me through! My friend's upstairs...'

Nobody was listening. Layla tried to resist the human barrier but more hands were upon her. A couple of male students she knew, as well as Helen and the other girls, surrounded her, preventing her from seeing. She found herself being half carried further along the street, away from the house. The doors of the ambulance flung open, spilling harsh light into the dark street.

Helen's voice, low, tremulous, reached Layla. 'It's Danni. She... fell out of the window.'

'*Fell?* What're you talking about?'

Layla shook off the hands that held her, tried to break away so that she could get to the house and bring Danni out. She ran straight into the tall, broad figure of another police officer.

'No, miss. You can't go in there.'

'I have to find my friend. You don't understand...'

The officer shook his head. Layla turned, silently appealing to the others for help. Nobody came forward. A hush had descended on the scattered groups. Stunned faces. All eyes trained upwards towards the house. Layla looked, and saw a window, fully open, the casement pushed right the way up. Just as she had left it.

'She didn't fall,' somebody else said, looking at Helen. 'She jumped. That girl who was upstairs. Went a bit crazy earlier.'

'We don't know that for certain,' Helen said. 'Layla...'

Jumped?

Layla shook her head. 'I left her asleep. She was well out of it. This is all wrong.'

A sob broke from Helen's throat. 'There were people outside, on the pavement. They saw. *I* saw... We couldn't have stopped her.'

Layla gazed around, bewildered. She could feel her mouth opening and closing but no sound came. She looked back at the gaping window.

No. This was madness. Something had gone badly wrong here, because whatever people were saying – and it wasn't only Helen; she could hear the same words, being bandied around – they had all got it wrong. They were hammered, and they'd made a mistake. A rumour had started. Chinese whispers. Danni was here, somewhere, amongst the crowd. But, in that case, why couldn't she find her? And why was Helen, as she could see now, holding Danni's phone in its Barbie-pink case?

A flash of blue light from a police car seared Layla's eyes, as she scanned the groups of students for any sign of her friend. Already she knew it was hopeless. Adrenaline surged through her. She felt its power, lifting her feet from the ground, sending her hurtling through the crowd, elbowing people aside, until she arrived in front of the house. This time, nobody stopped her. Gripping the railings with both hands, she peered down into the dark well of the basement. Luminous jackets merged into one acid-yellow mass, preventing her from seeing properly. She was vaguely aware of another figure mounting the wall at the side. Then a camera – *flash, flash, flash* – each spurt of light adding one more piece to the scene.

Layla's mind grabbed at the fragments crossing her vision, hustling them into a whole, like a tragic jigsaw puzzle. A figure lay motionless on the concrete, head twisted to one side, blonde hair fanned out, hiding the face.

The face she knew was Danni's.

Layla heard a deep, inhuman sound coming from somewhere. From inside her. A second later, or it might have been a lifetime, she felt a hand on her arm as gentle words were spoken, words she couldn't understand. Resisting the pressure to be led away from the scene, Layla turned, and stood facing the house directly, training her eyes on the window above. The room was in semi-darkness, with just a glimmer of light presumably coming from the open door inside. And set against that light, she saw a shadow, a shape. The pale oval of a face, and something white, below it. The shape melted away, as the person backed into the room. It was only a glimpse, but it was enough to tell who it was: *Nathan*.

Layla woke with a start. Her eyes snapped into focus, taking in an unfamiliar room, a strange bed, an unusual amount of space around her. So much space she could reach out on either side and touch nothing. She seemed to be wearing just her knickers and bra. Her heart racing, she tried to sit up but her spine felt like rubber, her limbs as loose as wet sacks. And her head – what was wrong with her head?

Hangover. That must be it. The mother-and-father of a hangover. Water. She tried again to move, this time managing to haul herself into a sitting position. Shuffling across the expanse of white sheet, she swung her legs over the side of the bed.

And then she remembered. Piece by piece, the events of last night drifted and shifted, then slotted into place, revealing the whole devastating story.

Ambulance. Police. The open window above. The scene below.

And after; a stranger's coat round her shoulders. Tea. More police. Questions. A car ride. Lights – bright, harsh. Then dimness. A small, quiet room. A curtain drawn back. A white sheet. Pale hair, smoothed unnaturally away from her face.

'*Yes. It's her. It's Danni Morland.*'

The bedroom door opened, startling her afresh. 'Ah, you're awake.'

Layla stared at the familiar face. Familiar, but weirdly out of context. She began to shake. Every part of her quaked, from the tips of her fingers to her toes.

'Hey, it's all right, Layla. It's Judith, from last night. Remember?'

Last night. Of course. Judith, the university's pastoral care tutor.

'You came with me, to...'

It was coming back to her now. The shaking subsided. A mug of tea was set on the bedside table. It seemed very far away.

'When you agreed to identify her, they sent for me. You were brave, so brave, Layla. But try not to think about that any more now. Pop back into bed while you have your tea.'

Layla obeyed. Judith handed her the mug, then sat down on the side of the bed and folded her hands in her lap.

'What time is it?'

'Twelvish. Midday.'

Midday? Layla looked at her wrist. She was wearing her silver bracelet but no watch.

'Is this your house?'

'Yes. It's not far away from where you were.'

'Thank you,' Layla said.

'You're very welcome.'

Layla's brain formed a question, a shoal of questions, but she couldn't catch hold of them, couldn't quite bring to mind what it was she wanted to know. Her head felt so muddled. And then she knew what she needed to ask.

'I don't understand how it happened. How she... I left her sound asleep. I was going back for her, to take her home. Was it my fault because I left her so long? Or because...?' She didn't dare think about the open window, or the door jammed with the wedge. Did Danni try to get out of the room? Was that why she went to the window, thinking she was on the ground floor? 'Was it my fault?'

'Of course it wasn't your fault, Layla. You were looking out for her, like friends do. The police understood that. I was there when you were questioned, remember? So, no more talk about that, understand?' Judith gave Layla a motherly smile, and patted her hand. She got up from the bed and glanced out of the window, between the half-drawn curtains. 'Drink your tea, there's a good girl, and then we'll sort you out.'

But Layla knew Judith was only saying what she thought she wanted to hear. Of course it was her fault, firstly for leaving Danni at the party in the first place to go to Harvey, and then for trapping her in that room when she still had drink and drugs in her system.

And then there was Nathan. She hadn't told anyone she'd seen him at the window, nor that he and Danni had had words earlier in the evening. Not the police, not anyone. For one thing, she couldn't be certain it was him. Or anyone at all. It could have been a trick of the light.

But if it was Nathan, if he had somehow slipped into the room while she was settling Danni and she'd locked him in with her... No. Nathan wouldn't have done anything to hurt Danni; Layla didn't believe that for one minute. By mentioning him possibly being in the room, she'd be implying he played a part in Danni's death. She wouldn't do that, because it wasn't true. There was no need to drag a perfectly innocent boy into it.

This – Danni's death – was entirely down to Layla herself. There was no doubt about that.

She drank a drop of tea, then put it down. She wanted to cry. She should be crying, sobbing her heart out. Instead, she felt numb, solid as a plank of wood. Judith was saying she should phone her parents and tell them what had happened. When Layla explained that there was only Mum now, Judith just nodded. April would have been there like a shot – Rowan, too, probably. But what was the point? There was nothing they could do that would make this any better. Nobody, nothing, could do that. They would want to take her home but she couldn't leave. Not now. She couldn't abandon Danni yet again. It was unthinkable.

She could tell that Judith thought she should go home by the way she was speaking, while not voicing it directly. Without dismissing the tutor's kindness, she needed to be out of here. She looked around for her clothes, and saw them neatly laid out on a chair in the corner. The jade green sleeveless dress with silver sparkles and the flimsy black shrug – her party outfit – looked incongruous in the light of day, slightly sleazy. Her black thin-heeled sandals were on the floor beneath the chair, next to her bag.

'Take your time,' Judith said kindly, then told her where the bathroom was, and left her to it.

Judith drove her back to her student house. The boys were out. All was silent. Layla trod carefully up the stairs, clutching the handrail. The door to Danni's room was closed. If she trained her mind, concentrated really hard, she could make herself believe that Danni was sleeping behind that door, or at uni, working in the library, or... Yes, she could just about manage that – she had to, because there was no other possible direction for her thoughts.

In this dreamlike state of pretence, Layla shut herself in her own room, sat down at the desk by the window and sent a text message to Harvey. No pretence about that.

She waited. Unsurprisingly, her phone trilled. She heard his voice, hurt, disbelieving, strung through with damaged pride. Then her own voice, unemotional, flat, as if it came from a distance. *I'm sorry, but it's over... No, I'm not overreacting... I love you but I can't be with you any more. I'm sorry.*

Afterwards, she took off the dress and shrug, and stuffed them and the shoes in the bottom of the wardrobe, out of sight. She pulled on a pair of leggings and a jumper, then lay down on her bed and tried to cry. Willing the tears to come. Eventually, they did, and she cried as if she would never stop.

She had sometimes wondered, in a vague, half-serious kind of way, whether she shouldn't have been so dismissive of the offers of support from the university counselling service, and the tutor who had scooped her up that night and taken care of her. Instead, she'd palmed them all off with a promise to seek help as soon as the exams were over. A promise she'd had no intention of keeping.

One thing only had been allowed to occupy her mind – her finals. Everything else had been firmly shut out. She had to do well, and come out of university with a decent degree. It was the only thing in the world that mattered. All there was left.

She got a First.

This is for you, Danni.

THIRTY-EIGHT

Layla's eyes were drawn to the wall above the round dining table. Her graduation picture was gone. In its place was a photograph of Danni, aged about seven or eight, standing on the middle bar of Foxleigh Farm's entrance gate, wearing a green-and-white gingham dress and white knee-socks. She had a disarming grin and funny, sticky-out plaits.

Melody noticed her looking. 'That was taken on her first day at the junior school. We had it enlarged.' Melody laughed. 'Danni was so looking forward to being one of the "big girls", wasn't she, Reece?'

'Yep. Couldn't get there fast enough.'

'It's a great photo,' Layla said. 'I love it.'

It was a grey, wet Saturday morning, not long after ten – the earliest Layla had ever arrived at Foxleigh. But, as she'd explained on the phone, she'd be heading home this afternoon, if they didn't mind, because she was on duty at the Manor tonight. Melody had merely said *fine*, in a way which showed that she meant it; there'd been no note of complaint in her voice. However, she had insisted they all sit down to a second break-fast the moment Layla arrived. So here they were, the three of them, with freshly-brewed coffee and golden croissants, warmed in the oven.

Layla had also said that she needed to talk to them, about something important. Now, seeing Melody so relaxed and Reece with his jokey avuncular manner in place, she wondered if this was, after all, the right time. But only for a moment. It had to be done. And it had to be today.

'So,' Reece said, dabbing a flake of pastry from the corner of his mouth, 'it's off to the US of A for you. New York had better watch out, that's all I'm saying.' He winked.

Again, the prickle of anxiety every time somebody mentioned New York. She'd had to tell them she was leaving. It was, after all, one of the reasons she'd come. To say goodbye.

She smiled. 'I'm very lucky. It's a great opportunity.'

'It certainly is,' Melody said. Then, 'What did your mother say about it? She'll really miss you, won't she?'

'Don't put a damper on it, Mel,' Reece said, but his conspiratorial grin at Layla removed any trace of remonstration.

'Mum's okay with it. She said it'll be an excuse for her to hit New York for a big shopping trip.' She laughed. 'I expect she will, too. And my younger sister can't wait to get her room back, so everyone's happy.'

Nobody spoke for a minute. The rain lashed noisily at the window. Beyond, the branches of the trees rose and dipped in the wind. The distant hills sulked under a bank of purplish cloud.

Melody made a face towards the window. 'What a dreadful day! You'd never believe it was August.'

'In England, you would,' Reece said.

Layla stopped thinking about her own feelings, and thought instead about theirs. The removal of the graduation photo, Melody's determined cheerfulness, the easy way they'd brought Danni into the conversation – all the pointers of change were heartening, but there were no quick fixes. For any of them.

Melody turned to Layla. 'We wish you all the luck in the world, with New York and the new job, and everything. Thank you for coming all the way here to tell us. It means a lot.'

'Yes, yes, it does,' Reece agreed.

'Do you think,' Layla said, after a moment, 'we could go through to the other room?'

Melody and Reece exchanged looks. Layla felt a fraud. They'd thought she'd come to tell them she was leaving, and that was all. As if that wasn't enough.

'Yes, let's.' Melody was on her feet. 'It'll be more cheerful than out here.'

They went through and sat down, Layla on the yellow sofa next to Melody, Reece in the armchair. Melody reached behind her and switched on the lamp. 'That's better. Lamps on in the middle of summer! Whatever next?'

Reece was silent, looking down at his feet, his hands clasped in front of him. He knew there was something more to come. They both did. The problem was, how to begin?

'I can't believe it. I can't believe that all this time you've been blaming yourself for what happened to Danni. Oh, darling, don't cry.' Melody leaned towards her, putting both arms round her.

It would be so easy to let herself be held, to cry her heart out on Melody's shoulder. But wrong. No more tears. She had to be strong. If ever there was a time when she had to be strong, this was it. Gently, she extricated herself.

'I'm not crying, not really.' She rubbed her eyes with the cuff of her cardigan.

After a moment, she said, 'Why are you being kind to me? Why don't you understand that what I did, running off to my boyfriend, then leaving Danni in a strange room with the window wide open while I sat in a café drinking coffee was the biggest, stupidest mistake? I should have known she was still in a state. Should have realised she could still do something stupid. What I did was tantamount to, well...' She wanted to say *killing Danni*, but they were chilling words, impossible words, words that had no part to play in this. Except inside her own head, where they belonged.

I killed Danni. It was me, all me.

She looked from one to the other. Melody, so upset on her behalf; Reece all at sea, confused, astounded. Both of them perplexed as to how this had come about. Both wanting desperately to lift the burden from her shoulders. Why couldn't they accept what she was saying, rage at her, throw her bodily out of the house?

'Layla,' Reece said. 'Layla, look at me.'

She realised her head was bowed, her hands clasped to her face. Eventually, she looked up, but she couldn't meet his gaze.

'*Layla.*'

She looked, properly this time, and the sorrow and compassion she saw in his eyes almost floored her.

'Our daughter was out of control, out of her mind, with alcohol and the drugs she'd taken. Even if you'd stayed with her at the party, there was nothing you could have done to save her, and I think, deep down, you know that.'

Reece shook his head slowly. His eyes told of a struggle going on inside. After a moment, he reached forward and took both of Layla's hands in his. 'If it was anyone's fault, it was ours. Mine and Mel's.' He glanced at his wife.

'*Your fault?* What do you mean? How could it have been your fault, either of you? You weren't even there.'

Layla gazed at Reece, appalled, confused. He let go of her hands and looked pointedly at Melody. 'I think it's time she knew.'

Melody gave a single nod. 'Let me.' She turned to Layla. 'Layla, darling, this might be hard for you to take in, after everything, but you've been honest with us and now we must be honest with you. You see, Danni was pregnant when she died.'

Pregnant? Layla stared at Melody.

'No, she couldn't have been. I would have known. She would have told me...'

'It's true, Layla,' Reece said. 'Our daughter was pregnant. Only a few weeks, but definitely pregnant – the post-mortem confirmed it. She'd made up her mind to have a termination. We had a right royal argument about it, the last weekend she came home. We wanted her to take her time, think it through properly, but she wouldn't hear of it. We never thought it would be the last time we saw her.'

His voice had grown husky. He looked at Melody.

'When I was eighteen,' she said, 'I fell pregnant and I had an abortion. I won't go into the details. Suffice to say, I came to regret it later, especially when it took us so long to have Danni. She was so certain her life would be ruined if she had a child, but knowing what I did, I couldn't bear her to have the same regrets. That was why we argued so strongly against it. I wanted to make her understand the enormity of what she was doing.' Melody paused for breath. 'We would have supported her in the end, of course, whatever her final decision. She was our daughter, and we'd have done anything to make her happy. But she'd only just told us and we were in shock. She went back to university without us having made our peace with her.'

How sad, Layla thought. But Danni knew her parents loved her, and she loved them. Melody and Reece knew that, too.

'Why didn't she talk to me?' Layla spoke in a half whisper, as if she was speaking to herself. 'I was her best friend. I might have been able to help.'

'If it's any consolation,' Reece said, 'she probably wouldn't have told us, either, only we'd arranged to take her on holiday straight after her final exams. To Rome, somewhere we'd always said we'd go. We'd booked it as a surprise for her, only it was us who got the surprise...' He smiled ruefully. 'When she said she couldn't go, that's when we knew something was wrong. She had to tell us, then.'

'I think, also,' Melody said gently, 'that she might have felt too ashamed to tell you. She thought the world of you. She would have found it hard to admit how stupid she'd been.'

'Yes.' Layla nodded. 'Maybe.'

She could understand how Danni might think that. She'd have been completely wrong, of course.

She remembered the time her friend had come back unexpectedly early from a weekend at home. She'd been determinedly cheerful, but brittle and on edge. She hadn't looked well on the night of the party. Layla should have questioned it, got Danni to talk.

So, who...? Nathan. Of course. She hadn't been seeing anyone else.

Layla thought back to the party, though it hurt like mad to remember. How must Danni have been feeling when she rejected Nathan's attempt to win her back, knowing he was the father of her child?

Melody interrupted her thoughts. 'No more guilt, Layla. Not for you. And not for us, either. It won't go away, what happened, and the part we played in it. If we can learn to live with it, then so can you, because you, Layla, you were her best friend and you did nothing wrong. Nothing at all.' Melody smiled sadly. 'Love – or what we sometimes see as love – has a lot to answer for.'

'You don't think' – Layla hardly knew how to say this but she had to ask – 'you don't think she did what she did on purpose, hoping that she'd lose the baby?'

'No, we don't,' Reece said. 'She may have thought that by drinking, doing drugs, going a little bit crazy, she could pretend it wasn't happening, or that she could say she'd done those things and she needed the termination – we'll never know that now. But jumping out of the window, no. There was no ulterior motive behind that. It was a heat of the moment thing, a crazy stunt gone wrong. A tragic accident, as the coroner said.'

'We know – knew – our daughter,' Melody added, 'and we're sure about that. As sure as we can be.'

Then, as if they'd spent the last half hour making idle chat, Melody pointed towards the window and said, 'Oh look, the rain's stopped. The wind's dropped, too.'

Layla looked. The trees were still. The cloud had lifted, leaving patches of bright blue sky.

'If you don't mind, I'd like to go outside,' she said.

'Shall I come with you?' Melody smiled. There was relief in her expression.

'I'd like to be on my own for a bit, if that's okay.'

'Of course,' Melody said.

Layla walked along the gravel path, puddled from the rain, towards the converted stable holiday lets. To her left, the fish-pond with its tattered fringe of reeds and sloping grassy bank inset with rockery stones. To her right, the irregular-shaped lawn, emerald-bright from its recent dousing, and edged with a tapestry of cottage-garden flowers.

She hadn't been able to breathe inside the house, as if so much emotion had used up all the air. Still, she couldn't believe how wonderfully understanding the Morlands had been. Both were mortified at the long, drawn-out punishment she'd inflicted on herself for something which, according to them, she had never been guilty of in the first place. She felt as if she'd been trapped in a room to which the door was stuck, but not locked, as she'd thought. One hard shove and she would have been free.

It wasn't that simple, of course. Melody's ever-more pressing invitations to Foxleigh, Reece's attempts to jolly everyone along and make it all seem perfectly normal when clearly it wasn't, had impacted on her conscience at a time when she had been most vulnerable.

And now, this new piece of the tragedy had shocked her deeply – she hadn't dared show them exactly how much, for fear of upsetting them further. Two lives were lost that night, not one. Layla couldn't think about that now, not in any depth – it was too much to bear – but she would later, and she would give way to grief again, but not for long. Danni and her unborn child were as one; she'd already mourned enough for both of them.

The path opened out into the courtyard bounded by the three holiday lets. The pretty little dwellings were deserted, their tenants off somewhere enjoying their holidays. A thin, brown tabby cat shot out of the trees behind the stables and streaked diagonally across the yard to disappear into the under-growth. She had seen cats here before; they came from the working farm along the lane.

As a place to grow up, Foxleigh was a picture-book paradise; Danni must have loved it. She'd never said, but perhaps she'd taken it for granted, which you would if you'd never known anything else. But Warbler's Way had its good points, and Maybridge itself, well, that was pretty special, too. She was beginning to realise how special, now that she was leaving.

Her next thought stilled her feet, rooted her to the spot. Not only was she leaving, she was running away; that was the plan. Only now, there was nothing to run away from, was there?

She pushed the thought away. If anything, her reasons for going to New York were stronger because they were genuine. She was doing this for herself, to make something of her life. There was no turning back. And anyway, she wouldn't be gone for ever. Maybridge would still be there when she came back.

And Morgan, would he still be there, waiting for her to fling herself into his arms and tell him she'd made a colossal mistake?

Of course he wouldn't. He'd given her every chance to explain, to put things right between them, and she'd pushed him away. He'd want no more to do with her now. It was far too late.

Her eyes filled with tears. She forced them back. Resort to self-pity and she was lost. Taking a deep breath, and giving her head a little shake, she turned and walked back along the path towards the house, to find Melody coming towards her. She was waving, smiling. She looked happy. Layla waved back and broke into a jog.

'I'm going to look at my roses,' Melody said, when they met at the fork in the path. 'Coming?'

Melody was born and brought up in Birmingham, she told Layla. An only child, she lived with her parents in a third-floor flat with no garden. The walk to school took her past large, mock-Tudor houses in tree-lined avenues.

'It was my favourite part of the walk because I loved looking at the gardens, especially in the summer when all the flowers were out. My favourite garden was one full of roses. There were pinks and creams and crimsons and yellows, so many you couldn't count. They hung off the bushes, right over the front wall.' Melody stopped halfway along the brick path and gazed dreamily into the middle distance. 'They were so pretty, and the scent, oh the scent; so strong and sweet, like nothing I'd ever smelt before. I used to put my face up close and stand there for ages, looking and sniffing.

'Then one day I picked one, a bud that was about to open. Snapped it off, just like that. It was a pink one. It smelt like sugar and I wanted to eat it, it was so delicious.' She laughed. 'I didn't, though. I held it in front of me, by the stem, all the way to school. It gave me a very special feeling, as if I was holding the future in my hands. But you know what happened the next day?'

She turned to Layla. 'The front door opened and an old woman came out. She must have been watching for me from behind her net curtains. She shouted at me to clear off, and said if I ever went near her garden again she'd fetch the police. And I thought, what was the point of growing beautiful flowers if nobody was allowed to enjoy them? It was incomprehensible, the stupidest thing.'

Melody continued along the path, Layla following. 'When Danni was born, of all the things I wanted to give her, I wanted most of all to give her roses.' She smiled. 'Isn't that silly?'

'Of course it's not silly,' Layla said. 'I think it's lovely. And you gave her the name.'

Melody smiled. 'Yes. Danni Rose. Danni Rose Morland. Look, these are Danni's roses. They were one of the first I bought, when I was making the garden. I chose them because they suited her, I thought. The bush has been replaced since then, of course, but you can still get the variety so I pretend it's the same one.'

The roses were pale pink, the flowers delicate and unshowy, and wonderfully scented.

'They're beautiful,' Layla said. 'Like her.'

'Yes, they are, aren't they? They've taken a bit of a battering with the rain.' Melody touched one of the blooms, bowing on its stem. It fell apart, scattering pink petals on the dark soil below. 'Never mind. There are plenty more. We must cut some for you to take home. Roses are for sharing.'

Reece peered out of the kitchen window and rubbed his hands together. 'You should get home in the dry, if it lasts.'

Melody stood beside him, emptying the dregs of tea into the sink, rinsing the mugs under the tap. She'd offered to make lunch, but Layla was both too full from the croissants and too nervy in her stomach to eat anything else.

'Oh, I didn't tell you, did I?' Melody said. 'I've got a job. I'm starting next week, at the animal charity shop in the village.'

'Are you?' Layla was surprised. She wouldn't have associated Melody with racks of old clothes and dog-eared books. Nor voluntary work, for that matter.

Melody slapped her playfully on the arm. 'It's quite a posh one, as charity shops go. It might sell old tat, but it's clean old tat.'

Layla laughed. 'I'm sure it is.'

'I was passing the other day and nipped in for a chat with Gwen who runs the shop – I've known her for years. She said was I free for a couple of mornings a week, and I said I was, and I thought, why not? If I'm to go back to work at some point, I'll need to start off gently.'

Reece raised his eyes. 'Yes, we don't want you overtaxing yourself, do we?'

This was so good to see. The Morlands, joshing with one another, a real partnership again. And Melody, ready to return to the world. Layla's heart went out to them.

Melody picked up a tea towel and began briskly drying one of the mugs. 'Yes, I thought it was time I talked to some real people for a change. About ordinary things. Not that Kate wasn't real, and she helped me a lot, but I don't need to be cloistered any more.'

'Kate?'

'My therapist, down at Haverstone. Anyway, I'm going to be busy. I shan't have time to trek all the way down there.'

'What was she like?'

'She was nice, helpful, as I said. Young, not much older than you. She had freckles, and lots of lovely hair, all red-gold curls, like "Annie", I always thought. Why?'

'No reason. I just wondered.'

Kate. It had to be her, didn't it? Morgan's ex. All along, the connection had been there, an invisible thread, weaving them all together.

'Are you okay, Layla?' Melody threw her a concerned look.

'What? Oh, yes, I'm fine. Just thinking, that's all.' She smiled.

The roses Melody had picked for Layla to take home were on the kitchen counter, their stems wrapped in newspaper.

'They're gorgeous,' Layla said, picking up the bunch and holding them to her face to take in the scent. 'Thank you.'

Melody looked doubtful. 'I should have nipped off the thorns. I wouldn't want you to get scratched.'

'They're fine as they are. I'll be careful,' Layla said.

Nobody spoke for a moment. The long-case clock in the hall ticked on.

Reece broke the silence. 'Send us a postcard, let us know how you're getting on.' He smiled.

'I surely will,' Layla said. Then, 'There's something... before I go...'

She hurried through to the other room and fetched her bag. Opening it, she brought out an envelope containing the cheque and handed it to Reece. Glancing inside the envelope, he gave one firm nod.

'Is this what I think it is?' Melody picked up the envelope and looked for herself. 'Layla, you are very welcome to keep this. You know that, don't you?'

'I do, but it wouldn't feel right. Please?'

'Of course. We understand.'

She took the envelope across to where letters and papers stood in a rack and dropped it in amongst them. Then she returned to Layla and gathered her into a hug.

Outside, more hugs, kisses, promises to keep in touch. Layla waved as she turned the Fiesta in the direction of the gate. The Morlands waved back. Reece's arm was round Melody's shoulders, hers around his waist. Together. Where they belonged.

THIRTY-NINE

Monday morning. Rain was forecast for later, but now the air was muggy and still, the sky screened in low white cloud. Traffic slunk across the bridge with muffled engine sounds. Along the banks of the May, the fronds of the willows drooped despondently into the moss-green water. Moorhens upended silently, their foraging activities barely disturbing the perfectly described reflections.

Attached to their moorings, *Lady Tabitha* and *Princess Delilah* idled, coloured flags hanging limply above the scrubbed decks. The rowing boats, gleaming with fresh blue paint, rocked gently alongside the jetty. The kiosk was still shuttered. No call for drinks, ice creams and tickets for the boats yet, although it wouldn't be long before they came straggling down to the river: tourists; local families in search of school holiday amusement for the children; and the older generation, to gather in chattering groups in the café.

The café was where Morgan was bound for now, intent on helping Maureen and the other assistant open up and begin the food preparation. Connor came out of the office and headed him off.

'Leave them to it. They can manage. Let's go while we've got the chance.'

A few minutes later, they arrived in front of a small, red-brick cottage with green-painted window-frames and a walled front garden spilling over with pink hydrangeas. Ted's house. The old man had suffered another stroke, this time a major one; he wouldn't be coming home for many months, if ever. Last week, Connor and Gina had seen him settled into a nursing home, a short distance from Maybridge.

'The houses along here used to get flooded quite regularly. But not any longer, since they did something to the banks,' Connor said, turning the key in the lock and giving the door a shove with his foot. It opened with a creak of protest.

The front door opened straight onto a living room with dated but homely furnishings, and a 1930s curved, red-tiled fireplace surrounding an ash-strewn black grate. Morgan followed his friend through the door at the end into a bright and cheerful kitchen.

'Nan was always on at him to have the place modernised,' Connor said, 'but the stubborn old devil insisted he liked it as it was, and that was that. He let her have a new electric cooker, but that was back in the eighties. He had the house re-wired, though, so it isn't a death-trap, and it's got storage heaters as well as the fire.'

The house might exist inside a time warp, but it was cosy and quiet. Morgan liked it, very much. He'd had no luck so far in his search for a place of his own, and the bungalow seemed more crowded every time he set foot in it. A move was well overdue. There was, however, a slight feeling of wrongness about using Ted's illness to his advantage.

'Are you sure, though, about me moving in?'

'To be honest, you'd be doing us all a favour, mate.' Connor picked up an empty milk carton from the wooden draining board, scrunched it up in his hand and dropped it into the waste bin. 'If you were living here, I wouldn't have to check up on the place, and the rent will be useful for Grandad.'

Connor had already named a sum that was well within Morgan's reach.

He could write here, late into the night if he wanted to; that had been his first thought. The boathouse was great in summer but was only really useful during the day, and even then, it would be decidedly draughty in the chillier months. He could buy a desk and set it up in front of the window in the living room, or perhaps upstairs in one of the two bedrooms, where he'd be able to see the river.

A new writing place for a new novel, the next in the Poodle Chafferty series. His agent – Fiona's friend, whom he'd met up with in London a fortnight ago – seemed convinced that the sale of his first book to a publisher was only a matter of time.

'Right then,' he said. 'You're on. But on one condition.'

'What's that?'

'You let me take you and Gina out for a meal tonight. Somewhere decent, anywhere you like.'

'You don't have to do that,' Connor said, 'but since you ask, thanks, that'd be cool. If we made it the Swan, it would be a kind of tribute to the old man, seeing as he's spent so much time in there.'

'The Swan it is then.' Morgan's palm met Connor's. 'I do appreciate this, and for letting me stay at the bungalow and everything.'

'Don't be daft. Here...' Connor threw Morgan the keys to the cottage. 'Move in whenever you're ready.'

'So, you haven't tried phoning or messaging again?'

'No point. She made that all too plain at the time. Anyway, I promised I'd leave her alone.'

They'd left Ted's house and were walking along the riverside of the road, passing the Swan and the bridge. Morgan had wondered when Connor would raise the subject of Layla again. Since he'd been told the story – not that there was much of one to tell – he'd been surprisingly silent on the subject, and Morgan had rather hoped he would remain that way. But now, having found him a place to live, it seemed Connor was on a mission to sort out the rest of his life for him. Well, he needn't bother, Morgan thought uncharitably. He was fine as he was.

'No matter. The personal touch is always the best. You don't know her address, right?'

'Right.'

'But you know where she works.'

'So?'

Morgan was being deliberately obtuse, he knew. He stuffed both hands in his jeans pockets, effecting a nonchalance he didn't feel. Along the riverbank, in the middle distance, the jagged profiles of the broken priory walls stood out darkly against the paper-white sky. The site, not only of a ruined priory but of a kiss that led to his own downfall.

'So, take the afternoon off,' Connor said, making it sound as if he was stating the obvious.

Morgan kicked out at a handy beer can. It bounced off the pavement and landed with a clatter halfway across the road. He shook his head.

'I've moved on. And even if I hadn't, even if I wanted to rake all that up again, there's no way I'd be setting foot inside Tidehall Manor. That'd make me look like a stalker. Or desperate.'

'Which you are.'

'No, I'm not.'

Morgan felt exasperation rising within him like flood water. Connor meant well, but he didn't want this conversation.

'Okay, desperate's a bit over the top, but you can't get her out of your head. Am I right?'

Morgan gave a noncommittal shrug. Connor was right, of course. Layla had taken up permanent residence inside his night-time dreams, and his waking ones; had never left them, in fact. She was installed in the wings of his life like a prompt in a stage play. No matter how hard he tried to ignore her, she wasn't going anywhere. But, in time, even the bad stuff went away. In time. He had to believe that.

They had reached the path leading down to the river. Connor stopped walking, the better to emphasise his next bit of advice.

'Don't leave it till it's too late, that's all.'

Stopping, too, Morgan took his hands out of his pockets.

'It was too late ages ago. I'm not going to Tidehall. She knows how to find me if she changes her mind. Which she won't. Even if I did manage to speak to her, it wouldn't make any difference. You didn't see her, mate. The way she looked at me, like I'd really scared her. I wouldn't want to put her through that again, whatever it was about.'

They carried on walking, past the yard and the sheds, down to the kiosk and the jetty. Pete, the worker with the tattooed head, was attempting to steady a rowing boat into which a portly middle-aged man and his chubby female companion were gingerly stepping. The woman's arms flapped out at her sides as she struggled to keep her balance. Morgan and Connor grinned at one another. The boat rocked perilously as the couple made the descent to the seats. The man took up the oars with surprising efficiency, and the little craft with its load moved smoothly out into the middle of the river.

'It sounds to me,' Connor said, as if there had been no break in the conversation, 'as if you need to tie it up one way or another. Find out what's in her head. You'll never get any peace otherwise.'

I can't be with you. I can't be with anyone. The cryptic message was still there, locked inside his phone. He didn't read it any more. He'd stopped puzzling over what it meant, wouldn't even be thinking about it now if it hadn't been for Connor. But he hadn't deleted it. If Connor only knew, his well-meaning advice had had the opposite effect from what he'd intended.

Morgan's hand was on his phone even as he left Connor at the jetty and headed for the office. By the time he'd let himself in and sat down at the computer, the message – the whole of that last conversation – had been erased and her name wiped from his contacts list.

Switching on the computer, he turned his attention to a note Maureen had left for him with a list of supplies to order for the café. By the time he'd looked up from the screen, the sky had turned a dull, misty grey. Holiday season or not, the river wouldn't be the main attraction today. The accounts and the orders were up-to-date; there was nothing else that couldn't wait for another day. He had planned to move into Ted's cottage tomorrow, or the day after, but why not today? Suddenly, he couldn't wait to be there.

He looked at his watch. Quarter to eleven. If he went back to the bungalow now, he could load his car with his few possessions and be settling himself into his new home by lunchtime.

FORTY

Monday. Layla had the day off – a relief after working a long shift yesterday on top of a frantically busy Saturday night. There was some sort of bug doing the rounds and they were short-handed. Layla hoped she wasn't going down with it, too. But the slight wobbly sensation in her stomach was more likely to be left over from Saturday's visit to the Morlands, which was still fresh in her mind. So much so that she was finding it impossible to think about anything else.

Worrying about the Morlands, and her relationship with them, had become ingrained in her system, so much a part of her life that she felt strangely bereft now that it was over. It would take a while for the feelings to subside, the kinds of feelings she used to dread, but now she must concentrate on the new feelings, the new understandings that all three of them had reached. She was free, now, to remember Danni – grieve for her still, if needs be – in her own way.

Driving home from Foxleigh, she had thought about telling her mother, and possibly Seth, the truth about Danni – her pregnancy; the battles with her parents and with her own conscience; her fear for the future that had sent her hurtling over the edge of reason and into the arms of the unscrupulous Art. But by the time she'd pulled up in Warbler's Way, she'd decided there was nothing to be gained by telling them. If there was the smallest chance of Mum or Seth thinking any less of Danni because of what she told them, she couldn't do it. It was Danni's secret and she would keep it for her. As for herself, she didn't want or need sympathy. The rest was up to her now, as it was for Melody and Reece.

All this ran through Layla's mind as she sat on the back doorstep, her second mug of tea of the morning in her hand. It was warm out here – the kind of warmth Mum described as 'close' – but not sunny. The trees stood stock still. From over the fence came the subdued cackle of hens. Inside the house, Finn ran riot with some kind of toy space vehicle that spent half its time in unfathomable, sharp pieces which were scattered around the house ready to spear an unsuspecting foot, and the other half – as it was now – being propelled at speed up and down the legs of the polished mahogany dining chairs.

April had gone to work at the supermarket, Jadine was still sound asleep in bed – her usual position on a Monday morning when the salon was shut. It was Rowan's day off, too; she was upstairs getting ready to take Finn to the out-of-town mall to shop for new school uniform for him, and, no doubt, yet another new outfit for herself with which to impress Jeff on their next date night.

Finn hadn't yet been told that his mother was seeing Jeff again, which Layla agreed with April was a good thing. Rowan seemed happier by the minute, and altogether calmer, which in itself was good for Finn, and enough for now.

Jadine, on the other hand, seemed permanently on the precipice of melodrama involving, naturally, Smart Alec. They were young, too young for a relationship of such length and intensity; both had, in April's words, other fish to fry, which was exactly how it should be. Alec had twice now stood Jadine up –

not exactly left her waiting, but cancelled their date at the last minute with what her sister termed a pathetic excuse. When Alec did come round to the house, Layla couldn't help but notice a certain friction between them. She wasn't the only one.

'Rub two flints together and what do you get?' April had whispered to Layla in the kitchen one evening. 'Those two'll catch fire in a minute. Have you been listening to them?' She raised her eyes.

Layla had, and what she'd heard came into the category of too much information. Jadine had been complaining to Alec that all he thought about was sex — pots and kettles, Layla thought — and Alec had flung back that at least it was free, and if Jadine wanted clubs and pubs every night she'd have to part with some of the massive tips she was always boasting about.

Layla had raised her eyes back at her mother and said, '*Que sera, sera*.' She wasn't getting involved. If her little sister wanted her advice, she could ask for it. She laughed to herself; a more unlikely scenario she couldn't imagine.

She glanced at her watch. Ten o'clock. Tired though she was, she should do something with her day, something to take her out of her pensive mood. Tonight she was meeting Seth and some of his mates at the Tidehall Arms, the pub near the hotel, where a band that Seth knew was playing. But there was no need for her to hang around the house all day.

The river. She could go for a walk by the river. There were at least a dozen reasons why she shouldn't go anywhere near it; Layla dismissed them all, because that was exactly where she wanted to be. Soon she'd be in New York, a tiny dot on a side-walk among the seething traffic and the skyscrapers, one of millions of other tiny dots. Maybridge was her home town. She wasn't going to let a little thing like not wanting to set eyes on a certain somebody prevent her from making the most of it while she still had the chance.

Okay, bumping into Morgan wouldn't be a little thing. It

would be hugely embarrassing, and possibly upsetting, but if he was anywhere near the river today he'd be busy working, doing whatever his mate employed him to do. If she kept clear of the places he was likely to be – the boathouse included – she'd be fine. She couldn't live her life in fear of ever meeting him again.

Upstairs in the bedroom, Jadine's form rose and fell rhythmically beneath the pink duvet. Layla changed her shorts and T-shirt for a sleeveless cotton dress patterned with tiny blue and orange flowers. It had a fitted top, and flared gently from her waist to below her knees. It felt floaty and feminine. Her hair she left loose, smoothing it back with Jadine's brush. Downstairs, she collected her shoes and denim jacket from the hall, then, seeing how the sky had begun to darken, put Mum's umbrella into her bag and slipped out of the front door.

Morgan called at the café to update Maureen on the orders and to check there was nothing else she needed from him. It was still quiet, the only customers being an elderly man with a black Labrador and the couple who had taken out the rowing boat earlier. Next he went to find Connor. He was on board *Princess Delilah*, sitting in the covered part of the boat with his feet up on the seat in front, reading the daily paper. He seemed pleased to hear Morgan's plans and told him not to bother returning to the yard today. They'd meet up in the Swan tonight.

As Morgan set off for Connor's house it began to rain, a miserable, light drizzle that barely disturbed the surface of the water. He turned up the collar of his jacket and strode along the riverside path, hurrying in his eagerness to begin the move to his new home. Rather than head in the opposite direction from his destination in order to cross the river at the road-bridge, he continued along the nearside bank. There was a wooden footbridge some way past the boathouse. If he crossed there, it was only a stone's throw to the right-of-way which led to the bungalow.

It was as he happened to glance across the river that he saw her. Layla. Or rather, he saw part of her, because her head and shoulders were completely obscured by a bright green umbrella, pulled well down as if she wanted it to hide her as well as protect her from the rain. She was walking along the opposite bank, a little way back from the river and slightly ahead of him, but even at this distance there was no mistaking her.

In his mind, he executed a kind of double take while his feet, instead of stalling on the path, took even longer strides as if they had a will of their own. Heat engulfed him. His stomach was shot through with nerves, yet he kept on walking, as she did, on the other side.

He hurried on for a few yards, passing the bench where the two of them had sat on warm, sunny days, then he glanced across again and saw that she was standing still. Ducks were congregating on the grass bank in front of her. Presumably she'd stopped to look at them, though he couldn't tell exactly what she was doing because of the angle of the umbrella. He thought of calling out but the river was too wide. She wouldn't hear him, and even if she did, she would turn tail and run.

She walked on. The river curved, the path with it. Panicking for a second as he lost sight of her, he picked up speed. And then she reappeared with a flash of bright green. He forced himself to slow down. It was ridiculous to be chasing her, literally; he should give it up, as he had given up the virtual chase. So many times he'd imagined seeing her again, running into her by accident. He had a script, well-rehearsed. But words that seemed eloquent at three in the morning became ludicrous in the honest light of dawn.

The boathouse was just yards in front of him now. The key was in his pocket. The sensible thing to do – the decent thing – would be to hide out until she'd gone, then forget he'd ever seen her. He jogged across the muddy grass towards the boathouse steps, but even as he reached them, his thoughts had spun off in a different direction. He couldn't let her go. Whatever the outcome, here was his chance to make it right with her; possibly his only chance.

Holding onto the newel post, Morgan took several deep, sustaining breaths. Then he turned and ran, faster than he'd ever run before, back towards the boatyard.

FORTY-ONE

Light rainfall had freshened the air and taken the mugginess away. Layla felt refreshed, too, and energised. She'd already walked a fair distance before she'd reached the May, having decided to leave the car at home, but her legs carried her on, powerful as pistons.

Passing through the old part of the city, she'd stopped off at the Spice Emporium to say goodbye to Raj. He'd deliberately made her laugh by putting on a comically sad face, coming out from behind the counter to present her with a parting gift – a poppy-seed loaf, wrapped in rustling brown paper. As she walked, she could feel the bulk of it inside her shoulder bag.

Reaching the river, she'd experienced a bout of nerves. She'd hurried across the road-bridge, averting her eyes from the boatyard below while keeping the umbrella tilted to one side, like a shield. She felt safer here on the riverside path, but kept moving, keeping her gaze straight ahead. This was harder than she'd imagined. Perhaps she should have turned left after the bridge and walked in the opposite direction, but along here was the most scenic stretch of the river.

She passed the backs of the Tudor cottages, their black-and-white picture-postcard prettiness always a draw for the tourists, and then the path wound around the riverside gardens where roses bloomed in the flowerbeds. Layla thought about Melody, and then, of course, she thought about Danni. But it was all right. Really it was. She was getting better at thinking about Danni without succumbing to sinking despair.

Another time, she might be wishing it would stop raining, but today the umbrella had more than one use. She kept it well down, its handle her comforter as she gripped it. Opposite now would be the bench where she and Morgan had sat gazing at the river and idly chatting. As if they knew she needed the diversion, a flurry of ducks waddled on splayed orange feet across the grass bank towards her, a brown-feathered throng livened with flashes of emerald. They squawked as she approached. Their squawking and flapping made her laugh. They were after food, but they weren't getting the poppy-seed loaf. She was sorry to disappoint them.

She remembered coming down here as a child, with Mum or Dad, sometimes both, and Rowan, to feed the ducks with chunks of stale bread. When Jadine arrived, they'd brought her, too, and she'd sat in the pushchair and chewed on the lumps of bread instead of throwing them to the ducks. On impulse, Layla took out her phone. Clamping the handle of the umbrella under her arm to keep it securely in place, she took several photos of the ducks before walking on.

The clipped grass banks gave way to rougher grass, and trees – tall ones to the left, dipping willows at the river's edge. Here was the bend in the river; round the bend, across the water, the boathouse. Even with the umbrella in place, it was impossible to avoid a glimpse of it, in its raised position among the trees. Layla gave in to temptation and lifted the umbrella a little so that she could see. A deep sensation of longing filled her, and she regretted ever coming on this walk. Why had she thought she could get away scot-free? She wasn't made of stone.

Drawing on the little breath she had left, she resolutely tugged the umbrella down and hurried on.

A few minutes later, a sound reached her. A voice? Calling her name? Other sounds, splashy, watery, coming nearer. Puzzled, she lowered the umbrella fully. The sight that met her eyes sent shock waves through her stomach. Laughter rose inside her; hysterical, inappropriate laughter. Throwing down the umbrella, she clapped both hands to her mouth.

A little blue rowing boat was heading towards her, casting ever-widening ripples across the water as its occupant levered the oars, his shoulders pumping for all they were worth, as if he was in a race. One oar was pushed out towards the clumps of tall reeds as he tried to make contact with the muddy bank, but the boat drifted further out into the river. He tried again, and this time managed to manoeuvre it closer to the bank. A rope was thrown towards her, along with a smile which tore Layla's heart in two.

'Catch the rope, will you? Quick, before I capsize the bloody thing,' Morgan yelled.

How she'd managed to haul on the rope so that the boat came within distance and then clamber aboard, she had no idea. But somehow she had negotiated the mudslide while Morgan kept one hand on an oar and clutched at the reeds with the other to try and close the gap. One foot was wet and mud-stained, as was the hem of her dress. The umbrella hadn't made it into the boat with her. It had bowled into the undergrowth, where it lay tangled like a fallen bird. At least it had stopped raining now.

'I can row quite well but I'm not that good when it comes to parking,' Morgan said, pulling on the oars and arrowing the boat out towards the centre of the river. He grinned and flashed his eyes at her.

'You don't say.' She looked away. No smile.

She wasn't going to make this easy for him, whatever it was he had in mind. Yes, she was the one at fault, but she had ended it, with no room for doubt, and still he'd had the audacity to virtually drag her into this daft little boat and sail away with her. Row, then. It was all the same.

She shifted position on the uncomfortably narrow wooden seat and felt the ends of her hair. They were wet, too, but that would be from the rain. Around the boat, the brownish water swirled in the wash from the oars. She tried not to think about how deep it was out here.

'You look like the Lady of Shalott,' Morgan said.

'What?'

'The Lady of Shalott. You must have heard of her.'

'Of course I've heard of her. Well, I hope I don't come to a sticky end like she did.'

'She was very beautiful.'

'And very dead.'

Layla scowled. She yanked her bag onto her lap and clutched it to her with both hands, like a shield. Morgan seemed not to notice her disapproval of the situation, or if he did, he chose to ignore it.

'Soon be there,' he said cheerfully, his chest heaving from the effort of rowing.

Oddly enough, she hadn't thought to ask where he was taking her. She did so now.

'The boathouse. We need to talk.'

Ha. Obvious, wasn't it? The boathouse, the scene of the crime. Had he no sensitivity at all? She retracted the unfair thought. Morgan Hampshire was the most sensitive man she knew. She loved that about him. *Loved.*

A bubble of panic rose within her. Despite making her peace with the Morlands, despite her new thoughts about Danni and everything that had happened to spin her world around, she needed breathing space to settle down and be herself again. Morgan was one complication she could well do without. Yet here she was with no more than a few planks of wood between them and her defences crumbling faster than cheesecake.

She should have ignored him, turned her back on him and walked away. Or run. Except she'd had enough of running.

It only took a minute or two to reach the boathouse. It seemed a lot longer. Morgan steadied the boat as she stepped out, far more easily than she'd stepped in. Retrieving his jacket from beneath the seat, he tied the boat to the mooring post and ushered her politely across the grass and up the steps in front of him. Neither of them had spoken a word since he'd announced his intention to bring her here.

Once they were inside, he stood before her in the centre of the room, his smile uncertain, his chest rising and falling heavily beneath his grey T-shirt, and she saw how nervous he was.

'Layla...'

'Look, I...'

Their voices collided. They laughed, then fell silent. She had no idea what was supposed to come next, and by the expression on Morgan's face, neither did he. So much for talking, then. But they were marking time. They weren't ready.

She wanted to picture how it was when he found her. 'You saw me walking, while you were out in the boat? Not the sort of weather for it, I'd have thought.'

'No, well, it wasn't quite like that.'

He rubbed his chin. He had a habit of doing that, when he was thinking, or unsure about something. She wanted to ask what it was like, but thought better of it.

Another silence, then she said, 'It feels funny being here again. Funny-nice, I mean, not funny-peculiar.'

He smiled, raised his eyebrows, his demeanour a little easier. 'You have such a way with words, Miss Mackenzie.'

'I didn't mean to come here. I told myself I'd never come

here again, ever. I don't even know why I agreed to get into that damn boat.'

'Because you thought I might drown in the attempt? Anyway, whatever the reason, I'm very glad you did. Thank you.'

He glanced down at the floor, mildly embarrassed by his own words. She decided to help him out. Lifting her bag from her shoulder, walking across and putting it down on the desk, she gazed around.

'There's more stuff than before.' She was looking at a small, leather armchair, cracked and creased with age. 'Oh, and I love the little typewriter.'

She spotted a red plastic bucket in the corner by the tall cupboard 'What's that for?'

'Have a guess.'

'No!' Surely he wasn't using that for...

'I live here now. Had to do something. The trek to the bogs in the middle of night wasn't an option.'

She saw his face, the grin he was trying to hide. It broke.

'Okay. It's for the leak in the roof. I have moved into my own place, or rather I will be, today as it goes. Not here, though. That'd be a bridge too far, even for a dosser like me.'

He told her about the cottage, belonging to Connor's grandfather. She knew those cottages; they were lovely. She wondered if she would ever see it from the inside. And then, when she asked about his writing, he told her with some excitement about the agent who had been sufficiently impressed with his first Poodle Chafferty book to sign him up, and how he hoped a publishing deal wouldn't be far off. She was delighted for him. He deserved success.

When she'd finished congratulating him, he asked, 'Would you like some tea? The biscuit tin's empty but there's milk for the tea.'

'No, thanks.'

'Well, at least sit down.' He indicated the leather chair. 'I got it from a charity shop. It's very comfy.'

She hesitated, then sat down. The leather creaked beneath her. Rather than taking the office chair, Morgan perched on the edge of the desk. His eyes locked with hers. She wanted to look away, but found she couldn't. Heat travelled up her spine. She felt it reach her face. He still had the same effect on her, shockingly the same. She wasn't supposed to be here, or anywhere, with him. Only now she was, suddenly it felt impossible to be anywhere else.

'I did apologise. Only by text, I know, but it was all I could do at the time. I need you to believe that,' she said.

'I know you did, and I do believe you. It's me who needs to apologise, for rushing things, for putting you into that situation. For scaring you. I don't know how I managed to do that, I only know I did, and I'm so sorry, Layla.'

'You didn't scare me. It wasn't you. I wanted to be with you, so much, and then when we nearly... well, I did get scared, but that was because of something that had happened in the past. To do with Danni, the night she died.'

Finally, finally, she could say those words without her eyes filling with tears.

'I see,' Morgan said thoughtfully. 'Would it help to tell me about it? Maybe not now, but some other time?'

Some other time. When would that be? She couldn't bear to think about that now.

'Yes,' she said quietly. 'I do want to tell you. Now, if that's all right with you.'

Morgan got up from the desk. He went to the cupboard in the corner and brought out the checked picnic rug and the cushions, arranged them on the floor and sat down. Layla took off her denim jacket and hung it over the arm of the chair, then got up and joined him. He sat cross-legged, waiting for her to begin, and when she was ready, she told him the whole story, from the night of the party right up until her last visit to the Morlands.

When she'd finished, Morgan just nodded slowly. And then he moved closer and put his arm around her shoulders, resting his head against hers. She leaned in, her body remembering his, the warmth of him.

'I can't stop thinking about you,' he said, after a while. 'I've never stopped.'

'Same for me.'

'Really?' He raised his head to look at her.

She smiled. 'Yes, really.'

And then he kissed her, and her arms went around his neck, and her fingers strayed into his hair as she kissed him back.

'I love you,' he said, kissing her again.

'And I love you. But it's not that simple.'

'Yes, it is. I love you. You love me, you said...'

'I do. I do love you.'

'Well, then, we can be together. How much simpler can it get?'

Layla made some space between them, dropping her gaze, aware that she may be about to break Morgan's heart a second time. And hers, too. But she couldn't hold out on him any longer. It wasn't fair.

'I'm leaving, Morgan. In less than two months, I'll be gone. I'm moving to New York. I have a place to live and a job all lined up. It's always been my ambition, my dream. I can't give up on it.'

She wanted to add 'even for you' but that would have sounded cruel, even though it really wasn't. He would never ask her to give up her dream. She knew him enough – loved him enough – to know that without a shadow of a doubt. And yet, he hadn't spoken. She looked up at him. He was smiling, a little sadly, but his eyes shone with emotion and excitement. Excitement on her behalf, for her great adventure.

'What difference does an ocean make? It's only geography. If I can let you go, knowing you love me and we'll be together properly, one day, then I can live with that.' He kissed her again, tenderly, his forefinger lifting her chin. 'Of course I'll be right behind you, on the next plane, so none of it matters anyway.'

'What?'

'I can write anywhere. It's the best thing about it.'

Layla put a finger to his chest. 'Let's not plan too far ahead, make too many promises.'

'No, okay, but—'

She silenced him with another kiss. She loved him. He loved her. It was enough, for now.

He pulled her to him and kissed her again, his lips hard on hers. Kneeling up, she reached for the hem of his T-shirt, tugging it up, running her hands over the smooth skin of his back. He pulled off the T-shirt completely, and helped her take off her dress. Then they lay down on the rug amongst the scattered cushions.

Later – a long time later, it seemed – they lay on their backs, fingertips touching, and the light in the room became brighter, patterning the wooden ceiling with ripples reflected from the river.

'Christmas,' Morgan said, still gazing upwards. 'I'll come to New York at Christmas.'

'The flight will be expensive, and I'll probably be working.'

'Not every minute, though.'

'No, not every minute.'

'Happy Christmas, then,' he said.

'Happy Christmas.'

They turned to one another and smiled.

FORTY-TWO

A year later

Melody and Reece strolled, hand in hand, beside the lake in the grounds of Foxleigh Court, the same walk they'd taken with Layla on one of her visits. It was quiet, hardly anyone about, which suited Melody's mood. They came to a place where the path narrowed between the trees, and they dropped hands and walked in single file, Melody in front.

She stopped, turning round to Reece.

'This is where Danni nearly fell in the water. Do you remember? It was just here, on the bank, by the willows.' She chuckled.

Reece laughed, too. 'She wanted to feed the ducks, only they weren't even there. They were right across the other side of the lake. It had been raining and the bank was slippery. She slid on her bum right down to the edge and I had to catch her. She got a shoe full of water, as I remember.'

'She did, and mud all over her dungarees. She must have been two or three, I think, at the time.'

Melody tilted her head to one side. 'Funny, I only remembered that just now, but I didn't the other times we've been here.'

'I did,' Reece said. 'I remembered before.'

'Did you? That's good, then.' Melody smiled, took Reece's hand and they continued along the widened path.

A few minutes later she said, 'Oh, I forgot to tell you. I had an email from Layla this morning. They've found a new apartment. It's not so far out of the city as their current one, so less travelling for her to get to work. And it's got an extra room for a study for Morgan. She sent me the address. I'll write it in the book. There was a photo, too, of her in her chef's uniform, gutting an enormous fish.'

'I knew those two couldn't stay apart for long.'

'Layla and the enormous fish?'

'Layla and Morgan, idiot. Morgan's been in New York, what, six months now?'

'Something like that.' Melody squeezed Reece's hand. 'They're having their adventure together. Isn't that lovely?'

Reece laughed. 'Yes, Mel. Lovely.' The sky had clouded over and a breeze struck up, rippling the surface of the lake. 'Come on, let's go home.'

Dear reader,

Many thanks for reading *The Night She Died*, I hope you were hooked on Layla's journey. If you want to join other readers in hearing all about my new releases and bonus content, you can sign up for my newsletter.

www.stormpublishing.co/deirdre-palmer

If you enjoyed this book and could spare a few moments to leave a review that would be hugely appreciated. Even a short review can make all the difference in encouraging a reader to discover my books for the first time. Thank you so much!

Thinking about what inspired this book, it wasn't one thing, but came from snippets of conversation, random memories and life experiences in general. In other words, a hotchpotch of ideas that I hope melded into a decent tale in the end! When a young person dies, it is, of course, desperately sad and tragic, whatever the circumstances, and I began by burdening Layla, not only with grief but with tremendous guilt. I often write about family and motherhood, so there's plenty of that in *The Night She Died*, too. A boat trip on the beautiful River Dart in Devon gave me the riverside setting and the boathouse, and I hope my descriptions were vivid enough to take you there too.

Once again, thanks for reading, and for being part of this

amazing journey with me. I love to hear from my readers, so do get in touch via the links below.

Deirdre

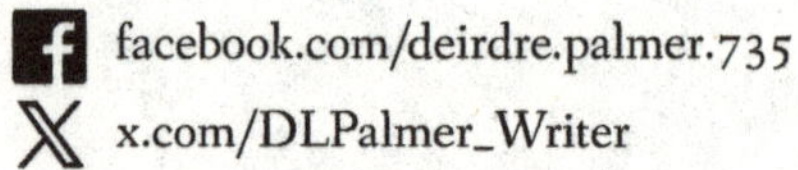
facebook.com/deirdre.palmer.735
x.com/DLPalmer_Writer

ACKNOWLEDGMENTS

My grateful thanks to Kathryn Taussig and the marvellous team at Storm for their wise guidance and amazing effort in bringing this book to fruition.

And heartfelt thanks, of course to my family and friends, in real life and online, for their constant support, post sharing and general all-round loveliness.